TRAITOR LODGER
GERMAN SPY

TONY ROWLAND

The moral rights of Tony Rowland as the author have been asserted.

Front cover image courtesy of Bernard Nock, Military Wireless Museum.

This is a work of fiction. The characters, places, events and procedures are either used fictitiously or are a product of the author's imagination.

A catalogue record for this book is available from the British Library

ISBN 978-1-91230-947-4

APS Publications,
4 Oakleigh Road,
Stourbridge,
West Midlands,
DY8 2JX

www.andrewsparke.com

For my wife and family

At 21.31 hours on Sunday 3rd November 1940, the teleprinter at 57-58 St James's Street, London, burst into life and MI5 Night Duty Officer, Flight Lieutenant Charles Cholmondeley, received the following message from Special Branch:

URGENT:
At 15.00 hrs today enemy parachute, complete with harness, overalls and flying helmet found behind hedge next to bridle path on Hill Farm, Haversham, Bucks. Inside camouflaged parachute was paper wrapping for chocolate made in Belgium, and packet containing white tablet, believed concentrated food. No trace of crashed aircraft, with parachute undoubtedly deliberately deployed. User appears to have landed uninjured and is still at large. Police enquiries continue together with Home Guard and military units.
Message ends.

This is the story of what followed, based upon now declassified Security Service documents, the author's further researches and some speculation. While trying to distinguish between the two, the reader is reminded that truth is often stranger than fiction.

1
CAMBRIDGE

To a hungry man the approach of a waitress should have been a welcome sight. To the spy it spelt potential disaster. He started to panic.

Sitting in the dining room of the Station Hotel in Cambridge, Dutch traitor Engelbertus Fukken was starving. His arrival by train the previous evening had been too late for a meal, and he had been looking forward to breakfast. Until he realised he had no idea what to order. He was struck by the irony of the situation. Although trained to transmit Morse at twenty words a minute, tell the difference between a Spitfire and a Hurricane and put a bullet into the heart of someone at ten paces, English food had not been on the syllabus of the spy school in Hamburg and remained a mystery to him.

Fukken glanced around the shabby room. Once a spick and span establishment, the Station Hotel was now showing signs of the neglect forced on it by the war. Regular redecoration had ceased when tins of paint disappeared from the shelves of Barratt & Sons, the local hardware shop in St Andrews Street. There was always the black market but the redoubtable owner, Miss Brown, would have no truck with the spivs who were flourishing in such times.

Although many of the men in the room were in uniform the spy was confident his neat, three-piece suit was the equal of those in civvies. He knew he spoke with a Dutch accent, but at least he was fluent in English. His confidence began to return.

Out of the corner of his eye, he saw the waitress walking towards him, pencil and pad at the ready. His fears resurfaced and he became convinced that the other diners were listening intently for what he would have to say. His heart pounded as he waited for the question that might expose him.

The waitress smiled at the tall, smartly dressed young man, with wire-rimmed glasses and the small moustache. 'Good morning Sir. What can I get you for breakfast?'

Fukken froze. What could he have? If he said something silly, it would expose his ignorance and could bring his mission to an end before it started. His worries were interrupted by an impatient voice. The smile had also disappeared. 'Your breakfast order. Sir?'

He looked around and in desperation nodded towards the next table. 'The fish looks nice, I'll have that please.'

Fukken hated kippers, but ploughed his way through them if only to satisfy his appetite. His ears pricked up when diners at a nearby table discussed the likelihood of an invasion. He wondered what they would have said if they knew he had trained initially to be part of an advance party to reconnoitre landing grounds and then support the invading troops.

After completing his meal he passed the reception desk on the way back to his room. The young lady on duty tried to catch his attention. 'Mr Ter Braak. I've got your bill here for you.'

At first the spy failed to recognise his cover name, and it was only when the receptionist called out again that he returned to the desk and apologised to mask his mistake. 'Sorry, I didn't hear you. I was wondering where I might find a letting agent. I need to organise some permanent accommodation.'

'You'll need to walk into town. Haslops in Green Street should be able to help you. Here's your bill,' and she handed over the account which he paid, at the same time offering up a silent prayer of thanks for having been so thoroughly taught the intricacies of pounds, shillings and pence.

In his room, Fukken opened the 1938 edition of the Cambridge street plan he had brought with him, and checked the location of Green Street. Although keen to take the shortest route, he decided on a slightly longer detour to avoid passing the police station in St Andrews Street.

Leaving the hotel, he set off down Station Road. At the junction with Hills Road, Fukken noticed the statue of a soldier, a memorial to local men killed in the Great War. He wondered what sort of monuments the Third Reich would erect to celebrate what he saw as their inevitable victory. Concluding that it would undoubtedly be something very grand, he pulled his cap down over his face, and strode on carrying his two cases, keeping a look out for a phone box so that he could make that all important call.

Surprised not to find the extensive bomb damage he had been told to expect, he soon reached the crossroads and the Catholic Church of *Our Lady and The English Martyrs*. Promising he would return when he could and make his peace with the Virgin Mary, he turned left. By the time he reached Trumpington Street his arms were sore from the weight of his cases, especially the one containing the radio set. His legs were also aching and the hole in his left shoe felt as though it was getting bigger with each stride. He cursed himself for not getting it mended before leaving Hamburg. To make matters worse, there was still no sign of a phone box.

Passing Addenbrooke's Hospital, with its sandbag protection around the external walls, Fukken soon reached Green Street, and turned right into the narrow cobbled lane. On one corner, the Whim Tea Rooms were just opening, and from the other side of the street came the enticing smell of newly baked bread from Matthews and Son. He continued walking, and at number 4 spotted his goal, the offices of G W Haslop & Co., Estate Agents. Pushing open the door, he approached the receptionist and after carefully reciting his cover story, asked for details of available accommodation.

'For how long, Sir?' asked the young lady.

The spy hesitated. Even if he completed his mission to find Maud in a matter of days, he knew he was trapped until the invasion took place. 'I'm not sure; a few months at least,' he replied.

The receptionist pulled open the drawer of her wooden filing cabinet, and took out one of the cards. 'Are you a smoker?' Fukken had puffed a pipe for a number of years, but anxious to get himself a room as soon as possible, shook his head.

The young lady smiled. 'This may suit you then. Mr and Mrs Serrill at 258 St Barnabas Road. They have one room for a non-smoker. Their last tenant was thrown out the other week, when they caught him puffing away in his room. They want one pound ten shillings a week for bed and breakfast, and evening meal. Will that do?'

Fukken readily agreed, and made his way out into the road, struggling as before with his luggage. It was not long before he was sitting on a bench overlooking the grass and trees of the Victorian park known to locals as Christ's Pieces, close to where some building work was taking place. Consulting his street map he soon located St Barnabas Road and anxious to be free from his incriminating radio set, he pressed on, passing Parkers Piece, where the sight of army lorries, a couple of anti-aircraft gun emplacements and a pillbox, surrounded by coiled barbed wire, left him in no doubt that this was a country at war.

Striding out, he spotted what he was looking for, a red public phone box. Approaching, he saw someone inside, in the middle of a call. The spy weighed up his options and decided that to stand around and wait might provoke awkward questions, so he kept walking until he reached St Barnabas Road, with the church of the same name on the corner. Reaching number 258, Fukken cursed when he realised he had now carried his two suitcases virtually back to the railway station.

The front door to the neat terraced house had a small coloured glass panel at head height through which he could see movement inside. He put down his cases, knocked and waited to see who would answer the door, at the same time repeating under his breath, 'My name is Jan Willem Ter Braak, Jan Willem Ter Braak...'

2
LONDON

To the casual passer-by, 57-58 St James's Street was a building in search of a new tenant, as announced by the 'Office To Let' sign outside. To those in the know, this was merely a front to hide the London office of the security service, MI5.

On the third floor, two men were deep in conversation. The senior of the pair was Guy Liddell. Bald-headed, with a round cherub like face, he was a quiet man with an intuitive talent for his role as director of B Division with responsibility for counter-espionage. The other was the handsome and extrovert Major Thomas Argyll Robertson, head of section B1(a) dealing with special agents, and known to all by his initials.

Tar Robertson completed his update on the missing parachutist. 'I've just checked with special branch, army units and the home guard, and so far they've all drawn a blank. A stranger wandering around country lanes ought to result in some sightings, so either this man is very good or just lucky.'

Liddell nodded. 'Not good enough to bury his parachute, so at least we know he's here.'

'I suppose that's a blessing in disguise. The fact that the 'chute was camouflaged certainly confirms we're dealing with another Abwehr agent. It's worrying that we didn't get the usual advance warning. Do you think Major Ritter has rumbled us?'

'Let's hope not. Perhaps we'll have more news in time for tonight's meeting with the DG.'

Both men grimaced at the thought of the tongue lashing they were likely to get from the recently promoted acting director general of MI5.

3
HAMBURG

Major Nikolaus Ritter greeted his visitor with a broad smile. 'My dear Karl, I'm delighted to see you. I really thought you'd bought it this time. Do tell me what happened.'

Hauptmann Karl Gartenfeld, the Luftwaffe's most experienced 'special ops' pilot frowned. 'It's kind of you to worry about me, but could it be you're more concerned about my passenger?'

'I'm anxious about all my agents but why the delay in getting back?'

'I have to admit this was the hairiest trip so far. We reached the drop zone without any trouble, but as we set course for home, a night fighter got onto our tail. I managed to lose him, but by then we'd drifted further south so I went for plan B and made for Rennes. Ran into some anti-aircraft fire on the south coast, but eventually made it. Needed some repairs before I could get back to base.'

'And how did the drop go?'

'That guy was the most gung-ho man I've ever flown. He showed no fear when it came to the jump. My dispatcher says he even shouted, 'Maud, here we come' as he was about to leave the plane. So who's Maud, then?'

Ritter glared at the pilot. 'Maud is no-one you need worry about. In fact, it's a name you and your crew must forget. If I ever hear it mentioned again...'

Gartenfelt had been involved with special operations for long enough to know not to ask any more questions. He saluted smartly. 'Instructions received loud and clear, Major.'

Once the pilot had left, Ritter dispatched the following message:

STRICTLY CONFIDENTIAL
Priority to Admiral Canaris, Tirpitzufer 72, Berlin.
Search for Maud commenced.
Ritter (Major), Hamburg.

4
CAMBRIDGE

Walking back into town in the late morning sunshine without his heavy luggage, Ter Braak, as he now thought of himself, enjoyed his newfound freedom. Not having the radio set with him was also a great weight off his mind. To be caught with such incriminating evidence could only lead to the hangman's noose and it had been a relief to lock it inside the wardrobe in his bedroom.

Thinking back over the morning, he reckoned he had been fortunate to have ended up on the doorstep of the Serrills who seemed a kind and caring couple, but more importantly, had accepted his cover story without question. His bedroom at the back of the house was ideal, with its window overlooking the garden and from which he could hang his radio aerial when transmitting. There were also some gas pipes to which he reckoned he could connect the earth wire from the set. His forged passport and registration card had passed muster, together with his ration book which Mrs Serrill had kept for her daily provision of meals that they had agreed should start tomorrow.

These achievements put a spring in his step, and retracing his earlier route, he made his way back into town, looking for somewhere to have lunch. All thoughts of food were forgotten when he came across another phone box, this one empty. At last he could call the local contact he had been given by his spymaster. He opened the door and stepped inside. Checking the details from the note in his wallet, he dropped two penny coins into the slot, dialled the number, and waited. A voice soon responded. 'Professor Carpenter's Office. How may I help you?'

Ter Braak pressed button A. 'May I speak with the professor please? I have a message from Dr Rantzau,' responded the spy, quoting the cover name.

'I'm sorry Sir, Professor Carpenter is away at present but should be back next week. May I take a message?'

Ter Braak tried not to sound as dejected as he felt. 'No thank you, I'll call again later.' He left the phone box feeling very lonely. He had been banking on this contact to guide him to his target. How was he going to find Maud now?

Forcing himself to focus on finding somewhere to eat, he hesitated outside the Post Office on the corner of St Andrews Street and Petty Cury, where a sign announced the presence of a '*British Restaurant*'. Unsure what to expect, he decided to see what else was on offer and, walking on, chanced upon Dorothy's Café next to Hobson's Passage.

He was amazed by the size of the premises, which could clearly accommodate many hundreds, but the separate entrances and exits on both Sidney and Hobson Streets persuaded him this was the place to choose; ideal for losing any unwanted followers. Making his way up the curved staircase to the restaurant, he found a seat close to the piano, but panicked once again when confronted by a waitress.

This time, with no-one close enough to copy, he blurted out, 'I'll have what you would eat yourself. Your favourite.' Praying he would not be presented with another plate of kippers, he hurried to pass himself off as a Dutch refugee who'd escaped via Dunkirk and was now working for the Dutch Free Press.

The young lady, in a smart black dress with white apron, already considered anyone involved with Dunkirk a hero. She smiled graciously. 'I'll get you mince and mash.'

Ter Braak left a tip when he left which, although only a few pence, seemed to be gratefully received. Descending the stairs and reaching the street, he wandered aimlessly, eventually sinking down onto a bench, and putting his head in his hands. Staring at his feet, he remembered the hole in his shoe, and the need to get it mended. His mind turned to the well-worn clothes he had brought in his second suitcase. The spy had always liked nice things, but until now had not had the funds to buy them. It did not take him long to persuade himself that the risks he was taking justified some reward. After all, he was not being paid a salary for his services to the Third Reich. Fingering the bulging wallet in his jacket pocket, he resolved to sort out his shoes and buy some more clothes. His mission to find Maud, whoever Maud was, could start when the professor returned.

Comforted by this decision, Ter Braak spent the rest of the day trying to come to terms with the layout of the town that was to be his home for the immediate future. Wandering along Wheeler Street, he glanced up at one of the grander buildings, and stopped. Carved over a large doorway were the words *Free Library*, together with a coat of arms and the year *1884*. He knew that in such places daily newspapers, reference books and local directories could be viewed, all free of charge.

Entering the library with a feeling of anticipation, he found himself in an impressive Reading Room. Below the lofty domed glass roof, people were studying books at several of the polished wooden tables, and many others were standing in front of lecterns reading daily papers. Around the edge of the room the walls were covered from floor to ceiling with book-laden shelves, which spilled into several annexes. All was quiet except for the rustle of pages being turned and the occasional cough.

Locating the librarian he asked in hushed tones where he might find a directory of the town. He was pointed to one of the annexes and went off in search of information which he hoped would help him trace the mysterious Maud.

Running his eyes along the shelves, he came across *The Blue Book, Cambridge Directory 1938,* and next to it another volume with a brown cover called *Spaldings Directory 1939*. Not knowing which to choose, he carried both to a nearby table. Opening up the Blue Book first, he felt a tingle down his spine. Here was a complete list of Cambridge residents and businesses. Flicking through the index, he located the page of surnames beginning with M and looked for the name Maud. Nothing. Worse still, Christian names were limited to initials only.

He opened the Spaldings Directory, hoping that would be of more help. Again, there were no surnames given as Maud, and even though full Christian names were stated, he realised it would take forever to search for that as a first name. In any event, there must be many of them and which one would it be? His optimism vanished.

His next idea was to check who lived at 7 Oxford Street, the address on his forged registration card. Quickly turning the pages of Spaldings, he was shocked to find there was no Oxford Street, let alone a number seven. The realisation that anyone local was likely to know Oxford Street did not exist made him wonder if Hamburg was trying to set him up. Deciding he would have to watch out who saw his card, he closed the book and replaced both volumes on the shelf.

Making his way back along Trumpington Street to his lodgings, he lost his way in the blackout, and wandered into one of the smaller roads next to Saxon Street. As he was wondering which way to go, the clouds cleared and a weak moon illuminated a row of ramshackle buildings. Suddenly, the door to the Cross Keys pub burst open and out spilled a rowdy group. The majority made their way back towards the town centre, except one red-haired young woman. She sidled up to Ter Braak, unbuttoning her coat as she did so, to reveal a low-cut blouse and ample breasts. 'My name's Marge. Want a good time, deary?' she enquired.

Ter Braak was taken completely by surprise, and found himself unable to protest when Marge, with practised fingers, began to undo his fly buttons. Rising to the occasion, he let Marge lead him all the way down Gothic Street to her shabby first floor bedroom. It was some sort of way to celebrate his safe arrival in Cambridge.

5
HAMBURG

In a purpose-built concrete bunker, a few miles north of the city, radio operator Heinz Valenti sat with headphones clamped to his ears, listening for a message from the latest agent to be sent to England. He had been involved with teaching Fukken the intricacies of Morse, and knew that he had left on 1st November. However, four days later, static was all that could be heard on his allocated frequencies.

Valenti thought back to his lessons with Fukken. He had seemed different to the other trainees. His mastering of Morse had certainly been quicker than most and the radio man knew he would have no difficulty in recognising his distinctive touch, or fist. But there was something else that had set Fukken apart from his peers; his blind faith in Hitler and in resounding victory for the Third Reich. Not that Valenti had ever discussed this with Fukken. He knew that even an innocent remark could be reported as treason, and too many people had received a visit from the Gestapo before disappearing for ever.

Valenti reminded himself that it often took some time for new agents to settle in before beginning transmissions, and he decided there was nothing to worry about...yet.

6
CAMBRIDGE

Making his way carefully in the blackout to St Barnabas Road, Ter Braak could not stop dreaming about Marge; how tender she had been; how kind; how seductive. His thoughts turned to his darling Neeltje, the fiancé he had left back in the Netherlands. He knew he should feel guilty, and convinced himself it had been a one-off lapse in trying circumstances. He strode out and was soon standing in front of the door to number 258, which opened before he had time to knock.

'Hello, Mr Braak. I'm glad you're back at last.' Mrs Serrill had a smile on her face, but the tone of her voice conveyed obvious annoyance at being kept up. 'I think, Mr Braak, you'd better have a front door key, so you can let yourself in when you're going to be late back.' She handed him the key and gave him a stare which suggested that nice people did not stay out to this hour.

Thanking her, Ter Braak made his way upstairs to his room. Once inside, he locked the door, and after carefully closing the curtains, switched on the light with its puny 60 watt bulb. Unlocking the wardrobe, he took out the suitcase housing the radio he'd been given just before taking off from Schiphol airfield, and for the first time swung open the lid. He had feared that this would be an unfamiliar set but it was the same type he'd used during his training - an SE/88/5.

He looked again. Something was different. At first, he could not work out what it was. Then he realised, the labels for the various dials and plug sockets were all in English. He laughed at what he saw as a futile attempt to persuade anyone finding the set that it was not German. How would he be able to explain away the set itself?

Doing his best to put that problem out of his mind, he checked the contents of the case. Noting the pentode valves, and day and night-time crystals, he reckoned he had everything he needed, but then his eyes rested on the coil of wire that was the aerial. His heart missed a beat as he remembered that it needed to be matched to the wavelength. Not being able to recall the formula for calculating the correct length of wire, he concluded there was only one way to find out.

He settled on his first message as '*Capture successfully evaded. Now established Cambridge. Prof not yet available.*' To show he was not under enemy control he signed off with the letters *HH*. If he was forced to transmit with a gun to his head he knew to add *Heil Hitler* in full.

Just as he had done many times in training, he plugged in the aerial and without opening the curtains, lowered the coil of wire out of the window. The earth he connected to the gas pipe serving one of the redundant wall lights. Then there was a sharp knock on his bedroom door. His heart nearly stopped and he held his breath.

'Hello Mr Braak, you're not asleep are you?'

'No, Mrs Serrill. What can I do for you?'

'Sorry to bother you, but I forgot to say that I'll leave a jug of hot water outside your door in the morning. Will eight o'clock do?'

'Yes, that'll be fine, Mrs Serrill. Thank you very much.'

He listened with relief to the sound of his landlady slowly making her way across the landing to the front bedroom. Taking a moment to calm down, he realised he was simply too tired to continue. Putting his coding details back in their hiding place, he disconnected his earth wire, recovered the aerial, and shut the case before locking it inside the wardrobe, content that Hamburg would not be concerned by a delay of a few days in making contact.

Ter Braak lay back on the bed, and tried to gather his thoughts. He smiled at the memory of his time with Marge, but forced himself to focus on his present position. He was relieved to have made it to Cambridge without any mishap, and promised himself he would establish contact with Hamburg tomorrow night. His deliberations then turned to his mission to find Maud. The more he thought about it, the more he began to relax. The professor should be available quite soon, and in the meantime he had ample funds in his wallet. Ter Braak started to look forward to the coming weeks, and his shopping spree. He would buy some new shoes and get the hole in his others mended. After that, maybe another suit, some shirts and underwear. Then he would look for Maud.

Ter Braak was soon fast asleep.

7
LONDON: MI5 HEADQUARTERS

Behind the blackout curtains of 57-58 St James's Street Brigadier Oswald Allen Harker, the Acting Director General of MI5, was at his desk. Sitting opposite him were Guy Liddell, and Tar Robertson, the latter now wearing the regimental tartan trews that dated from his time with the Seaforth Highlanders, and which had resulted in him being christened *passion pants* by the ladies of MI5.

Harker, known by all as Jasper, made his usual point of staring disapprovingly at the unorthodox trousers for a moment before opening the meeting. 'Gentlemen, I realise it's very late but I need to know the latest position on this missing agent, the one whose parachute was found yesterday at...?'

'Haversham, Sir. Tar has the details.' Liddell, gestured to his colleague and Tar took over.

'To recap, Sir, the parachute was discovered by a Land Army girl at 15.00 hours yesterday, the 3rd November. It had been hidden behind a hedge on Hill Farm, near Haversham, a small village just south of the new radio intercept station we're setting up at Hanslope Park. Of more concern, it's only a few miles north of Bletchley Park. The local police were called, and as soon as they realised this 'chute wasn't one of ours, they passed the matter onto Special Branch. We received an Express Message from them at 21.31 hours last night confirming the find and that their search for the parachutist had so far drawn a blank.'

'What steps have been taken to find this man?' barked Harker.

'Air intelligence, field security, together with all searchlight and RAF units in the area were alerted, together with the radio security service, and of course all regional security liaison officers in adjacent areas. In addition, the military at Bletchley, Stony Stratford, Whaddon, Winslow, Lathbury, Hanslope and Cold Brayford are still searching, together with home guard units in those areas.'

Guy Liddell continued. 'As you can see Sir, we're all fully aware of the danger of this man remaining at large. It must be assumed he has a transmitter and we can't have him sending back intelligence which contradicts the false information we're feeding to Germany through our small band of double agents.'

'Who in the Abwehr might be this missing man's spy master? Will he be another of Ritter's merry men?' asked Harker.

Tar nodded. 'Seems most likely, Sir. Major Ritter appears to have been involved with all ten of the agents sent over to date.'

Harker rose and paced the room. The eyes of his subordinates followed him as he circled the perimeter of his office. 'Remind me, Liddell, how close have all the previous agents been dropped to their intended targets?'

'Not brilliant, Sir. I think 'could do better' would be my progress report on their pilot.'

The brigadier sat down again. 'So, where do we think this man was heading? From what you say, it would seem he only landed near Bletchley and Hanslope by accident, rather than by design.'

'That's also my view, Sir,' agreed Liddell. 'The problem is, he could have been aiming for anywhere. The only possible lead we had was the sighting, by a porter at Wolverton railway station - a man struggling with two suitcases who boarded a train on the branch line to Newport Pagnell. Unfortunately no-one remembers seeing him at the other end, so that trail seems to have gone cold.'

'What about the ticket office clerk? Did he sell any tickets to foreigners around that time?'

Tar checked his notes. 'It was a woman, Sir. First day on the job, but she didn't recall anyone strange asking for a ticket. The local bobby on duty at the station over that weekend also confirmed he didn't see anyone suspicious.'

Liddell looked worried. 'Sir, while the search goes on, I propose Tar visits station X at Bletchley to warn them of the possibility of a spy in their area. I will liaise with our new Y station at Hanslope Park myself.'

Harker closed his file to indicate that the meeting was over. 'Approved. Let me know how matters develop. We have to find this man, and silence him, one way or another.'

'Am I to take it, Sir, that we are to treat him in the same way as SNOW in the event of an invasion?' Liddell was referring to the cover name given to the Welsh double agent, Arthur George Owens. Recruited during the early 1930s by MI6 to report upon what he saw during business trips to Germany, Owens had felt he was underpaid by the British and had sold his services for a higher price to the Abwehr, the German secret service. Interned at the start of the war, he had admitted to having a transmitter/receiver which he agreed to use for MI5 providing, of course, that he was released.

The weight of responsibility resting on his shoulders was reflected in the brigadier's voice. 'Yes, you have my authority to liquidate. Ideally this new man should be captured and squeezed for as much information as possible, but if the only way to stop him is a bullet to his head, then so be it. At least it would save us the charade of a trial before his execution.'

8
CAMBRIDGE

After his best night's sleep since leaving Hamburg, Ter Braak went down to breakfast feeling refreshed and looking forward to a relaxed meal. He knew he would not be faced with making a choice with only tea and toast available, and butter if the rations allowed.

The greeting he received from Mrs Serrill came as a shock. 'Mr Braak, that ration book you gave me yesterday was out of date.'

The spy's mind raced. Why? he wondered. And then it came to him. It could only have been the extra tuition that delayed his departure. How careless not to have checked before he left. Whatever should he do now?

He was about to make some lame excuse when, to his amazement, Mrs Serrill said, 'You really should sort this out yourself, but don't worry, I'll drop it into the Food Office in town and get you a temporary card. Then I expect you'll have to write off for a new one.'

'That's very kind of you Mrs Serrill. By the way, there's one ration I won't need. I don't take sugar in my tea.'

This delighted his landlady and banished any criticism of the out of date ration book. 'Good. I can collect your allowance, and that'll make our ration go much further.'

Her husband, sitting in his usual chair reading the morning paper, looked up and also smiled. 'You've made our day, Mr Braak. Now, as I explained, my years on the footplate have wrecked my lungs, so as long as you don't start smoking, you're very welcome here.'

'Thank you, Mr Serrill. That's very kind of you, and I can assure you your lungs are safe with me.' Ter Braak had expected the strain of the last few days to have driven him to the comfort of tobacco, but it dawned on him he had not missed his pipe at all.

Recalling his thoughts of the previous afternoon, and knowing he had no idea where to buy what he wanted, Ter Braak asked, 'I need to buy some more clothes as I didn't manage to bring much over with me. Can you tell me the best places to shop, please? I can't spend a fortune, you understand.'

'Quite so, Mr Braak. Now let me think. It's a long time since Elsie and I bought anything for ourselves. We have to be careful. 'Make do and mend' as they say on the wireless. With the pension being what it is, and everything getting more expensive since the war started, we've no choice. That's why we let out your room, you know.'

At this point Mrs Serrill butted in. 'I know, Bert, aren't there all those men's tailors in Petty Cury?'

'So there are. That's your best bet, at least to start with.'

The spy was grateful. 'Thank you very much, I'll walk into town and see what I can find. By the way, I'm going to get myself another pair of shoes, so that I can get the sole of this one repaired. It lets in the rain. Do you know a good shoe shop and a repairer?'

Mr Serrill thought for a moment. 'Yes, there are also a few shoe shops in Petty Cury, and there's a shoe repairer in a small road just off Castle Street. Jack Overhill's his name. He fancies himself an author but does a good cobbling job, as long as you don't mind putting up with anti-war nonsense.'

Ter Braak's walk into town the previous day had avoided the police station. There had been a number of constables walking about the town on their defined beats, but none had given him a second glance. With growing confidence, he decided to pluck up his courage and walk along St Andrews Street into town.

Arriving at the catholic church in Hills Road, Ter Braak took a deep breath and walked straight on into Regent Street. Before long, he found himself in St Andrews Street with the feared police station on the left. It was impossible to miss as the whole of its stone-faced ground-floor frontage had been protected with sandbags, and a bobby stood on duty outside, gas mask bag slung across his shoulder. Staying on the opposite side of the road, the spy marched resolutely past, constantly reminding himself to keep walking, not look round and to keep his head up.

Inside the borough police headquarters, Chief Constable Robert Pearson had recently received the 'All Forces' message warning of the missing enemy agent, whose parachute had been discovered near the small village of Hanslope. But even if he had looked out of his window at that moment, as Ter Braak walked past, with no description to help him, the chief constable would have had no reason to suspect the man striding along the pavement.

Not knowing this, Ter Braak dreaded hearing a whistle or a shout. However, none was forthcoming and he soon reached Petty Cury. Turning left past the Midland Bank, it struck him that this road had been designed to cope with the horse and cart, but now had to deal with cars, the odd bus, not to mention the ubiquitous bicycle. Continuing down the narrow street , he found the type of shop he sought, Thirty Shilling Tailors, nestling next to the Musical Box Café. Strolling on, he reached Falcon Yard. Instead of well-kept shops he saw children with ragged clothes playing in a debris-strewn street, surrounded by dark, dingy dwellings. Overwhelmed by this depressing sight, Ter Braak quickened his pace, and soon reached the junction with Market Hill. Realising he had only been looking at the shops on his side of the street, he crossed over and began his journey back on the north side of the road.

This was much more encouraging. The second shop was Montague Burton the Tailors, followed by the Dolcis Shoe shop. Further on and sandwiched between the Empire Meat Company and Joe Lyons confectioners, he spotted Fifty Shilling Tailors. Confusion reigned when another branch of Montague Burton appeared. His shopping options increased even more when he encountered Hepworth Tailors and, just before the junction with St Andrews Street, the True Form Boot Co.

Deciding a rest was called for, Ter Braak made his way to Dorothy's Café. In spite of his gaffe about what to eat, he had felt comfortable there on his visit the day before. It had been busy, but not excessively so. The last thing he wanted to be was a customer sitting on his own.

Walking up the curved stairs, he was pleasantly surprised to be able to take a seat at the table he had occupied before, just by the piano. He ordered a cup of tea, and sat back to mull over what to buy, and from which shop.

His first decision was straightforward. The shoe in need of repair was from True Form, which had been the only English shoes in the Abwehr store to fit him. He liked the style and, apart from the hole, they were comfortable, so he resolved to get another pair from the shop of the same name.

Where to buy a suit was another matter. He reminded himself it had to look smart, but not too smart. It must look the part, but not stand out.

He had no knowledge of any of the tailors he had seen, and for no particular reason, decided to rule out both Burtons and Hepworths. That left the Thirty Shilling and Fifty Shilling Tailors and upon the basis it was not his money he was spending, he opted for the dearer one.

After paying for his tea, he made his way back to Petty Cury, and taking a deep breath, pulled open the door to the consumer world of Cambridge.

9
STATION X BLETCHLEY PARK

Tar Robertson was one of the few people in the country who knew what went on at Bletchley Park. Arriving at Bletchley railway station, Tar rang the telephone number he had been given, and a disembodied voice at the other end told him to wait for the car which would collect him.

The journey only took a few minutes, and he was comforted to find armed guards at the entrance gate, and a tall perimeter fence topped with barbed wire. His pass was inspected thoroughly before the car was allowed into the long tree-lined drive that led up to the manor. A lake with a small island soon came into view, together with an imposing Wellingtonia tree. Numerous timber huts were dotted around the grounds.

Greeted by a pretty young Wren, Tar was shown into the surprisingly modest ground-floor office of Commander 'Alistair' Denniston, a veteran of Room 40, the centre for code breaking during the first world war. The man in charge of Bletchley Park greeted his visitor and the two sat down in a pair of old, but comfortable easy chairs located in the large bay window, through which the tree and lake could be seen.

The major had not met Denniston before and judged him to be in his late fifties, a quiet and reserved man but with an incisive manner of speaking. Tar's gaze then fell upon a hockey stick hung on the back wall.

The commander smiled. 'That's the one I used in the London games. Managed to get a bronze medal with the Scottish side.'

Nodding his appreciation of the feat, Tar got straight down to business. 'Thank you for seeing me, Commander. I'm sorry to say that sometime towards the end of last week, one of Canaris' spies dropped in to see us. He left his parachute behind a hedge up at Haversham, a small village some six miles north of here. The problem is, we don't know where he is, and it's always possible he's interested in this place.'

Commander Denniston felt his stomach turn over. All his waking hours were focused upon breaking Enigma, the coding machine used by the Germans. He had gathered together some of the best brains in the country and significant progress had been made, but that could now be at risk. 'I'm very sorry to hear that major, but before we go any further, I need to ask how much you know about what we do here. We work on a 'need to know' basis.'

Tar explained that he was fully cleared for Ultra, the cover name given to Enigma decodes. 'I therefore appreciate the dire consequences of this man getting inside here, and finding out for himself,' he added.

'That's a relief, at least. The problem of keeping our work here secret is nearly as difficult as breaking the codes themselves. It was easier in the early days, as we could then recruit people known personally to us, but we've expanded so much that we've had to cast our net much wider.'

'I presume they all sign the Official Secrets Act?'

'Naturally, and I always have the process supervised by a rather fierce chief petty officer, who's under instructions from me to frighten the living daylights out of them by stressing the consequences of any transgression.'

'I have to say I was impressed by the thoroughness of the guards at the gate.'

The commander sighed. 'A lot of resources have gone into physical security. So, for example, we have a system of passwords that are changed at regular intervals and which our people are required to give to the military police who patrol inside the grounds after dark - we work a 24 hour shift system, you know. The problem is, some of the boffins can't be bothered with such trivialities, and on more than one occasion, they've been marched to the guardroom as a suspect intruder.'

'That's good to hear, but how about security when all these people are outside, in their digs, or at home?'

'So far, only one problem. One of our young girls, and out of the *top drawer* as well, mentioned to her family what she did here, and that was repeated by a relation at a cocktail party a few weeks later. Luckily for us, one of our senior men was present, and steps were taken to ensure this knowledge went no further.'

'What happened to her?'

'I have to say, I don't know. All I wanted was her out of here.'

'What do the locals think?'

'It must be obvious that something is going on here, but thanks to the majority of my people being on a different intellectual, and dare I say it, higher social plane, the townsfolk just don't ask. But tell me, major, what have you done to track this man down?'

'As soon as the significance of the parachute became apparent, all possible resources have been involved. The problem was the 'chute was only found by accident, and apparently some time after it'd been hidden. If this man had only had the sense to bury it, we'd never even have known he was here.'

'All a bit worrying if you ask me, but surely if the Germans know enough about this place to send in a spy, wouldn't it be simpler to just bomb us out of existence?'

'Hopefully Germany doesn't know about the Park, and you weren't this man's specific target. It's quite possible he may have landed off course and won't chance upon you as he makes his way to wherever he was supposed to be going.'

'And where might that be?'

'Impossible to say. As you know, your success in cracking the Abwehr codes has given us a window into their activities, and so far we've had advance notice of any new arrival. But not in this case. On the face of it, this area is already well served by previous agents, at least all those we know about, which might suggest this man was dropped well away from his intended target. But who knows?'

10
CAMBRIDGE

Sixty miles away, Ter Braak emerged from the Fifty Shilling Tailors with a parcel containing the jacket and trousers of his new suit. The waistcoat had required slight alteration, and he had been told to collect it on Friday. He had wondered if it had been wise to leave his name and address when asked, but reckoned to refuse would have aroused unnecessary suspicion.

He decided to have some lunch at Dorothy's and then spend the afternoon sorting out the rest of his wardrobe.

After a walk around the centre of the town in his new shoes from True Form, which turned out not to be quite as comfortable as the old ones, he settled upon Joshua Taylor, the large and rather grand outfitters on the corner of Market Street and Sidney Street. The staff were even more stuffy than those at Fifty Shilling Tailors, but he eventually escaped carrying parcels of shirts, collars, ties, suspenders, woollen socks, and some rather nice woollen vests and underpants, both long and short. His ability to only give his collar size in centimetres caused a slight stir, but the use of a tape measure in feet and inches soon resolved the problem.

His confidence was now such that he walked boldly past the policeman on point duty at the corner of Sydney Street, on his way to

Johnsons, where he treated himself to a hat, sized six and seven eighths, whatever that was. Stuffing his old cap into the pocket of his raincoat, he put on the trilby at a jaunty angle and walked out into the street feeling very much the English gentleman.

Ter Braak then set out to find the boot repairer recommended by Mr Serrill. He knew from his map that his shop was off Castle Street, and crossing the river, soon reached the traffic lights at the junction with Northampton Street. His heart nearly skipped a beat when he heard the sound of running feet. He looked up and to his horror, saw a police constable running for all he was worth down Castle Street towards him. He started to panic. He had the bags with his recent purchases in both hands, and without thinking, dropped those in his right hand, which he thrust into his raincoat pocket. His searching fingers soon found the comforting shape of the butt of his Browning, which he grasped, flicking the safety catch off as he did so.

The policeman came closer and closer, the steel tips on the toes and heels of his boots clattering on the pavement as he ran. With his pulse quickening even more, the spy braced himself to shoot, regardless of a mother with two small children about to cross over the road towards him but, in an instant, the now puffing and blowing bobby ran past him without a second glance. Still holding the butt of his gun in his pocket, Ter Braak slowly turned his head to see who, or what, could be the subject of the constable's attention. He was both relieved and mystified to find the policeman standing inside a blue box, with a blue light flashing on top of it. He had opened a door in this mysterious structure, and could be seen inside talking on the phone, in between getting his breath back.

Looking more closely, Ter Braak saw *Police & Public Call Box* written over the door. He breathed a sigh of relief, and carefully re-engaged the safety catch on his gun. Taking his hand out of his pocket, and with a very sweaty palm, he picked up the bags he had dropped. Glancing back, he could see the constable still talking on the phone. Dismissing as an optical illusion the fact that the police box looked bigger inside than out, and trying to look as if he did not have a care in the world, the spy continued his walk up Castle Street.

Ter Braak knew from his street map of the town that the shop he sought was in the fifth road on the left. Carefully counting the entrances, he turned into Castle Row. Peering down the narrow street, he was delighted to see the words *Boot Repairs* painted on one of the windows. Entering what turned out to be a very small shop, he found the proprietor with his back to the door, typing away at an impressive rate. Guessing that this would be Jack Overhill, the cobbler and aspiring author, and having decided to have both shoes re-soled, he handed over the pair and was told to collect them on Friday. He made the mistake of not leaving the shop quickly enough and was treated to the tirade of anti-war rhetoric Mr Serrill had predicted.

As he walked back to St Barnabas Road, the spy reflected on the past few days since his arrival in Cambridge. He reassured himself again that his encounter with Marge had been a one-off and that his heart still lay with his fiancé. His main worry had been to pretend to be a non-smoker but to his continued surprise, he had found it possible to survive without his pipe and reckoned he might soon be able to say goodbye to it forever.

The comfort gained from this small achievement was soon swamped by the nagging fear of being exposed by his out-of-date ration book. He cursed Hamburg for being so careless, and berated himself for not spotting the problem before he left.

Although Mrs Serrill had promised to get him a temporary card, he wondered how many of those he would be allowed to have.

11
CAMBRIDGE

The Honourable Nancy Cox often thought back to that dinner party, and what at the time had seemed a chance meeting with a very nice man. That *very nice man* had turned out to be a member of MI5, and before long she had found herself recruited, working alongside other girls of a similar social background, handling the highly confidential files of the security service.

As a career, this did nothing to affect her social life, other than to impose on her a duty not to tell anyone what she did. Nancy discovered she actually enjoyed pretending she worked in a very dull ministry, doing very dull secretarial duties. Then came the war, and the setting up of a network of regional security liaison officers by Guy Liddell. This came at a convenient time for Nancy, who was dreading the imminent transfer of MI5 to the recently vacated Wormwood Scrubs prison. When she heard there was a post of secretary to the new RSLO at Cambridge, she jumped at the chance.

Nancy was surprised to find the regional office was located over a wool and needlework shop in Regent Street, not far from the town centre. The security liaison officer turned out to be Major Cyril 'Dickie' Dixon, who was soon joined by Captain Jack Hester of the radio security service. It would have been difficult to find two men who were such different characters. Dixon was a veteran of the first war and always dressed in an immaculate uniform, while Jack Hester was the complete opposite. Formerly a development engineer with the radio firm Philco, he wore wire rimmed glasses and had the look of a boffin. He had been made a temporary captain, but his uniform hung off him in a baggy sort of way. Major Dixon had tried to smarten him up, but to no avail. However, they both played golf and this common interest helped them work in close proximity, even though the junior of the two had the lower handicap.

As usual, Nancy arrived at the office just after eight in the morning. Her journey into town had been typical for early November; cold, with a hint of rain in the air. Climbing the stairs to the offices on the first floor, she let herself in through the double locked door, and glancing towards the teleprinter, spotted a message. Tearing off the paper, she scanned it, expecting to see a reminder for Captain Hester to submit some return or other. To her surprise, it was an urgent message to the major from a Flight Lieutenant Cholmondeley confirming the discovery of a discarded parachute from a suspected enemy spy.

When she read details of the location, between Hanslope and Bletchley, Nancy's pulse raced. She was trusted with confidential material, and knew from her work with Jack Hester that some new base related to his work was being set up at Hanslope. She was also aware, from memos she had typed for Major Dixon. that something important went on at Bletchley.

Nancy knew the major would not arrive until later in the day, following his meeting with other RSLOs at Blenheim Palace, the so called 'country office' of MI5. Thinking back to the previous spy who had been brought to their office just over a month ago and wondering how many agents the Germans would send over, she settled down to catch up with the typing. Her concentration was such that she was surprised when, just after lunch, in walked Dickie Dixon.

'Good afternoon major, I'm glad you've arrived. There's a top secret message for you. Seems there's a German spy at large.'

The major picked up the printout. 'Yes, this was on the agenda at today's meeting, but I'd be surprised if this man is heading in our direction. I reckon we've had our quota of spies for this part of the world and I'm sure the Abwehr will want to cover as much of the country as they can.'

Dixon sank into his chair. 'If he does come here, as a foreign refugee he'll have to register with the aliens office, and I know I can rely on Superintendent Wilson to let me know when anyone suspicious does that. Anyway, better let the captain know as well, so he can keep an ear out for any local transmissions.'

The news of a possible spy in the area made Jack Hester frown. At the start of the war, it had been realised that help would be needed to monitor enemy transmissions, and radio hams were recruited as voluntary interceptors, or VI's as they became known. He had just heard that his VI in town had succumbed to tuberculosis. He vented his frustration on his colleague. 'He must be replaced as soon as possible. Perhaps now they'll give me the okay to recruit young Ray Fautley.'

12
HAMBURG

As a senior officer in the Abwehr, the German secret service, Major Nikolaus Ritter was entitled to the use of a staff car, but frequently chose to walk to his office in Sophien Terrace. He found it useful to think things over, which usually involved trying to solve the latest crisis threatening one of his agents abroad.

At the outbreak of the war, Ritter already had one spy active in Britain. Operating under the cover name *JOHNNY*, Welshman Arthur Owens had established regular radio contact, and was considered something of a star in Hamburg. On the back of this success, Admiral Canaris, head of the Abwehr, had handed Ritter the task of infiltrating agents into England to support the planned invasion. In what became known as Operation LENA, he had been given only a matter of weeks to recruit, train and insert the spies and this had resulted in mixed results.

Ritter thought back to the ten LENA agents dispatched so far. He was sure that the four he had sent in by boat on the south coast during August, Jose Waldberg, Karl Meier, Stoerd Pons and Charles van den Kierboom, must have been caught. After all, the second transmission from one of the pairs warned of their imminent arrest. Changing to parachute drops for Gosta Caroli and Wolf Schmidt, the next two spies dispatched in early September appeared to have paid dividends, with both sending back regular reports.

The major cursed himself for abandoning what seemed to be a successful system and using a seaplane and dingy for Karl Drucke, Werner Walti and Vera Erikson. Inserted up north on the Moray Firth at the end of September, none of the trio had ever made contact, and he had had to accept that they too must have perished.

It had been an easy decision to revert to the use of a parachute for Hans Reysen, the last LENA man, dispatched in early October. What appeared initially to have been a successful mission changed however, when his communications stopped abruptly.

The spymaster had mixed feelings about this latest setback. He had an enviable reputation within the Abwehr, having been the man who had acquired details of the top secret *Norden* bombsite from the USA in 1937, but his current standing in the Abwehr depended on how many active agents he had. The distinctive fist of the person now sending the Morse messages was clearly different to Reysen, the man he had trained, suggesting he was almost certainly under enemy control. Ritter knew that to report this could lead to charges of defeatism and he was glad his dilemma had been resolved by the sudden cessation of transmissions.

Convincing himself that he had done the best he could in the limited time allowed, Ritter turned his thoughts to the latest agent to be dispatched, Engelbertus Fukken. Recruited originally as a LENA spy, he had been given extra training, equipped with forged papers and, on the orders of Admiral Canaris himself, sent on a special mission to find someone called Maud who was developing a new super weapon in Cambridge.

The major persuaded himself there was no need to panic just yet. It was only two weeks since the Dutchman's departure, but the importance of this mission weighed on his mind. Fukken had to make contact soon, otherwise Ritter knew his own survival would be at risk.

13
CAMBRIDGE

'What's your uniform, please, Mrs Serrill?' asked Ter Braak, when he came down to breakfast.

'Oh, I'm in the WVS, that's the women's voluntary service, although my Bert says it stands for "women of various sizes." We help out where necessary.'

'I see. Is there a similar organisation for men?'

Mr Serrill nodded. 'Yes, I'm in the home guard. I originally joined up when we were called the LDV, local defence volunteers. It was Winston Churchill who changed our name to the home guard. Good job too, because by then people were saying LDV stood for, ' Look, duck and vanish!'

'Have you any weapons?'

'Not yet. We drill with pitchforks, brooms and pikes, but we're promised some proper guns soon. And then I suppose we'll have to learn how to use them.'

'Pardon me for asking, but aren't you a bit old for all this?'

'There's supposed to be an upper age limit of 65, and as you've no doubt gathered, I'm well past that. I just put 64 on the form, and nobody said anything. But enough of me. I presume you'll be sorting out an office for your work?'

This took Ter Braak completely by surprise. Nothing of the sort had been mentioned during his training, but it occurred to him that this would be a useful place for keeping any confidential papers he might obtain. 'Yes Mr Serrill, but I'm not sure where to look.'

'Well, if it was me, I'd start with Haslops, the agents who put you on to us. Even if they can't help, I'm sure they'll know who can.'

'That's a good idea. I'll pop in, when I'm in town.'

Mrs Serrill got up. 'I can't sit here all day nattering, I must finish my cleaning.' With that they went their separate ways, Ter Braak into town, Mrs Serrill into the parlour, and Mr Serrill, who had nothing better to do, into the garden.

The pretty receptionist in Haslops was most obliging. 'If it's only one room you're after, I may be able to help. We've a spare room upstairs. It'll cost you two pounds a month. Here's the key, go and have a look.'

He ran up the stairs, unlocked the door, and looked in. The room was small and empty, and very dusty. He looked out of the window, and reckoned his aerial might work, even though there were buildings all around. Forgetting to check for a suitable radio earth connection, he made his way downstairs again, and announced, 'I think it'll do, but there's no furniture, and it's very dusty.'

The young woman smiled. 'That's no problem. We'll get it cleaned, and you can rent what furniture you need from Coopers & Son. Shall I telephone them?'

'That's very kind of you. I'll need a desk, chair, table and also some sort of cabinet I can lock.'

The girl picked up the phone, dialled a number, and spoke to someone at the other end whom she clearly knew well. After a few moments, she put her hand over the mouthpiece. 'They've got a kneehole table, wooden armchair, a lockable cupboard and a davenport, which you can have for one pound ten shillings a month. If that's OK, they'll drop them off for you tomorrow. They want the cash up front, but you can leave that with me if you like.'

Ter Braak had no idea what a davenport was, but keen to bring negotiations to an end, he agreed and paid for three months' room and furniture rental before leaving.

Back in St Barnabas Road, Mrs Serrill was busy dusting the front parlour. She was disturbed by her husband. 'Hey Elsie, I've just been chatting to Edwin from next door, and he says we've got to report our foreigner to the police.'

'You'd better pop down today, then, before they clap us in jail,' replied his wife.

Sitting at his desk in Cambridge borough police station in St Andrews Street, the assistant aliens officer was having a bad week. There had been a renewal of 'Fifth Column' warnings on the wireless, and as a result he had been inundated with reports of suspicious persons, all of whom he had to record for his colleagues on the beat to follow up. The arrival of Mr Serrill to report another foreigner was all he needed.

Having heard the details, he reached for the required form, but then realised there were none left, and that he had forgotten to order replacements. Knowing a report on the wrong piece of paper would bring the wrath of the superintendent down on his head, the assistant aliens officer paused and with a sigh, looked at Mr Serrill. 'Oh, I'm sure he'll drop in and report himself. He sounds genuine enough, I wouldn't worry about him.'

Over supper that night, Ter Braak nearly choked on his meal when Mr Serrill recalled his visit to the police station. 'It seems you've got to call in and register,' he told his lodger.

'Of course, Mr Serrill, I'll pop in tomorrow,' replied the spy, knowing he would be a dead man if he did.

Friday dawned cold and bright, and after his usual morning routine, Ter Braak made his way into town. It was a relief to be able to leave Fifty Shilling Tailors with the waistcoat duly altered. Going northwards, he soon found himself inside the war-hating Mr Overhill's shop. He took his shoes, paid the requested amount of two shillings and three pence and this time managed to leave before the cobbler could bend his ear again.

Making his way back into the town centre, he noticed a group of fed-up soldiers drilling on one of the side roads. He was then held up for quite some time at the traffic lights, as a long convoy of RAF buses drove past down Northampton Street.

Dorothy's Café had become his regular lunch venue. Served by his usual waitress, he reckoned he was at last coming to terms with English cooking and actually enjoyed his simple meal of braised tongue and carrots and peas, followed by treacle tart with watery custard. After leaving his usual tip and with nothing better to do, he decided to stroll back up Sidney Street towards the peaceful grass of Parker's Piece. Much to his annoyance, his progress was halted by a large crowd. Wanting to know what was going on, Ter Braak lingered on the edge of the throng. An elderly lady turned to him with an envious look on her face. 'Doesn't she look smart in her uniform.'

Ter Braak explained he was a Dutch refugee and did not know who he was looking at.

'Oh, that's the Duchess of Gloucester, she's just opened a new servicemen's club.' At that point, the royal visitor was ushered into her car and driven off, with waves from the crowd.

Back at St Barnabas Road, Ter Braak mentioned the encounter to Mrs Serrill. 'Oh, you must have seen Princess Alice. She married the Duke back in 1935 and she's now head of the Women's Auxiliary Air Force.'

'Surely women don't fly planes?'

'No, I don't think so. At any rate my friend Jane's daughter doesn't. She's in the WAAF, and was originally packing parachutes until they discovered she spoke German. Then they sent her off to Bletchley. No idea what she does now, but the main thing is, she's doing her bit.'

Ter Braak recalled changing trains at somewhere called Bletchley on his way to Cambridge. His conversation with the porter while waiting for his train had made him wonder if something special went on there and the posting of someone speaking German sounded promising. 'I've seen all these posters telling us *keep it under your hat*. Surely she shouldn't have told anyone where she'd been sent.'

'Certainly not, but she didn't say so in so many words.'

'What do you mean?'

'She wrote to her mum and said she'd fallen on her feet, and was billeted with her Aunt Joan, and only had a mile to ride her bike to work.'

'I don't understand.'

'Her Aunt Joan is innkeeper of the Shoulder of Mutton, a lovely old thatched tavern in Old Bletchley, about a mile from Bletchley itself. By all accounts her aunt isn't too hampered by rationing, and they all live very well. Anyway, since you're back early, here's the local paper. You might find it interesting.'

Ter Braak had seen the *Cambridge Daily News* lying around the sitting room on previous days, but had considered it rude to pick it up uninvited. Now, he sat back to digest its contents. *RAF heavy blows at Krupp's Engineering Works in Essen*, he read, followed by another upbeat report of a blaze at an oil plant in Cologne.

He realised this was a good way of finding out how the war was progressing. 'Mrs Serrill, I do find this paper interesting. Would you mind if I had a look at it each day, when you've finished with it, of course?'

'Certainly Mr Braak, I'll push it under your bedroom door when we've read it. But make sure you put it in the box out the back when you've finished with it. We've got to save it for the war effort, you know.'

It took Ter Braak a few days to realise that the headlines were always about some success in the war, however minor, with only the briefest of mention of any setback. He reflected that Dr Goebbels was not the only one manipulating the news.

14
LONDON: MI5 HEADQUARTERS

Waiting for news of the missing parachutist was putting a great strain on Brigadier Jasper Harker. 'Winston is going to have my guts for garters if this man isn't found very soon,' he admitted to Guy Liddell, as they met for their regular review meeting.

Liddell had considerable sympathy for his boss, but was unable to give him any good news. 'I'm sorry Sir, but there's still no trace of him.'

'Why do you think this one got away when all the others were rounded up very quickly.'

'This is the first time we haven't had some advance warning by way of the Bletchley decodes of Abwehr radio traffic. Added to that, all ten of the previous agents were notably lacking in knowledge of day to day life over here, with some of them not even speaking English.'

'Not to mention the deliberate mistakes we included in the documents sent over via SNOW.'

Liddell smiled. 'Yes, I couldn't believe our good fortune when Ritter asked Owens for sample ration books and registration cards for the Abwehr to copy. The forgeries carried by our earlier visitors included the mistakes we deliberately included on the documents Owens passed over, but it's ironic that they were exposed by their behaviour well before they had to produce their papers. But, as you say, Sir, if the missing man is carrying similarly flawed documents, he'll hopefully be trapped when he presents them.'

The brigadier still looked worried. 'This man seems to be a cut above his predecessors.'

'True. Although we've congratulated ourselves on the early capture of those previous men, it has to be admitted they were easy prey. This man shows the extent of our difficulties when what appears to be a better trained agent is put up against us.'

'Any news from the regional security liaison officers in the areas surrounding the landing site?'

'No Sir. They're always on the lookout for misfits, and we mustn't forget that Major Dixon in Cambridge already has to his credit the two who arrived in September and Major Naylor in Northampton can claim that last man who arrived in early October.'

Harker picked up a file from his desk. 'Ah yes, that last man, Hans Reysen. I've had a note from the lawyers about him. It seems that as we've used him, albeit somewhat briefly, as a double agent they take the view that we can't now put him on trial as a spy.'

'I agree, if only to avoid the risk of details of his handling coming out in court.'

Harker frowned. 'I wonder now if it was a good idea to use him as an obvious double agent?'

'I was working on the basis that the Abwehr must expect to have some men caught and turned, but it seems we overestimated their skills. Even though his messages were clearly being sent by a man with a different fist, there was no reaction, so I could see no alternative but to close him down.'

'Where did he end up?' asked Harker.

'He was sent to the camp at Huntercombe and will stay there for the duration.'

'Good. Now back to our missing man. What more can we do?'

'I accept that we might be clutching at straws, but I suggest we send young Cholmondeley to the landing site, and let him put his fertile imagination to work, to see if he can figure out what this man might have done.'

The brigadier had no better idea. 'Agreed. Get him off there immediately and let me know if he comes up with anything.'

Flight Lieutenant Charles Cholmondeley, the officer on duty when news of the discarded parachute had arrived, was delighted for the chance to get out of his poky office. His train to Wolverton arrived on time and a taxi took him to Hill Farm at Haversham in a matter of minutes. After telling the driver to wait for him, the flight lieutenant took the bridle path running north to the point where the parachute had been found. The plane that had been chased by a night fighter during the early hours of Saturday 2nd was the most likely to have delivered the parachutist. Cholmodeley stood next to the hedge, trying to imagine what it must have been like for the spy. Weather records showed it had been raining, with cloud cover masking a crescent moon so he reckoned it would have been a miserable and muddy arrival.

He asked himself what he would have done. None of the spies captured so far had any decent maps on them when arrested. Even if this man had been better equipped, he would still have had to lay low until daylight. What landmarks could he have seen?

Just as he was looking for a possible answer, Cholmondeley heard a train whistle, and staring in that direction saw a wisp of smoke from the locomotive rising above the trees in the distance. Even if there had not been a whistle, he reasoned that the missing spy should have seen the same sort of smoke, and with no other landmarks around, would have made his way towards the line in the hope of following it to a station.

Getting out the Ordnance Survey map he had brought with him, the flight lieutenant checked his position, and established that he was about midway between Wolverton and Castle Thorpe stations. Making his way back to the waiting taxi, he found the driver had nodded off. Waking him up, he ordered him to drive to Castle Thorpe, the northerly of the two stations and was soon chatting to the ticket collector, an elderly man of the village who was adamant he had not seen any strangers recently, adding with a smirk that he would soon spot any newcomer as he knew not only the name of every local who passed through his station, but what they did, where they lived and, with a meaningful wink, 'who was doing you know what with who!'

Realising the missing spy had been fortunate not to head for Castle Thorpe station, Cholmondeley set off again in the taxi back to Wolverton, but when the cab reached the right turn to the town, he decided to walk the rest of the way. Paying off the now totally mystified driver, he strode out and before long was crossing the bridge over the River Ouse, with the railway viaduct in the distance. Passing the heavily camouflaged railway carriage and engine works, he wondered if the spy, if indeed he had come that way, knew the works were now repairing Whitley bombers, and converting vans into armoured cars.

Arriving at the station, he made himself known to the stationmaster, and was shown into a small office. After a few moments, a very nervous young woman entered. Cholmondeley put out his hand. 'It's very good of you to spare the time to see me,' he said, smiling in an attempt to put her at ease. ' It's Violet, isn't it?' She nodded.

'I'm sure you've been told already, but what I need to talk to you about is confidential, an official secret in fact, and you're not to mention it to anyone else. That includes your husband, or fiancé, mother, father, brothers, sisters. You do understand?'

'What have I done wrong, Sir?' she asked, on the verge of tears.

'Nothing. Nothing at all. It's just that we think you may have sold a ticket to a German spy. Now, please think back to your first day once again. Can you recall anyone who might fit the bill?'

The young lady looked petrified, and said nothing.

The flight lieutenant prompted her. 'Someone who had difficulty with the money, spoke with a funny foreign accent, or perhaps didn't know where he was?'

Violet thought back to that first day, and the strain she had been under. 'No Sir, but it was quite busy and I was trying very hard to get it right, if only for Percy's sake.'

'Percy? Ah yes, your predecessor, who's now doing his bit on a parade ground somewhere. What about the tickets you sold? Can you remember the destinations?'

'There were so many. A lot going north. I know there were some to Rugby and Stafford. Also quite a few down to London, and a couple to Bedford, one to Oxford, and another to Cambridge. Oh, and a couple to Newmarket, if I remember correctly.'

'Any to Newport Pagnell?'

'Not that I recall. Hardly anyone travels there during the day. They all arrive in the morning, and go back again at night. Most of them work in the railway workshop, but I shouldn't be telling you that, should I?'

The flight lieutenant patted Violet on the arm. 'Don't worry, my dear, I've forgotten already. Thank you, you've been most helpful. That will do for now, but if you think of anything else, just tell the stationmaster. He knows how to get hold of me.' With that, he was gone, leaving a very worried Violet, wondering how she was going to keep to herself the knowledge that there could be a German spy in their midst.

On the train journey back to London, Cholmondeley thought back over the interview, and in particular, the apparent absence of any tickets being sold for Newport Pagnell. Could the man seen struggling with his cases have boarded a train to there by mistake? That seemed a reasonable assumption. Upon that basis, the spy must have intended to travel south, so all travellers going north could be ruled out. But that still left the numerous stations to the south, including London, a proverbial haystack with plenty of places for a needle to hide.

15
GIRTON, NORTH WEST of CAMBRIDGE

A man also searching for something just as elusive as a needle in a haystack was Dickie Dixon. The Cambridge RSLO was enjoying a rare game of golf at Girton golf club with his colleague Jack Hester. Both men had now come to terms with the club house having been requisitioned by the pioneer corps, but still felt annoyed by the presence of sheep on the fairway and the wire fences to keep the animals off the greens. They did however agree that such things had been a small price to pay to prevent the whole course being returned to farmland as had been sought initially by the war agricultural committee.

Dixon had hooked his ball into the rough on the difficult third hole. He knew it could not be far away, as he had seen it drop in front of a nearby tree. Spotting it in some long grass, the major took a six iron from his bag, and settled himself. Although the overhanging branches restricted his backswing, he hit a clean shot and was delighted to see his ball land well down the fairway. Joining his partner, whose last shot was still some distance away, the two took advantage of their isolation and obvious lack of eavesdroppers to discuss the recent discovery of the spy parachute.

Captain Hester voiced his fears. 'When I first heard about that parachute find at Haversham, I was concerned that they'd come to have a look at the new 'Y' Station we're setting up at Hanslope, which is not far away. But that's not my only worry. As you know, my previous voluntary interceptor has succumbed to tuberculosis so now I've no cover in Cambridge itself.'

The major nodded ruefully. 'Yes, I remember, but I'd be surprised if this latest spy has come this way. The Abwehr can only have a limited number of agents they can send over here. I know they weren't aiming precisely for Cambridge, but I reckon the two men who dropped in during September must be our quota for this region.'

'I know all about that chap called Schmidt. Was he the first of the pair?'

'No, that was Gosta Caroli. He's Swedish, aged twenty-seven - a mechanic before the war. He was dropped at Denton in Northants on the 5th of September but managed to knock himself out with his radio when he landed. Sounds daft, but he'd strapped it to his chest and, not surprisingly the set bounced up and struck him neatly under the chin when he hit the ground. In his groggy state, he was soon picked up, and shipped off down to London. Initially he refused to co-operate but he eventually admitted to being a spy. He also mentioned that another man was to follow him. It seemed the men were great mates, and had even arranged to meet at The Black Boy pub in Northampton. Lt. Colonel 'Tin Eye' Stephens, who runs the camp 020 interrogation centre, then pulled a master stroke by offering to spare the life of this second spy if Caroli would help us. That did the trick, and Caroli, who's been given the code name SUMMER, agreed to co-operate and started to transmit messages drafted by us back to his masters in Hamburg.'

'Where's he based?'

'At the moment he's not far away. Recently he let slip that he'd been over here, acting for the Abwehr for some time prior to the war. He hadn't mentioned this before, and there's now some doubt as to his loyalty to us, so he's currently under guard at the Home for

Incurables. That's the cover name we've given to the Old Parsonage at Hinxton, which we've just taken over as a safe house.'

'Ah, yes, I know Hinxton, that's just south of Cambridge. So, Schmidt was the second of the two?'

'That's right, Wulf Schmidt, a twenty-six year-old Dane. He arrived on 19th September and landed near Willingham. Again, he was picked up very quickly. I interviewed him and passed him straight onto 'Tin-Eye', who broke him using the information extracted from Caroli. Poor old Schmidt thought that Caroli had sold him out, rather than saving his life. Schmidt has been christened TATE because Tar thinks he looks like the music hall star Harry Tate.'

The captain frowned. 'I must admit I didn't take much notice of who or what he looked like when he was brought back up here again to try out his transmitter.'

'Ah, yes, that weekend of, what was it, yes, 28th and 29th September. We didn't get much sleep then, and in my book, that was all your fault.'

Hester looked hurt. 'Why do you say that?'

'Because we set his radio up in your office, and it turned out the place was no good for transmitting. What did you blame it on? Bad screening?'

'Yes, but don't forget I tried to get a different building from yours when I was first sent here, although once you'd arranged the Regent Street location, that was never going to happen. We spend money on some daft things, if you ask me, but nothing sensible, like an out of town office for my work.'

'At least we did find somewhere else to try out Schmidt's set. It was fortunate that Nancy was able to persuade her friend, Captain Walker, to let us use his place at Steeple Bumpstead Hall, but that didn't work either if I remember correctly.'

'No, but as I was able to rule out any screening problem or the like, it confirmed my initial thoughts that it's down to the inefficiency of the aerials provided with sets with such a small output.'

'So, the trip up here wasn't a waste of time, then?'

'Not entirely. At least we now know we're going to have to *ginger up* the sets we've taken over, to ensure that our messages get through.'

16
CAMBRIDGE

Ter Braak was becoming concerned at the lack of any acknowledgement of his nightly covert transmissions. After the exhaustion of his first night in St Barnabas Road, he had managed to get off messages every evening.

Although he had mastered the knack of keying Morse code easily back in Hamburg, with his tutor Heinz Valenti rating him as one of his star pupils, he had always struggled to code his messages. He had just about coped with the cardboard disc issued to him during his LENA training, but the more advanced book code introduced when he had been transferred to Dr Praetorius had proved a step too far.

While he had managed to prepare the 'key for the day' by reference to pages within the books related to the date of transmission, the construction of a 'coding square' and the distribution of his wording within it always ended in a message which was undecipherable. The solution had been to take written instructions with him and follow them carefully.

This nightly routine eventually produced a degree of competence that he had never believed possible, but any satisfaction he could take from this success was removed by the lack of any response.

He always listened carefully, but silence was the stern reply.

17
HAMBURG

When the telephone rang in his office, Major Ritter suspected this was the call he had been dreading for days.

The cold, icy voice confirmed his fears. 'How is Fukken? Any news?'

'No Herr Admiral. He has yet to make contact.'

'Why the delay?'

'Difficult to say, Herr Admiral, but it's still only fourteen days since he left, and he may be lying low before setting up his radio.'

'I very much hope so, major. I would remind you of the importance of this mission.' With that Admiral Canaris rang off, leaving the Abwehr officer responsible for spies in Britain in no doubt about his own future should the silence continue.

18
CAMBRIDGE

It was after supper and Ter Braak had been reading that day's edition of the *Cambridge Daily News*, when he spotted details of the conviction of the landlord of the Crown public house in Wellington Street, for receiving stolen goods. A lance corporal of the Royal Norfolk Regiment had also been sent down for stealing the stuff in the first place. Poor devils, he thought, recalling the misery of his own prison sentence.

He checked the date on the paper - 14th November 1940. Fourteen days since his departure from Brussels, and ten undisturbed days in Cambridge. His feeling of smug satisfaction was suddenly banished by the undulating wailing of the air raid siren in Mill Road.

Hampered by her stiff right knee, Mrs Serrill slowly rose to her feet. 'I wonder if I'll ever get used to the horrible sound of that warning. It makes my stomach churn. Come on, let's get down to the shelter. I'll grab something to eat on the way, just in case we're in for a long one.'

Mr Serrill ran upstairs, shouting. 'I'll fetch it while you get down there.'

Wondering what *it* might be, Ter Braak made his way down the garden path to the earth covered curved sheets of corrugated iron that formed the Anderson shelter. Looking up into the dark sky, he wondered who the bombers were targeting. Raids on Cambridge had been relatively limited since his arrival, although planes had passed over, en-route to the industrial areas of the Midlands. He hoped, somewhat selfishly, that it was their turn again.

'In you go, Mr Braak,' urged Mrs Serrill limping down the garden path as fast as she could, carrying a thermos flask of tea and a bag which contained some bread, an open tin of corned beef and a knife. 'Bert should be along in a minute, once he's got it from the bedroom.' She made no attempt to explain further, but Ter Braak assumed she meant the red box which Mr Serrill carried under his arm as he left the house, carefully locking the door after him.

Seeing the look of surprise on his face, Serrill explained. 'Can't be too careful, even now. Old Jack down the road was burgled during the last air raid. You'd think that even thieves would take time off during a war, especially as they can be hanged if they're caught.'

As they all sat inside the shelter, illuminated by the single 60-watt bulb that hung from the curved roof, Mr Serrill carefully put down the red box. 'I wonder who's getting it tonight?' Seeing the quizzical expression on Ter Braak's face, he looked at his wife. 'I don't suppose there's any harm in telling Mr Braak what's in here, is there, Elsie?'

His wife shook her head in agreement. Given this seal of approval, Mr Serrill unlocked the red box. 'This is our deed box where we keep all our valuables,' he said with some pride. 'Not that we have much, but we've got our birth certificates, and of course our marriage lines.' Rummaging through the papers, he pulled out a well-used envelope. Clearing his throat, he tried to continue. 'Got a few keepsakes, and...' His voice tailed off and he quickly replaced the envelope, shut the lid, and put the box down again. Taking out his handkerchief, Mr Serrill wiped his eyes. 'Damn dust in this place,' he cursed.

His wife gently put her hand on his knee. 'Here Bert, have a cup of tea and a corned beef sandwich,' she said as she unpacked her bag of provisions.

Desperate to change the subject, Mr Serrill turned to their lodger. 'So what was it like at Dunkirk then, Mr Braak?'

The spy's stomach churned, and he felt sick. He had no idea, not having been there. 'Terrible, just terrible. I don't like to think about it, but please Mr Serrill, how long have you lived here in Cambridge?'

'I was born here, back in 1870. Just in time to have to go to school, but I was never much of a book person, so I skived off most of the time. Worked on the land until I was fifteen, and then started with good old Eastern Railways. Their line ran from London, through here to Norwich. Stayed with them after they'd become the LMS. By then I'd worked my way up to being a fireman. Finally retired after fifty years. Gave me a clock, they did, it's the one in the front parlour on the mantelpiece. Very proud of that, I am.'

Ter Braak nodded his appreciation. 'Are you local, Mrs Serrill?'

'Yes, I was born here as well. I wanted to be a pianist, used to play the accompaniment to the old silent films, but my father didn't think that's what girls should do, so he got me apprenticed to a hairdresser in town.'

Ter Braak had wondered why Mrs Serrill limped so badly when she walked, and felt that now was an opportunity to ask. 'I hope you don't mind me asking, but what did you do to your leg Mrs Serrill?'

'I caught it on an open cupboard door at work. The doctor gave it a fancy name, but as far as I'm concerned, I buggered the joint. As you'll have noticed, I can hardly bend it now, and it gives me real gyp in cold weather.'

The straight-forward response to his last question gave Ter Braak the confidence to find out more about the Serrills. 'You cope very well Mrs Serrill. How long have you been married?'

'Bert and I got hitched in 1890. We met when he came to see the good old silent films.'

'Yes,' added her husband, with a smile. 'I like a good film, but I must admit, I also liked the music that went with it.'

'You have no family?' ventured Ter Braak, keen to keep the questions away from him. When the pair fell silent, he regretted his inquisitiveness.

After a brief pause Mrs Serrill, in a soft voice, spoke. 'Yes, we had our Fred, but he joined up in 1914, as they all did. Killed at Ypres, in April 1915. We never heard officially, but a good mate of his who we saw after the war said it was a gas attack that did for him.'

Mr Serrill slowly reopened the deed box, and took out the envelope again. 'This is a lock of his hair, from when he was only five. Lovely blond curly hair he had, just like me when I was his age. I suppose he'd have gone bald if he'd lived longer,' he muttered as he ran his hand over his bald patch. Pulling himself together, and wiping a tear from his eye, Mr Serrill made another attempt to change the subject. 'What about you, Mr Braak, do you have any family? Did you have to leave them behind?'

Ter Braak sat quietly for a moment, as he turned over in his mind what to say. His basic cover story provided in Hamburg had not extended to any domestic background as his instructors had deemed such details unnecessary. As a result, he had not given the topic a second thought.

Reasoning that there was less chance of being caught out this way, so long as he did not use his own name, Ter Braak opted for the truth. 'My mother Elizabeth married very young, but she left her husband as he was violent. She left Amsterdam and moved to The Hague, where she met my father. I was the third of their seven children. Mother died giving birth to her eighth, another son, and he passed away as well. As my parents never married I kept my mother's name. Then, after my mother died, we moved to a little town on the coast where my father married the matron of the local military hospital. I couldn't get on with my stepmother, and then the war came...'

Mrs Serrill could sense his embarrassment. 'Well, all I can say is that the last war was supposed to be the war to end all wars, and now look at us.' At this point the *all clear* sounded, and the three stood up, stretched their aching limbs, and trudged back to the house, glad to have survived.

After such a disturbed night, it was no surprise that there was little sign of life from number 258 until later than usual. Ter Braak came down well after nine o'clock, to find Mrs Serrill setting the table for breakfast. 'Morning Mr Braak,' she said cheerfully. 'Sit yourself down and have some toast and tea. Sorry, no butter at all this morning, we've used up our ration for the week.'

He took his place at the table and then noticed Mr Serrill sitting in the corner, his head buried in that day's issue of the *Cambridge Daily News*, which he had walked down to the shop in Mill Road to collect.

'Morning Mr Braak,' he said, without coming out from behind the paper. 'It was Coventry that was bombed last night. Quite a few people killed, and they even got the cathedral,' he moaned. 'But Berlin got it as well,' he added with some glee.

Ter Braak did his best to look pleased at this news.

19
CAMBRIDGE

Raymond Fautley lived for radio. At sixteen years old, he had been the youngest in the country to obtain his *ham* transmitting licence.

Then the war has started, and had been forced to take down his aerial and hand in his set, or face the full fury of the law.

His was not the standard 'wireless' that the bulk of the population switched on each day to hear the latest, and invariably grim, news. It was one he had painstakingly designed and built himself, and was capable of not only receiving, but also transmitting Morse messages to other enthusiasts far afield.

Sitting in his bedroom, Raymond stared idly out of the window at the Cambridge college spires in the distance, and dreamed of the day when he could resume contact with his fellow *hams*. He began to sketch a circuit diagram that he was sure would improve the performance of his transmitter, when he realised his mother was calling him from downstairs.

'Raymond, there's an army captain here to see you. Says he can only talk to you on your own. Whatever have you been up to, my lad?'

The young man could detect the worry in his mother's voice, but could not recall anything he had done that would have attracted the interest of the army. Knowing he was still too young to be called up, he hurried downstairs into the parlour, to be taken aback by the appearance of his visitor, a tall thin man in a uniform that hung off him. He carried a briefcase, and gave Raymond the impression he was a desk bound pen-pusher, enforcing ridiculous regulations, and certainly not a front-line commander. This prejudice was further reinforced when he was asked to sign a piece of paper headed *Official Secrets Act*.

The captain looked intently at Raymond. It had been a long drawn out battle with officialdom to secure permission to approach someone so young, but at long last, he had the authority. 'Hello, Raymond, my name is Captain Hester. I'm sorry for arriving unannounced, but I believe you may be able to serve your country in a very important way. You should know that some background checks have already been carried out on you and your family, but I just need to ask you to confirm a few final points. Please tell me where were you born?'

'Here,' replied Raymond, who was by now intrigued by the man perched on the settee opposite him.

'And your parents?'

'Mum was born in Luton, and Dad here in Cambridge.'

'Thank you Raymond, I'm sure you appreciate I have forms to fill in. I also have to ask you this - do you now support, or have you ever supported, the Communist Party?'

'No, I don't have any interest in politics at all,' replied the mystified Raymond.

The captain smiled. 'That's good. Now, as you have a ham transmitting licence, I know you're able to read Morse code.'

'Yes, but you haven't let me transmit since the war started,' complained Raymond.

'True, although you'll appreciate that we have to control who sends messages these days. In fact, that's why I'm here. I'm the local liaison officer for the radio security service. We're responsible for monitoring enemy radio traffic and I'd like you to join us and act as a voluntary interceptor and listen in to Morse transmissions, logging what you hear. We can't force you at your age, but your skills are desperately needed, especially in this area, where we have a gap in our coverage. How does that sound?'

Raymond could hardly contain his excitement. 'Yes, when do I start?' then, after a pause he added, 'and where do I start?'

'Here at home, and as soon as possible after we've kitted you out.'

'How long will I be expected to do?'

'A daily shift of a few hours. We'll allocate you to a specific range of frequencies.'

'But what about the other times of the day? Won't there be messages all round the clock?'

'Certainly, but you're not alone. We aim to cover everything, 365 days a year. I can't tell you any more as we work on a need to know basis.'

The young Fautley suddenly looked worried. 'I know it won't be for some time, but what happens when I'm called up?'

'Don't worry. When your papers arrive just go to the recruiting office and tell them to call the telephone number I'll give you. You're now exempt from national service in one of the armed forces, but you'll be serving your country in a way that's just as vital.'

'Can I ask one more thing? How did you know about me?'

The captain smiled indulgently. 'I worked in the commercial radio sector before the war, and got to know who was who in the wireless world. As the youngest holder of a ham licence, you've quite a reputation.'

Raymond beamed with delight, but suddenly looked alarmed. 'What do I tell Mum and Dad?'

'Nothing. I'll let them know this is top secret work you'll be doing. Not a word to anyone else, you understand.'

On his way out, the captain spoke to a startled Mr and Mrs Fautley, and then disappeared, leaving an excited Raymond and a mother and father desperate to know more. Their son stuck to the letter of the Official Secrets Act and refused to say a word, but his parents naturally presumed it was all to do with his obsession with wireless. This conclusion was confirmed a few days later, when two men arrived with a receiver and a box containing various forms, some envelopes with SECRET stamped on them, and further larger envelopes with gummed labels addressed to PO Box 25, Barnet, Herts.

Raymond was soon into the routine of posting his daily log sheets to Arkley View, the country house hiding behind the mysterious PO Box Number and the headquarters of the radio security service, where they were collated and then taken by motorcycle courier to Bletchley Park for decoding.

20
CAMBRIDGE

After carefully counting the days, Ter Braak reckoned the professor should now have returned and with a mixture of anticipation and apprehension, he telephoned from the first phone box that was vacant.

The response was prompt and courteous. 'Professor Carpenter's office, How may I help you?'

'Hello. My name is Ter Braak and I called a few weeks ago. Is the professor back yet? I have a message from Dr Rantzau.'

'Yes indeed. Hold the line, and I'll put you through.'

After a slight pause, a cautious voice responded. 'Hello, this is Professor Carpenter. I understand you have a message from a Dr Rantzau. Who is he? Are you sure you have the right number?'

Ter Braak panicked and blurted out, 'Yes, yes, that was the name Major Ritter gave me. He was sure you would recognise it and be able to help me.'

Professor Carpenter froze. Major Nikolaus Ritter was indeed an old friend, and Dr Rantzau was his alias. But he worked for the Abwehr, the German secret service. Could this call be from MI5? Was it a trap?

In the end, caution ruled the day. 'I'm sorry Mr Ter Braak, I don't know a Dr Rantzau or a Major…what was his name? Ah yes, Ritter. I won't be able to help you. Good day.' With that the line went dead.

Ter Braak's heart sank. How was he going to find Maud now? With no idea where to look next, he left the phone box and walked without caring where he was going. Bumping into another person brought him to his senses. Looking up, he found himself not far away from Dorothy's Café. A few minutes later he was sitting at his usual table sipping a cup of tea and thinking.

Why had Professor Carpenter denied knowing Major Ritter? Perhaps his call had sounded like a trap. Yes, that must have been it. But, how could he show that it was not? He knew he was unlikely to get anywhere with his mission without help.

The spy's determination started to dissolve, and a feeling of loneliness swept over him. Then, it was if a light had been switched on. Since his original encounter with Marge, he had resisted temptation to return to her dingy dwelling, but he knew her bed was the only place where he would find some comfort. After paying for his tea he set off walking as quickly as he could to Gothic Street.

On the other side of town, Professor Carpenter was having second thoughts about the phone call. Perhaps it had been a mistake to deny all knowledge of Nick Ritter. What if that man Ter Braak had indeed been a German agent in need of help? Was that a missed opportunity to help Adolf Hitler win this war? Would Ter Braak get in touch again?

Marge welcomed her visitor warmly. 'It's lovely to see you again Jan, but what's the problem, my lover? Is this terrible war getting you down?'

Knowing it was impossible to explain the real reason for his surprise visit and his black mood, Ter Braak nodded. 'Yes. I can see no end to it. I might never see home again.'

Marge smiled. 'There are an awful lot of people in the same boat, but if you want my advice, you should live for today. There's no telling what tomorrow will bring.' With that, she began to unbutton her dress.

Ter Braak lay back and decided not to worry about the future, or his fiancé, for the time being.

21
CAMBRIDGE

Prompted by the lack of a reply to his nightly transmissions, and the gradual death of his batteries, Ter Braak decided now was the time to buy the ingredients for his secret ink, and start writing to the PO Box number in Madrid that he had been given, with his real message hidden behind some innocent text.

Opting for a chemist well away from St Barnabas Road, he was taken aback when told that one of the items, amidopyrine, was on the poisons list and that he would have to sign the poisons register, stating what he wanted it for. Having no idea what legitimate reason he could cite, he muttered something about checking his needs, and beat a hasty retreat, concluding that secret writing was not an option.

This piled further pressure on Ter Braak, and his feeling of isolation became almost unbearable. If only he could persuade the professor to help him, but maybe this person was not the saviour Major Ritter had led him to expect. These doubts plagued him for the rest of the day, until just before supper when his landlord took him completely by surprise.

'Mr Braak, do you think Preston North End will beat Manchester City again this weekend?'

'Sorry, Mr Serrill, I don't know what you mean.'

'Apologies, lad, I should explain. I'm talking about football, the real English religion. You know, if I have one real gripe with old Adolf, it's that he's put a stop to this season's proper matches. I can forgive him some things, but never that.' Calming down he scratched his chin, deep in thought. 'Preston beat them last week at home, but away…I doubt it. No, I'll put that one down as a home win. I'd better get my coupon filled in, buy a postal order and get them in the post. It would be nice to have a win just before Christmas.'

The spy's natural curiosity prompted him to ask, 'How do you celebrate Christmas in your country?'

'We used to have a really good time with lots to eat and drink, but that was when you could get what you wanted, if you had the cash, of course. Nowadays, what with all this rationing, I don't know what Elsie and I'll do, even if we have a win on the football pools. As always, we'll go to the midnight service at the Church at the end of the road on Christmas Eve, that's if it isn't cancelled because of the blackout. If it is, we'll go to the morning service on the 25th.

'The 25th of December?' asked an amazed Ter Braak.

'Yes, when else is Christmas?'

'We celebrate St Nicholas Eve on 5th December. That's when we exchange our surprises - what I think you call presents, but ours are all wrapped up to disguise what's in them and tradition has it that they should also be accompanied with a short bit of verse, but I'm not very good at that, so I usually leave it out.'

'But what do you do on 25th December?'

'Not very much,' replied the spy.

Mrs Serrill put her hand on Ter Braak's arm. 'Well, you're very welcome to spend it with us. As you know, we've no family now, but I warn you, it's not going to be a feast this year.'

Ter Braak was taken aback by this spontaneous gesture. His immediate reaction was to refuse. After all, the Serrills were the enemy. It then dawned on him that he no longer thought of the them that way. The spy surrendered. 'That's very kind of you, Mrs Serrill, I'll happily join you after I've attended mass at the catholic church in town, provided that isn't cancelled as well.'

'That's settled then,' responded a pleased Mr Serrill, who retired behind his paper once again.

The thought of spending Christmas with his landlord and landlady reminded Ter Braak that he needed do something about his hair. Not having had it cut before his sudden departure from Hamburg, it was now looking distinctly on the shaggy side.

As Mr Serrill had his head in the paper, he turned to Mrs Serrill, who was knitting a pair of socks. 'Do you know where I could get a haircut?'

He had completely forgotten she had trained as a hairdresser, and was stunned when she put down her knitting, pulled out a chair from the table, and in a voice that brooked no argument, told him to sit down. 'I'll give you a trim as fast as you can say Jack Robinson.'

He did as he was told, while wondering who 'Jack Robinson' was. Mrs Serrill produced an old sheet, which she tucked into his shirt collar and taking her comb and hairdressing scissors from the top drawer of the sideboard, was soon snipping away.

'It's good to have a nice head of hair to get my teeth into,' she muttered, while glancing across at her husband's bald patch. It was at this point that Ter Braak realised Mrs Serrill was trimming his neck with a cut-throat razor. He was about to protest, but thought better of it, and sat transfixed until she announced she had finished by removing the sheet with a flourish.

Glancing at himself in the mirror on the wall over the sideboard, he had to admit his hair looked much neater. 'That's very good of you, Mrs Serrill, how much do I owe you?'

'Oh, don't worry about it, it's nice to keep my hand in.'

Mr Serrill put down his paper. 'I'll tell you what. I've got to go to the doctors next Monday. My bunions are giving me hell. Now, Monday is washday, and I won't be able to help Elsie. Would you be able to stand in for me?'

Mrs Serrill looked hopeful. 'Yes, that would certainly get us out of a corner. I'll show you what to do, and a strong young man like yourself shouldn't have any trouble.'

Ter Braak was unsure what he would be letting himself in for. He had always been out on Mondays, to come back to the washing all done and ready for ironing the following day. Accepting that he could hardly refuse, he nodded. 'Yes, I'll do that for you, and thanks again for the haircut. You've not lost your touch.'

'Morning Mr Braak. Don't forget it's washday!'

The cheery voice of Mrs Serrill outside his bedroom door sent shivers down his spine. Regretting that he had not just gone to a barber, and avoided all this worry, Ter Braak got up and dressed. Descending the stairs, he found Mrs Serrill already in action.

'Just a mo, Mr Braak, while I put these in to soak.' She lifted the lid of the *copper*. Steam billowed out of the boiler, only to be smothered by the pile of coloured washing she dropped in. 'Let's have some breakfast now, while there're all doing nicely.'

As Ter Braak sat down to enjoy the meal, the absurdity of the situation suddenly struck him. He had been told by his spymaster to integrate with the locals, but...helping with the weekly wash? He managed to stifle a snigger.

The stop for tea and toast was all too brief, and the pair were soon back in action, with Ter Braak receiving constant instructions and encouragement. Heaving the wet sheets and other *whites* out of the rinsing water, turning the handle of the mangle, and repeating the process again and again exhausted Ter Braak. By the time it came to the final rinse and the addition of the *blue bag*, he was a physical wreck, and had to sit down to recover. Mrs Serrill, who was used to this weekly test of stamina, put a cup of tea in front of him. ' Drink that, and you'll soon feel better. Then you can help me with the pegging out.'

When Mr Serrill returned home, his wife explained that their lodger had been a great help, but had exhausted himself in the process, and been obliged to go for a lie down on his bed before supper. Discreet listening at his bedroom door verified he was fast asleep.

'I'm glad he was able to help. I felt bad at having to leave you on your own, especially on washday, but at least the doctor has given me some cream to put on my bunions.'

Mrs Serrill sighed. 'Yes, he was a help, but he's not as fit as you are, even though he's probably less than half your age. But you know what, I've just realised, I've never had any pyjamas or nightshirt from him to wash. You don't suppose he sleeps in the...'

'Nude, you mean? Well, he must do, unless he leaves his underwear on. But these foreigners have funny ways, so unless you ask him, or burst in on him while he's in bed, I don't suppose we'll ever know.'

22
HAMBURG

Major Nikolaus Ritter was becoming desperate. His deputy, Captain Boeckel, knew Ter Braak had left but had not been told of the special mission - he thought the Dutchman was still part of the LENA spy programme.

'Why do you think he's not made contact?' questioned the captain.

The major took off his wire rimmed glasses and polished them carefully. 'I wish I knew. He may have been caught but that would be very bad luck, especially after I took great care not to have his drop date announced to anyone in advance, including *JOHNNY*.'

'I thought *JOHNNY* had proved his loyalty, especially when he gave us the details of those ration books and identity cards.'

'I agree he earned his crust then, but suppose he's had a change of heart? Just think about it, he's got one of our radios and our codes and if he's passed those over, MI5 could be reading all our transmissions.'

'Surely the really important stuff is coded using an Enigma machine, which I am told is impossible to crack, with the number of permutations running into the millions.'

'Yes, it is indeed. One of the better things we've adopted if you ask me. But this silence from Ter Braak could be the death of me. If we don't hear something very soon, we must send someone else to fill his place.'

Boeckel found this a strange reaction. Other LENA spies had been lost and his boss had merely shrugged his shoulders. Why was he so concerned this time? In the absence of any explanation he knew not to ask any further questions.

23
CAMBRIDGE

Breakfast was normally a relaxed affair, but Ter Braak nearly had a heart attack when Mr Serrill put down his paper and casually announced, 'Oh, Elsie, I forgot to tell you, Edwin next door says he saw a radio detection van driving around the town centre the other night. You know, they have an aerial poking out of the roof.'

The spy felt sick, and made a supreme effort to control his features. He carefully put down his teacup. His hand shook, and the cup rattled slightly on the saucer. To give his trembling fingers something to do, he picked up his knife and carefully redistributed the sliver of butter around his piece of toast. He glanced across at his landlady and was surprised by the look on her face. She was also clearly perturbed. 'They must be checking up on who hasn't got a licence for the wireless. You have renewed ours, haven't you, Bert?'

A look of panic crept across her husband's face. He jumped up, and rummaged in the top drawer of the sideboard. Eventually, and with some relief, he flourished a small certificate in the air. 'Here it is. I knew I'd done it. Our ten bob takes us to the end of April next year, so it can't be us they're after.'

His wife relaxed. 'Thank goodness. But I wonder who they're looking for?'

'There's plenty around here who'd try to get away with it.'

'We're always being told to keep listening to the wireless these days. You'd think that they'd stop the need for a licence when there's a war on, wouldn't you?' complained Mrs Serrill.

'I suppose so. But, hey, what if it's a German spy that they're after. What do you think Mr Braak? You've had dealings with Germans before, haven't you?'

Ter Braak was not expecting to be drawn into the conversation, and nearly choked on his toast. He took a mouthful of tea to give himself time to think. 'I really couldn't say, Mr Serrill. I did my best to keep out of the way.'

'Quite right too. Oh, well, perhaps we'll find out when the boys in blue send one of their Black Marias round to collect the poor soul.'

The spy sat quietly, trying not to look as scared as he felt. He excused himself as soon as he could, and once in the solitude of his room, sat on his bed to contemplate what to do. He knew he had to get the set out of the house. But where to hide it? He then remembered his as yet unused office which would be ideal. But how to get the radio case out without being seen? He always went out after breakfast, usually in the full view of either Mr or Mrs Serrill. To leave suddenly with a suitcase would undoubtedly provoke awkward questions.

It took some time to work out what to do, but then it came to him. The Serrill's life was one of routine. They always did the same thing on each day of the week. Yesterday was wash day. Today, Tuesday, was the ironing. Tomorrow, Wednesday, Mr Serrill played at being a soldier with the home guard and Mrs Serrill disappeared off in her WVS uniform. That was it. Tomorrow was the day to hang around after breakfast and leave with the radio when the coast was clear.

Ter Braak spent the next twenty-four hours in a state of panic, but no-one arrived looking for his radio. He managed to get through breakfast, and as soon as he was alone in the house, he slipped out with his radio case in hand. Walking as fast as he could to the station he took one of the many waiting taxis to Green Street. Giving the girl behind the ground-floor counter of Haslops a cheery wave, he ran up the stairs to his office and locked the set in the cabinet.

Ter Braak had transmitted every night, and lived in hope that one day he would hear from Hamburg, but having to hide his set put an end to that dream. His mood became blacker each day, relieved only by the now regular visits to Marge, who confided to Jan that she considered him a friend rather than a client, although she still expected payment for her services. Having managed to overcome his earlier feelings of guilt towards his fiancé, Ter Braak began to wish that Marge would move to a better area, the dilapidated state of Gothic Street really depressed him.

Sitting in Dorothy's Café, sipping his cup of tea, he reviewed his position. By now, someone would probably have found the parcel he had left behind the hedge. But had they traced him to Cambridge? Routine anti- surveillance measures, one of the few skills he had been taught properly in Hamburg, appeared to suggest no-one was following him. He felt reasonably safe for the time being.

Ter Braak's thoughts then turned to Professor Carpenter. Suddenly he had a brainwave. He would see if the professor's home address was listed in one of the directories in the library. Then he could at least think about making contact again.

Sunlight shone through the domed glass roof of the public library as he made his way to where the almanacs were kept. Glancing along the relevant shelf he had a sudden flicker of fear when there was no sign of *Spaldings*. He grabbed the *Blue Book*, and retired to a nearby table.

With bated breath, he turned to the list of *Residents* under *C'* and then his heart sank. *Carpenter* was listed fifteen times. Taking out his notebook and pencil, he carefully copied down the addresses. Returning the *Blue Book* to the shelf, he quietly made his way from the library, knowing he had a long job in front of him.

After walking back to St Barnabas Road, he let himself in and was surprised to find both Mr and Mrs Serrill in the parlour with a pretty young woman whom he guessed was in her early twenties.

Mr Serrill introduced her. 'Mr Braak, this is Maud Thorpe. She used to live down the road until she married her Charlie. Now she's moved to Peterborough.'

Ter Braak froze at the name of Maud. Could this be the person he had been sent to find? How could he find out? He decided to sit quietly and listen as Mr Serrill started explaining that Mr Thorpe was now away in the RAF serving as air-crew.

Maud raised her eyebrows and stared at Mr Serrill disapprovingly. Keen to change the subject, she explained that letters had not always being forwarded from her previous address. 'It's all sorted out now. At least my Charlie knew where he should write to.'

'How is Charlie?' asked Mrs Serrill.

'He's okay. We've worked out a bit of a code, so he can tell me what he's up to, without the censor blue pencilling it.'

Ter Braak tried not to look too interested at the reference to a code, but blurted out, 'How do you do that then, if you don't mind me asking?'

'That would be telling, wouldn't it,' smiled the young lady. 'The silly thing is, I'm not able to write to him about my job as they never tell us what we're making. I often pass the time by imagining we're turning out a part for a new weapon that will win the war in days.'

Ter Braak looked carefully at Maud, but could not tell if she was joking or not. He tried another tack. 'So, what do you do? Make the tea?'

The reply was instant and indignant. 'No, I don't. My move to Peterborough was the best thing I've ever done, as I've been trained as a machinist. I operate a capstan lathe, and turn out whatever's needed. I can now work to an accuracy of one thousandth of an inch, I'll have you know!'

The spy looked suitably humbled. 'I'm so sorry, but in my country, Holland, women don't do that sort of work. Are there many of you?'

'Oh yes. Even though the skilled men were exempt from being called up, many wanted to do their bit. That left the firm short-handed, especially as they're now busier than before the war. So they took on lots of us women, and we've proved to be just as good as the men.'

'Sounds hard work. What sort of hours do you do?'

'It's bloody hard, I can tell you. My normal week is a twelve hour day, starting at seven in the morning, Monday to Thursday, with another ten hours on Friday. If that wasn't enough we're quite often asked, well, required to work overtime, sometimes up to another eight hours on Saturday and again on Sunday. There's another shift each day, so we're working around the clock.'

Ter Braak looked aghast. 'That sounds terrible. I hope you get well paid.'

'Not really, but there's a bonus scheme. We're given a target for each job, but most of the times are too tight to earn any decent money.'

'What about holidays?'

'I'm married, so I can have seven days off four times a year, when my Charlie's on leave. He's due some next month. I can't wait to see him again.' Blushing, she added in a soft voice, 'He signed his last letter NORWICH.'

Mrs Serrill giggled. 'And quite right too! Is today classed as a holiday?'

'No, I managed to swing a welfare half day, but I'm not getting paid for it. But here's me going on. I must catch my bus back home.' With that Maud stood up, said her goodbyes, and was off.

Mr Serrill was dumbstruck. 'I didn't know she worked those sorts of hours. I didn't do anything like that on the railways, but then us firemen had a good union to fight our corner, and I suppose there wasn't a war on. But over seventy hours a week...' His voice tailed off in sheer admiration.

Ter Braak sat quietly, but was obliged to acknowledge there was clearly nationwide support for the war effort, and his blind faith in a Nazi victory dimmed slightly. After a minute or two, he plucked up the courage and asked the pair, 'What does NORWICH mean? Is it part of a code?'

Mrs Serrill got up. 'My Bert will tell you,' and she left the room chuckling. Mr Serrill leaned forward and whispered in his ear. 'It's simple really, it stands for *knickers off ready when I come home*. I know knickers is spelt with a K but I suppose KORWICH doesn't sound quite the same.'

The spy burst out laughing, soon joined by Mr Serrill. The two agreed it was a clever piece of coding before playing a game of darts to pass the time until the evening meal. Ter Braak found it difficult to concentrate as he thought about Maud. Could she be the person he had been sent to find? She had mentioned a new weapon, but in Peterborough. Perhaps things had changed. After all, Maud used to live here in Cambridge. Was she joking or was that just a slip of the tongue?

His deliberations were interrupted by a cry from Mrs Serrill. 'Look, Maud has left her gloves and scarf behind.'

Looking at his watch, Mr Serrill groaned. 'She'll be well on her way back to Peterborough by now. We'll have to put them in the post for her.'

Mrs Serrill shook her head. 'She didn't leave her new address. We'll have to hang on to them until she calls in again.'

Ter Braak saw his chance to take a trip to Peterborough and see if this was the Maud he had been sent to find. 'I need to check on some of my countrymen in Peterborough, so I could take the gloves and scarf with me and drop them in to her at her workplace. Do you know where it is?'

Mr Serrill scratched his head. 'Now, she did tell me. Let me think... I'm sure it's Bakers something. Would you, Mr Braak? I'm sure Maud would be grateful.'

The spy smiled. 'It'll be a pleasure, I can assure you. I'll go there tomorrow.'

24
CAMBRIDGE

Arriving at the bus station in Drummer Street, Ter Braak soon spotted a cream and red single-decker Eastern Counties bus with the number *150* and *Peterborough* on the destination board. He climbed onboard, and came face to face with a pretty clippie, who handed him a ticket to Peterborough in exchange for the sum of one shilling and ninepence. Taking one of the rear window seats, he checked again that the scarf and gloves belonging to Maud were safe in his coat pocket.

It was a cold day, and the warmth in the bus meant condensation had formed on the inside of the windows. Wiping the glass with the back of his hand, Ter Braak peered out and was surprised to see workmen still labouring away on what could only be a pillbox or an air raid shelter. Feeling sure he had seen that building before, and in very much the same state, he wondered why it was taking so long.

Just then, the diesel engine of the bus burst into life, and pumped out a cloud of black oily smoke which drifted over the frost-covered grass of Christ's Pieces. The conductress closed the passenger door, rang the bell twice in rapid succession, which prompted the bus to move away, slowly.

It seemed to take forever to get out of the town, but soon they were bowling merrily along. The rhythmic throbbing of the diesel engine, and the slight swaying of the bus soon had Ter Braak's eyelids drooping. He had not slept well the night before, and had lain awake for hours, worried at the thought of his first venture away from Cambridge. Ter Braak was soon fast asleep, and only woke when the clippie tapped him on the arm as the bus reached Peterborough. The spy stepped out onto the pavement, not knowing where to go. His recent researches came to mind, and he knew he needed to find a library, and see if they had anything helpful in their reference section.

As he wandered towards what he took to be the town centre, he came across *Ellis Bell,* a smart menswear shop. Among the various items displayed in the window, Ter Braak was rather taken with a range of shirts labelled *Consulate.* Walking in, he was approached by a tall man in a black morning coat, who enquired how he could help.

'I'm looking for a shirt and I rather like the look of one of your brands, the *Consulate*. You have one in the window.'

'What size, Sir?'

'I'm sorry, I don't know.'

'Well, Sir, you look like a fifteen or perhaps a fifteen and a half. I'd better measure you. Please come this way.' He followed the man to the back of the shop, where he was duly measured. He then selected a rather natty blue striped shirt. He was just about to say that was all he wanted when he spotted some very smart hand-knitted sleeveless pullovers. Wandering over, he felt the material, which had the texture and softness of an expensive wool. Before he knew it, he had tried on a brown one. The man was a skilled salesman, and although he had no advance knowledge at all, hinted that clothing was likely to 'go on the ration sooner rather than later.'

The very mention of rationing, and by implication, ration books, sent a shiver down Ter Braak's spine, and he quickly agreed to buy two, without even asking the price. When presented with the bill, he had a sudden pang of conscience. Should he have spent over four pounds on a shirt and two pullovers? Parting with the cash, he convinced himself this was a reward for the risks he was taking.

On his way out, he turned to the salesman. 'I'm trying to find a factory called Baker something. I have some things to deliver.'

'Oh, you want Baker Perkins. They're at the Westwood Works. If you turn right out of here and make your way to the railway you'll see the factory on the other side of the line. It's enormous, you can't miss it.'

Following those directions, Ter Braak soon spotted the camouflaged buildings on the far side of the track, all surrounded by a tall wire fence. Making his way over the bridge, he arrived at the works entrance. Taking a deep breath, he walked purposely up to the gatehouse.

'Good morning, I'm here to return some belongings to Mrs Maud Thorpe,' he announced.

The gateman frowned. 'Mrs Thorpe, eh. Now what might those belongings be, Sir?'

Ter Braak took out the scarf and gloves and held them up. 'She left these behind at my house in Cambridge.'

'I see, Sir. Do you have any identification?'

Ter Braak held his breath and handed over his registration card. The gateman, making the most of his moment of power, stared at it studiously and noted the address of *Cambridge, 7 Oxford Street*. It never occurred to him that it was unusual to put the town before the street, and of course had no idea that Oxford Street did not exist. Handing back the card, he announced, 'Looks in order, Sir. However, I'm not allowed to let you in on your own, and you'll have to leave those parcels with me.'

Ter Braak handed over his purchases and did his best to appear relaxed as the gateman took his time to organise the necessary chaperone. Following his guide, his euphoria at gaining entry was suddenly shattered by a shout of 'Sir, please come back here.' Turning around, and fearing the worst, he duly obeyed, wondering how far he would get if he started running. Much to his relief, the gateman merely pinned a Visitors Badge on his coat, with an apology. 'Sorry Sir, I nearly forgot. We don't want you arrested as a spy, now do we?'

The spy agreed enthusiastically.

His escort led him to the door to the machine shop, and left him with a cheerful, 'There you are mate.' Once inside, Ter Braak was taken aback by the noise and smell of oil which assaulted his senses. He was amazed to see rows of women, leant over their machines, concentrating, all wearing blue overalls with nets over their hair. Approaching a woman operating a lathe, he stood patiently while she skilfully skimmed metal from a spinning rod, the ribbons of curly swarf spiralling away into a bin on the floor. Such was her focus that it was some time before she spotted the visitor. Hitting the stop button, she stood up, and adding to the greasy marks on her face by wiping her brow, she shouted to him., 'What do you want, then? You're not another of those work study bods, are you?'

Showing her the scarf and gloves, Ter Braak shouted back to her. 'I'm here to return these to Maud Thorpe. Where will I find her?'

'Over there,' the woman said, pointing to the far left corner of the workshop. 'Mind how you go. Don't get too close to the machines. Some of them will rip your arms off if you give them half a chance.'

With that warning ringing in his ears, Ter Braak picked his way carefully through the equipment, and soon recognised Maud, working at her lathe. Seeing him, she switched it off and greeted him with a beaming smile. 'Hello, Mr Braak, what are you doing here?' Handing over the gloves and scarf, he was thanked with a peck on the cheek. 'I didn't think I'd see these again. I realised I'd left them with Bert and Elsie as I was on my way to the bus station, but I didn't have time to go back.'

Ter Braak was about to say it had been a pleasure, when a wailing siren started up. Maud wiped her hands on her overalls. 'Another bloody air-raid. You'd better follow me. We're in D Shelter.' The pair joined the throng walking purposefully towards the exit door, and he soon found himself inside an underground bunker, along with many workers, mostly women machinists.

Ter Braak found it easy to sit quietly and listen to the general chatter. It was obvious he was not seen as a threat and he soon established that the main products being turned out were mobile canteens and definitely not a new weapon. It was inevitable that he was eventually asked how he came to be in England, and without thinking trotted out his cover story, reinforced by a vitriolic denouncement of all things German.

Comforted by the warm response this provoked, Ter Braak began to relax, when a young woman sitting opposite spoke up. 'My husband was rescued from Dunkirk. So, which ship picked you up?'

Cursing himself for his reference to the evacuation, about which he knew nothing, Ter Braak mumbled, 'I can't remember. It was so terrible.'

The young lady nodded. 'Yes, I suppose it was, but how did you manage to get on board, you being a foreigner, and perhaps a spy?'

Ter Braak's heart nearly stopped. He had no idea what to say. The likelihood of exposure faced him. Then, to his relief, the sound of a bomb exploding in the distance brought silence in the shelter. As further blasts grew closer, the structure shook and dust fluttered down from the roof. Ter Braak began to wonder if his salvation would also be his end but just as quickly as it had started, the air raid was over. The all-clear was greeted with a muted cheer, and making sure he stayed well clear of his earlier questioner, Ter Braak filed out along with the others. Finding Maud, the spy said his goodbyes quickly, and made his way back to the gatehouse to return his pass and retrieve his parcels.

Walking back towards the bus station, his mind still in a turmoil over his narrow escape, Ter Braak took a wrong turning and soon became lost. While wondering what to do he reached a church, identifiable from the notice board as *St Peters and All Saints Catholic Church*. He took this as divine intervention, and decided to sit in a pew and get his breath back.

Pushing open the door, he crossed himself as he stood at the top of the aisle. Looking around, he saw a priest with his back to him, changing the hymn numbers. Ter Braak's natural instinct was to turn and leave as fast as he could, but instead he stood rooted to the spot when the priest glanced round. 'Good day my son. Please don't go. If you wish to give your confession, I'm Father Patrick, and I'm here to take it. The confessional is over there to your left. I'll be with you in a moment.'

Ter Braak was about to say that he just wanted to sit quietly, but instead found himself making his way to the confessional. Father Patrick took his time following him. He always did his best to ensure his administration of the sacrament of penance was in private, and that he did not see the penitents. While he had seen the face of this penitent, he excused himself by the fact that he had no idea who it was. The foreign accent certainly came as a surprise, but nothing compared with what followed.

Father Patrick sat quietly, trying desperately to gather his thoughts. In all his years in the catholic church, he had never been so stunned. The man who had just left had confessed to being a German spy. He had claimed his role was no different to anyone else taking part in the war, and that there were undoubtedly English spies on the other side of the channel.

As a priest, Father Patrick had endeavoured to take the moral high ground. 'You may well be correct, my son, but not all actions in war are justified. National patriotism, or indeed obeying orders without question, can never be an excuse for an evil act. Wouldn't it be better to give yourself up?'

'If I did, I'd be hanged, that's for sure.'

Following the directions given to him by the priest, Ter Braak walked quickly back to the bus station. As he arrived, a number 150 bus was just about to pull away. Clambering aboard, he bought a ticket back to Cambridge, and slumped into the nearest seat.

The return journey was a blur, not due to the condensation within the bus, or the now darkening skies, but to the myriad of thoughts spinning around in his head. He had hoped that giving his confession would ease his mind, but instead it had left him in a state of confusion. That he was entitled to anonymity had been good news and helped justify the use of a false identity, but he had been taken aback when the priest had implied that his very confession of being a spy suggested he must have some feelings of guilt. He had argued that spies had been part of warfare for centuries, but did not feel he had been very convincing.

His thoughts then turned to poor Father Patrick. What else could he have done? He obviously had not come across an enemy agent before. Ter Braak was consoled by the fact he had been granted absolution. He was still asking himself why he had considered it necessary to admit to spying as a sin, when he fell asleep, only to be woken again by the clippie as the bus reached Cambridge.

Back in his room, Ter Braak lay on his bed, trying to regain some composure before going downstairs for supper. He had to accept that the day had been a waste of time, and he was no nearer to finding Maud.

He knew he needed the help of Professor Carpenter and vowed to start checking the fifteen names tomorrow.

25
CAMBRIDGE

Collapsing onto his usual chair in Dorothy's Café, Ter Braak thought back over his decision to return his radio to his bedroom. While it had been locked away in his office, there had been no further sign of the detector van, but the lack of a suitable earth connection had ruled out operating it from there. Having it available again for his nightly transmissions had been a relief, even though he had still to receive an acknowledgement of any of his messages.

He glanced down at his old shoes, which he was wearing again after being re-soled. The new pair had turned out not to be as comfortable as they had looked. He reckoned they should wear in eventually, but the miles he was walking around the town in search of the elusive professor were already taking their toll and the addition of blisters was something he was keen to avoid.

His street plan had made finding the various Carpenters listed in the *Blue Book* quite straightforward. He had trudged around the town to visit all fifteen, dismissing a few as not the sort of place where a university professor would live. It was only after he had worked his way through every address without any apparent success that he realised his judgement must have been wrong.

Finishing his tea he got up to start again, this time vowing to make discreet local enquiries or wait around and covertly look at the actual occupants before crossing them off his list.

It took some time to narrow his search down to a property in Clements Place, a short road off Park Street and near to the Round Tower. He had discounted this originally as a scruffy road, but it turned out that the place he sought was a thatched cottage right at the end. He had a gut feeling that this was where he would find Professor Carpenter, but he had to be sure.

Wandering around Park Street and Clements Place, Ter Braak watched carefully and eventually spotted a person walking purposefully, and carrying a bulging leather case. Judging that a professor would carry papers, he followed at a discreet distance. His theory was soon proved correct, as his quarry disappeared inside the thatched cottage.

The spy was then assaulted by mixed emotions. He was delighted to have found the person who could be his saviour. But what if Professor Carpenter was no longer a supporter of Adolf Hitler, or had been exposed and was being used by MI5 as bait?

Ter Braak kept an eye on the academic, and it soon became clear that Professor Carpenter had a regulated life, with tutorials taking up most of the working day. The exception was the afternoon when Ter Braak trailed his target to the entrance of the Arts Theatre, where posters announced the matinee performance of a comedy thriller, *Cottage to Let*. Following the professor into the lobby, he found himself in the queue for the box office. Deciding that to walk out now would arise some suspicion, he bought a ticket, and was soon settled into his seat in the circle just two rows behind the professor, who was now amongst a group of students.

He cursed when he realised that this could only be a study visit. Any thoughts of leaving were banished when the lights dimmed and the curtains opened. Ter Braak decided he may as well sit back and enjoy the performance.

It was not until after the first interval and the opening of Act Two that the penny dropped, and Ter Braak suddenly had to stop himself from laughing. The plot was all about British wartime secrets being betrayed to Germany, and the challenge was to spot the traitor.

However, the script cleverly implicated virtually everyone on stage. He eventually decided that a character called Perry was the villain with someone called Dimble being the MI5 man. His smug satisfaction knew no bounds when the ringleader of the German spy ring was indeed confirmed as Perry, who was shot by Dimble, the undercover British Agent. The genuine spy concluded that it took one spy to recognise another.

At the end of the play, the cast took their curtain call, and Ter Braak joined in the applause, not only to blend in with the remainder of the audience, but also acknowledging it had been an enjoyable afternoon, in spite of the irony. After standing to attention for the national anthem, Ter Braak made his way to the exit. Seeing that the professor was still surrounded by undergraduates, he set off to walk back to St Barnabas Road in the gathering gloom, realising he still needed to know if he could trust the academic. He decided to keep an eye on the thatched cottage for a few more weeks and see what happened.

Letting himself in at number 258, he was greeted by Mrs Serrill. who, as always, asked, 'Hello Mr Braak. Had a busy day?'

When Ter Braak had first moved in with the Serrills, he had feared she was suspicious, and was trying to trap him, but it soon became clear his landlady was just a naturally curious person. He normally gave her a straight faced, non-committal response, followed by what he had come to realise was a favourite British habit, a moan about the weather.

This time a grin played across his face, spotted immediately by Mrs Serrill.

'Mr Braak, you're smiling. Now what have you been up to?'

'I went to the Arts Theatre this afternoon and saw a play called *Cottage to Let*. I enjoyed it very much. It was all about an inventor, whose wartime discoveries were being sent to Germany by a spy.' Ter Braak pretended not to have guessed the identity of the spy. He then hesitated and could not resist adding, 'but then I don't know what a German spy looks like!'

'They say they'll all be dressed up as nuns,' joined in Mr Serrill, with a smirk on his face.

'And getting into bad habits,' chortled Mrs Serrill. 'By the way Mr Braak, I need a word with you about your ration book.'

The spy's heart nearly stopped, and it took a great effort to stay calm. 'Yes, Mrs Serrill, what do you need to know?'

'The nice man at the food office says you can only have a few more temporary cards, as he's not supposed to issue you more than six. I've now had four. That leaves only two more which will take us to the middle of December, so you must write to the office that issued your original card as soon as possible and get them to renew it for you.'

Doing a masterful job of not letting his voice betray the panic that was welling up inside him, Ter Braak smiled meekly. 'Of course Mrs Serrill. I'll write straight away,' knowing that was the last thing he could safely do.

Once in his room Ter Braak went through his usual routine of transmitting a brief coded message to Hamburg. He did his best to overcome the nagging fear that the low voltage from his depleted batteries meant a very much reduced signal strength, and that he was most probably wasting his time, but on the other side of the town, this time his efforts did not fall on deaf ears.

Young Raymond Fautley wondered afterwards why he had done it, and could only put it down to weariness. It had been at the end of his shift, and he had been busy noting down the transmissions on his allocated wavelengths. He decided on a final sweep, and began to retune, but went up the spectrum, rather than downwards. Just as he realised his mistake, and before he could return to his usual point on the dial, he heard a very faint signal. He listened carefully to a fist he did not recognise, and automatically jotted down the groups of five random letters, which soon stopped. Noting the wavelength as between 4508 and 4509 kc/s he wondered where the sender was located. The weak signal suggested to him someone either a long way away, or quite near but with a weak set probably due to the aerial, or screening from nearby buildings. The young VI knew he had to get details of this transmission off to headquarters as soon as possible.

After his hand to mouth existence in Holland, Ter Braak had found a wallet bulging with banknotes a great comfort, and was soon in the habit of buying almost anything he wanted without a second thought. His initial purchase of clothes had made the biggest dent in his funds, but the daily cost of his lifestyle, not to mention his regular liaisons with Marge, soon started to add up. The spy knew the time to cash some of his reserve US dollars was rapidly approaching.

As usual on Sunday he took a one pound and ten shilling note from his wallet, and handed them to his landlady. 'There you are Mrs Serrill, here's my rent. By the way, I'd like to change some American dollars. Do you know where I could do that?'

Mrs Serrill pocketed the cash and then shook her head. 'I can cope with real money like this, but dollars? I've no idea, you'll have to have a word with Bert.'

His landlord's response cheered him up. 'We have our account with Lloyds bank at the end of the road. I'm calling in there myself tomorrow so I'll take them in for you.'

Ter Braak decided to change five ten dollar bills at this point, and handed them to Mr Serrill, who looked at them with some curiosity. 'Tell me Mr Braak, just how did you manage to get all your money out of Holland, what with the jerries taking over so quickly?'

This was a question he had anticipated. 'I could see what was going to happen some time before the invasion, so I kept it all in a box under my bed, and just grabbed it when I ran. The dollars are what I get from the Dutch Free Press as expenses. They say they can't pay me in sterling.'

This seemed to satisfy Mr Serrill, but he was surprised at Ter Braak's reaction when he handed him the twelve pounds and ten shillings he'd been handed in exchange at the bank.

'Is that all?' questioned the spy. 'It works out at virtually a pound for four dollars.'

Mr Serrill reassured him that this was all he had been given. 'There's no way my bank would cheat you, so that must be the going rate.' Ter Braak felt obliged to agree, while worrying that his remaining stock of dollars was by no means as valuable as he had thought.

26
LONDON

The meeting in St James' Street was another late night affair. Around the table sat Brigadier Jasper Harker, Guy Liddell, Tar Robertson and Colonel John Worlledge.

The colonel, aged fifty-three, was a veteran of the Great War who had previously commanded a wireless company in Palestine before being appointed by the War Office to be controller of the radio security service. Known by its organisational reference of MI8(c), its brief was to '...intercept, locate and close down illicit wireless stations operated either by enemy agents in Great Britain or by other persons not being licensed to do so under the Defence Regulations 1939.'

Harker opened the meeting. 'Colonel, I understand one of your voluntary interceptors has picked up a suspicious transmission. Elaborate please.'

'We received some record sheets from a very young VI in Cambridge. He was certain it wasn't a fist he'd heard before. We checked the records of all other VIs in the county, and discovered that no one else had picked up this message. As my note confirms, the transmission was very faint. In fact, it was hardly audible, and I doubt we managed to get enough for Bletchley to be able to decode it. Anyway, we have to thank the young ears of the VI for picking up what he did.'

'You know we're still searching for a missing Abwehr agent. Do you think this could be him?' asked Harker.

'Although we haven't been able to triangulate it accurately, the fact that no-one else heard it suggests that we're dealing with a poor quality transmission somewhere in Cambridge itself. This could well be your man.'

Harker smiled at the thought that, at last, they were making progress. 'I presume you brought in a detector van to track down this man?'

'We did have Ga detector van in the town centre for a time, but I withdrew it when no rogue signals were detected,' said Worlledge.

Brigadier Harker nodded. 'Thank you for your help. I think this is a case for some boots on the ground. Leave it with us.' With that, the colonel rose and left the others to ponder the problem further.

Turning to Liddell, the brigadier asked, 'Have you thought of involving Special Branch?'

'Yes, I did consider it Sir, but as we have your authority to liquidate this man as soon as possible, I thought it best to keep it in-house, although it's not something I would want to order Dixon, or any of my other RSLOs to do.'

Jasper drummed his fingers on his desk as he thought over the options. 'I agree.' His fingers tapped rapidly on the desk. 'It goes against the grain, but I see no alternative to asking for some assistance. I'll have a word with C. He's still coming to terms with the reorganisation of special operations that took place back in the summer.'

Liddell had considerable sympathy for C, Sir Stuart Menzies, the head of MI6. 'Yes, he mentioned to me the other day that he reckons there's every sort of intrigue going on by people who would like to take over his set-up. And he's getting flak from all sides, particularly from those who don't know what they're talking about.'

Harker smiled ruefully. 'He's not alone, I can assure you. Anyway, back to our problem. C owes me a favour, and I think it's time I called it in. I'll speak to him directly.'

27
CAMBRIDGE

Ter Braak looked forward to reading the daily local paper. It gave him an update on local events and a window on world news, although he had come to accept that the headlines would invariably paint a rosy picture, from Britain's perspective.

Summertime clock settings still applied, and it was dark until just before 8.30am. For once, Ter Braak was up early and volunteered to collect the paper from Whites, the newsagents in Mill Road. As soon as he put his nose outside, he regretted his offer. It was a very cold day, with sleet blowing in the air.

Returning to the warmth of the house and finding the Serrills upstairs, he took the opportunity to take a quick look at the *Cambridge Daily News*. He checked the date – Tuesday 10th December, and congratulated himself for having been at large for over a month.

Scanning the front page he read reports of the British advances in various theatres of war. As usual, there was no mention of anything that had gone badly. Then his gaze rested on the next article on the front page.

'Spies Executed at Pentonville Prison.'

His stomach churned, and he felt faint. He forced himself to read on, with dread in his heart. The men were named as Jose Waldberg, Charles van den Kieboom and Karl Meier, all three of them his former colleagues back at Hamburg.

Their story was identical to his initial training as a LENA agent. Posing as refugees, their instructions were to await the invasion and then support the German troops. The article did not explain how they had been caught, but implied they had been poorly prepared for their mission, and stood no real chance of surviving. Their trial had been held at the Central Criminal Court under Mr Justice Wrottesley. A jury of 'twelve good men and true' had found all three guilty of espionage and they had been sentenced to death and duly hanged at Pentonville Jail.

Ter Braak now felt sick, and his heart raced. He took a number of deep breaths to try and calm himself down. Tears welled up in his eyes as he remembered shaking hands with four men when they left for their mission. What had happened to the fourth man? He prayed this meant Stoerd Pons was still free.

Ter Braak blamed Major Ritter. He had accepted those men for training but must have known their chances of survival were limited, to say the least, with poor old Jose Waldberg not even able to speak English.

Putting down the paper, Ter Braak sat back and closed his eyes, attempting to shut out the world and all the difficulties that went with it. What was he to do now? He had not heard a word from Hamburg, so presumably his messages were not getting through. In any event, his radio batteries had nearly run out. He dare not buy the ingredients for his secret ink, and at some point, when all his dollars had been exchanged, the spy was going to run out of money.

The seriousness of the situation hit him like a sledge hammer. These problems had been apparent for some time, but his comfortable existence as part of the Serrill household had cushioned him from reality. He wished he could share his worries with Marge. Relaxed as he felt in her company, he just could not bring himself to admit his true identity and mission.

Reading about the death of his fellow spies forced Ter Braak to face the facts and decide whether or not to confront the professor. He debated the pros and cons for some time, and eventually concluded he had no choice.

The knock echoed through the thatched cottage. Professor Carpenter's heart pounded. Neighbours had recently reported a man loitering outside on a number of days. Could this be MI5?

Another knock. This was a caller who would not go away. Taking a deep breath, the professor unbolted the front door and opened it slowly and was momentarily lost for words at the sight of a tall man with a small moustache and wire rimmed glasses. He was dressed in a smart three piece suit, with a raincoat over his right arm.

The visitor spoke first. 'Professor Carpenter, my name is Ter Braak. I telephoned you about a message I have from Dr Rantzau. May I come in please?'

The professor, after glancing left and right, nodded.

The spy was led into a book-lined study on the ground floor, and took the armchair to which he was directed. Keeping the raincoat on his lap, he looked around and was surprised to see a telescope on a tripod standing in one corner. The professor, who had begun to recover from the shock, sank into an upholstered leather chair behind a large mahogany desk, covered with a variety of papers and books, and stared intently at the visitor. 'If you're wondering about the telescope, I'm a keen amateur astronomer.'

Ter Braak relaxed at this remark, which he took to be the start of a convivial conversation.

The professor had other ideas. 'Now, tell me who you really are, why you're here, and what you want.'

The spy was surprised by this onslaught, but managed to reply in a clear steady voice. 'I've been sent to England by Major Ritter of the Abwehr. I understand he's an old friend of yours. He told me to contact you using his cover name of Dr Rantzau, as he was sure you'd be able to help me with my mission.'

'And what might that be?'

'To find someone called Maud.'

'That sounds very interesting, but what will you do if I say no?'

Taking his right hand from beneath his raincoat, Ter Braak aimed his Browning automatic at the professor. 'Then, I'd have to shoot you.'

Ever since that first phone call, the professor had regretted denying all knowledge of Dr Rantzau. The man sitting the other side of the desk certainly did not look or act like a plant by MI5. Any lingering doubts were swept away by the thought of helping a real life German spy.

'It's all right Mr Ter Braak, you can put down your gun. Nick Ritter is indeed an old friend, and I'd be delighted to try and help you.'

Relief swept over the spy. 'Thank you so much,' he gushed and began describing his landing and journey to Cambridge.

The professor held up a hand to interrupt. 'Thank you Mr Ter Braak. We can go into those details in due course. First of all, who are you really? I take it Ter Braak is a cover name.'

'Yes, I chose Jan Willem from Jan Willem Henny, the editor of a paper I used to work for. Ter Braak is the surname of another famous journalist. My real name is Engelbertus Fukken.'

'May I call you Engelbertus?'

'My family call me Beer, but my friends use Bertus.'

'Good. Now Bertus, how did you find my humble abode?'

'It was quite easy really. I looked up all the Carpenters in a book in the library, and checked them all out.'

'How did you manage that without asking the sort of questions that could have exposed you?'

'Simple. I followed them all to find out where they lived and worked. Luckily you were the only one going to one of the colleges. But professor, why did you take that party of students to the Arts Theatre?'

Professor Carpenter looked surprised. 'Oh, you mean *Cottage to Let*. You won't know, but it's all about spies, and ever since your first call, I've been somewhat captivated by the subject. I've given my undergrads the task of comparing modern spies to those in the Shakespeare plays, and I thought that would give them a basis from which to start, given that they can't ring up MI5 and ask them about the likes of you.'

'Yes, I know it's all about a German spy. I was sitting two rows behind you.'

This brought a smile to the face of the professor, who went to pour them both a glass of sherry. 'I'm sorry I turned you down when you called, but I really thought you might have been from MI5. Anyway I'm very glad you found me. Now, let's start at the beginning. What did you do before this nasty war broke out?'

'I was living in Noordwijk, that's a small village on the coast, west of Amsterdam. I went to the Zeevaartsschool in the Hague when I was sixteen, but couldn't get on with naval life. After that I started selling insurance...' Ter Braak's voice tailed off.

The professor frowned. 'Come now Bertus. If you want me to help, you must tell me everything. There can't be any secrets between us.'

'As I said, I sold insurance, but I didn't pass on the premiums I'd been paid. Times were hard, and I had to live. I was arrested for fraud, and went to prison for a total of nine months. After my release I managed to become a journalist with a weekly paper in Noordwijk, but that didn't last. I then got engaged to Neeltje van Roon, the lovely girl who lived next door. She and her family were very generous in helping me while I was unemployed.'

'How did you become involved with the Abwehr?'

'An old school friend of mine recommended me to the Abwehr in Brussels. Rittmeister Kurt Mirow, who ran that office turned up and offered me the chance to serve the Fuhrer.

'I presume he didn't give you any alternative.'

'He did, but only a one way ticket to a concentration camp.'

'No real choice then?'

'I didn't need one. I admire the Fuhrer, and jumped at the chance to contribute to his victory.'

The professor smiled. 'At least we agree on that, but what sort of training did you receive?'

Ter Braak grimaced. 'Not much. They have a spy school in Hamburg, called the Klopstok. It's run by a frightening lady, Fraulein Friede, but the lessons were by a Captain Boeckel. I was told he sold ladies stockings before the war, and I don't know how he got his job. He was hopeless, but we did have some fantastic nights out. He seemed to have unlimited funds, so we all took full advantage, and got drunk nearly every night.'

Professor Carpenter looked surprised. 'That doesn't sound like the best way to win a war. You said 'all'. How many others were there?'

'I only met those who, like me, were to be sent to England, under Operation LENA, in advance of the invasion. We were to reconnoitre suitable landing sites for parachutists and equipment, and then, when the troops were ashore, act as guides.'

'You're surely not the first to have been sent?'

'No. Before me in late August, four men landed in two boats on the south coast.' Ter Braak paused and clearly had to make an effort to continue. 'Three were caught, as their trial and execution was reported in the local paper. I don't know what happened to the other man, but it seems likely he also suffered the same fate. Two more were dropped a week or so apart in early September. I was told three more landed by seaplane up north. I never met them, but rumour had it that one was a woman. There was also a man who was parachuted in at the start of October.'

'How were you all to communicate with Germany?'

'We were all given a receiver/transmitter, but in spite of daily transmissions, I've failed to receive a reply. Now my batteries are virtually flat.'

'That's not good news, but you said you were here to find someone called Maud. What has that to do with the invasion?'

'Nothing, as far as I know. Maud, whoever that is, is supposed to be developing a new super weapon somewhere here in Cambridge.'

'This sounds like a very special mission.'

'Yes. It was only after I'd virtually completed my so-called LENA training that I was given this revised task. I was then transferred to a Dr Praetorius. He'd spent some time over here before the war and was able to explain lots of things, but especially all about the strange money. I think that's why I've survived as long as I have.'

Professor Carpenter's eyes opened wide. 'Are you saying the other LENA spies didn't have that sort of basic tuition?'

'No, and some of them didn't even speak English.'

The professor sat back in utter amazement. 'My God, and there's me thinking that German efficiency will easily win them this nasty conflict. Now, what about your journey here?'

Ter Braak thought back to the night of Friday 1st November and went on to describe his departure from Schiphol airport, the uncomfortable flight in the specially adapted Heinkel 111, and the skill of the pilot, Hauptmann Gartenfeld. 'I'd never jumped before, but I wasn't scared. In fact I found the whole experience quite exhilarating.'

The professor looked horrified. 'What, no practice jumps? That seems very risky to me. What if you'd frozen?'

'The dispatcher would have just thrown out my luggage and pushed me after it.'

'Luggage? What do you mean?'

'I had two suitcases, one for my spare clothes and the other hiding my radio. The set has been cleverly built inside a standard leather case, but it's very heavy.'

'How did you know when to pull the ripcord?'

My 'chute opened on a static line and before I knew it, I'd landed in a field. It was raining but I made it to a path, and then had a rest until it got light and I could see where I was going. I then discovered I'd not brought my spade to bury my parachute, so I rolled it up with my flying suit and helmet and hid the bundle behind a hedge at the side of the track.'

'Not a good start, if I may say so. If you'd buried your kit properly the authorities wouldn't know you're here. Instead, however, there's a good chance your stuff has been found and a search put in hand.'

The spy looked dismissive. 'Yes, I know, but that was nearly two months ago. They'll have given up by now.'

Professor Carpenter looked doubtful. 'I think that's highly unlikely. I reckon they're moving heaven and earth to find you and won't rest until they do, so you must keep your eyes open. Anyway, back to your journey. Where did you head for?'

'There were no landmarks to give me any idea where I was, so with the aid of my compass, I opted to walk north. It was a struggle with my two cases, especially with the heavy radio, but eventually I reached a stream, with a tall wire fence on the other side. I managed to find a small bridge which took me to a locked gate in the fence. There was a notice saying *Hanslope Park. Private. Government Property.* It was then that I heard voices.'

'What did you do then?'

'I threw myself and my cases into the bushes and held my breath. Two men were walking around the Park, on the other side of the fence. They were discussing things like rhombics and vee beam aerials, which must be something to do with radios. I waited for quite a time after they'd gone, but they didn't come back. So I got out the map that Dr Praetorius had given me. He said it was one he used when he was over here. It took some time, but eventually I managed to find Hanslope village with the Park nearby. It was then I realised just how far away from Cambridge I'd been dropped. I was between two railway stations, but I reckoned the nearest was at Wolverton, so I set off and managed to reach there without being stopped.'

'You said it'd been raining. After tramping along all those paths, weren't you a bit muddy?

Ter Braak grinned. 'Yes, but I tucked my trousers inside my socks until I reached the road. I then changed into a fresh pair, and used the dirty socks to clean my shoes.'

'Well done. So, I suppose you caught a train to Cambridge.'

'That's what I wanted to do, but I got onto the first train that arrived, which took me to the end of a branch line at Newport Pagnell. I just stayed on the train and went back to Wolverton. I eventually reached Bletchley, where I had to change for Cambridge. There was a bit of a wait between trains, but I kept my eyes open and it seemed that most passengers walked up a path next to another tall fence with barbed wired on it. I got chatting to a porter and he said they were going to a big old house called Bletchley Park.'

The Professor looked up. 'That's interesting. I wonder what they're doing there. Not playing games, I'll be bound.'

'No. Many of the passengers looked like boffins.'

'Boffins? That's curious. There's a railway line that goes from Oxford, through Bletchley and then on here to Cambridge. Not surprisingly, it's known as the Varsity Line. I wonder if what's going on at Bletchley might have anything to do with the two universities? I suppose your journey was straightforward after that.'

'No it wasn't. My train was stopped at Bedford due to an unexploded bomb on the line, so I had to get off, along with everyone else.' At this point Ter Braak paused, looking thoughtful. 'That reminds me. There were two RAF chaps who I think had got on with me at Bletchley. They were changing trains anyway and one of them said to his mate that there ought to be an easier way for them to get from X to Y. They both laughed, and I did wonder what they meant.'

Professor Carpenter frowned. 'Sounds like a mathematical joke, but I don't know any mathematicians with a sense of humour. Can you remember where they were heading?'

Ter Braak shook his head. 'No. I'm sure they did mention it, but I wasn't really listening. It was only the reference to X and Y which caught my attention.'

'Pity. So, what did you do in Bedford?'

'It was evening by then but luckily I managed to get a bed for the night with a very nice family who saw me wandering around, just as an air raid warning sounded. I caught a train to here the next day, Sunday, that was. Then, I stayed at the Station Hotel for the night. They recommended a letting agent in town who put me onto a nice couple, a Mr and Mrs Serrill in St Barnabas Road.'

'So, you've been here since the beginning of November. What have you been doing since then to find Maud?' asked the professor.

'I went to the library and had a look in a directory, but there was no-one with the surname Maud listed. That's also where I found your name and address.'

'Is that all?'

Ter Braak looked hurt. 'I also took a trip to Peterborough. I met someone called Maud who used to live in Cambridge, but had moved there, but she wasn't the one I was looking for. I've also been busy establishing myself here, buying more clothes, setting up an office, and generally getting accepted in the area.'

'I'm not sure you need an office, but I agree this is a difficult problem, especially with so little to go on. I'll give some thought to where we can start. I'll be busy from now until Christmas, and then there's the New Year. I suggest we meet again here in January. I know that's a few weeks away, but it just can't be helped. By the way, I think you should know that I had my own insurance policy against you being from MI5.'

With that the professor lifted a pile of papers from the desk to reveal a loaded Colt revolver. Ter Braak decided not to complain about the delay until the next meeting.

28
CAMBRIDGE

'I have a few friends who might be able to help with our Christmas celebrations,' announced Ter Braak at supper. 'I was wondering what would be the best things to look out for.'

'Anything, really,' replied Mrs Serrill. 'Things are getting scarcer by the day, and the problem is, I never know what's going to be on the counter, let alone under it. And all that queuing! You know, some people will join a queue without even knowing what it's for. They work on the basis that it must be something worth having in these terrible times.'

'We're okay for vegetables, as I've grown some in the garden,' joined in Mr Serrill, 'but we've nothing to wash them down with. I think we'd have to swap this whole house for a bottle of scotch, assuming you could find any.'

'I'll see what I can do,' promised Ter Braak, more in hope than certainty.

'That's very good of you lad, but don't go getting involved with those black market blokes - nasty types if you ask me,' said Mr Serrill, wagging his finger to reinforce his point.

Ter Braak was confident he could navigate his way through the underworld to secure the extra provisions he had promised, but was not sure where to start. Turning the problem over in his mind, he recalled the article he had read in the local paper about a pub landlord who had been sentenced for receiving stolen goods. Where was it?

He racked his brains, and then he remembered, the Crown in Wellington Street.

Making his way across town, Ter Braak found Wellington Street to be a particularly dingy backstreet, and the Crown even dingier. The loss of its previous landlord to prison had clearly not produced any positive results. Entering the scruffy public bar, all heads turned in surprise at a stranger, but soon returned to their pint glasses, filled with beer that was becoming weaker as the war went on.

Working on his habit of doing what others did, Ter Braak ordered a pint and started chatting to a man sitting on his own in a corner of the bar. After lubricating the conversation with several extra pints, he casually mentioned he was looking for some extras for Christmas.

The reply was guarded. 'The only person who can get what you want in time for Christmas is Lennie 'Scarface' Pearce. He runs most of the rackets in this county, let alone the town. You should be able to find him in the Blackamoors Head on Victoria Road. But watch your step, the bloke is dangerous.'

Upon entering the Blackamoors Head, Ter Braak was relieved to see just one customer, a bearded man sitting in the corner of the room. Walking up to the bar, he ordered a pint. 'I'm trying to find Lennie Pearce, I'm told he'll be able to help me with some shopping,' he said. Pushing a half a crown across the counter, he added, 'Keep the change.'

'And who wants him?' replied the barman, pocketing the extra cash.

Not wanting to give his real name, or indeed his false identity, the spy thought quickly. 'Tell him it's Dr Rantzau.'

'I knew you was a foreigner,' replied the barman. 'He's not here, but I'll pass on your message. I suggest you have another drink here about this time tomorrow.'

The next twenty four hours passed very slowly, but Ter Braak was back at the Blackamoors Head at the right time. The barman did not disappoint. 'Do you know Midsummer Common? Be there at eight tomorrow night. Take the path from Brunswick Walk, and sit on the seat half way along, and on your own, mind.'

The following night was windy, with low scudding clouds occasionally blocking out the moon. There was also a hint of rain in the air. Ter Braak arrived in good time and sat on the seat. He lifted his scarf up around his face, pulled down his trilby and waited. His breath hung on the cold night air.

Just after eight o'clock, a short stocky man holding a blackout torch appeared out of the gloom, and sat next to him. He wore a dark trench coat with the collar up, and a cap pulled down over his eyes. 'Dr Rantzau, I presume?'

'Yes, that's me. And you are Mr Pearce?' responded Ter Braak, but judged he had the right person by the long scar on his questioner's left cheek.

'Never you mind who I am. What's it you're after?'

Ter Braak handed over his list, which was received with a sharp intake of breath. 'This is going to cost you a lot. Have you got the lolly?'

Funds were not an immediate problem, as he still had much of the cash from his landlord's visit to Lloyds bank, together with a wad of still un-cashed ten and five dollar bills. Ter Braak decided to take a bold line, and hopefully avoid another visit to the bank. 'Certainly, but I can only manage American dollars. Will they do?'

This took Pearce by surprise. His activities had expanded substantially since the start of the war, and he now had deals across the county, and beyond. He had not met anyone before who traded in foreign currency, but was not the sort to display any such inexperience. 'I can handle that,' he said.

'So, how much?'

Pearce had no idea what the exchange rate between dollars and pounds might be. He reckoned he could charge at least £20 for what he was being asked to produce, so working on the basis one dollar must be about the same value as a pound, he added a bit for luck and said, '25 dollars. Cash up front.'

Ter Braak recalled he had only received one pound for four dollars when Lloyds Bank had recently changed his dollar bills. He realised the villain in front of him had made a mistake, but not wishing to look a gift horse in the mouth he replied, 'I'll accept the price, but I'll pay you when I get the stuff.'

Pearce was about to insist on his terms, but decided not to lose what he saw as a profitable deal. 'All right,' he grunted.

'When can you deliver?'

'I'll get them to you on Sunday 22nd. We need to meet somewhere quiet. Do you know Addenbrooke's Hospital?'

'Yes.'

'You don't want the main entrance, but the one at the back in Tennis Court Road. Look out for the boiler house. It's got a tall chimney, you can't miss it. Next to that is a gate. Go through there and to the left, behind the boiler house, is a small building, with *Engineers Store* written on the door. The hospital engineer is a good mate of mine. It's always locked , but I have a key. Meet me in there at eight o'clock in the evening, make sure you have the cash with you, and no funny business. People don't cross me and get away with it.'

'I'll be there,' Ter Braak replied. Letting the black marketer leave first, he then made his way back to St Barnabas Road, taking a roundabout route to ensure he was not being followed.

On the evening of Sunday 22nd December, Ter Braak managed to persuade Mr Serrill to lend him his precious Raleigh bike, together with its large leather saddlebag, which would hold the contraband. The bright light produced by the Sturmey Archer front wheel dynamo was now shrouded in accordance with the blackout regulations, although it still proved its value every day, as batteries for cycle lamps became more and more difficult to find in the shops.

The meeting had been scheduled for eight pm, well past blackout time, but there was a clear sky and a bright moon. Ter Braak arrived early, and from his vantage point behind a wall at the side of the street, he watched and waited. At a quarter to eight, the lights from the cloaked headlights of a car appeared, the white painted bumpers dimly visible. The vehicle did a three point turn, and pulled up next to the gate, a manoeuvre Ter Braak recognised as preparation for a quick get-away. The driver got out, and after checking the coast was clear, took a box from the boot, and went in through the pedestrian gate.

Ter Braak delayed his own entry until precisely the appointed time. Shutting the pedestrian gate behind him, he walked the short distance to the store, and tried the door. It had been locked when he had carried out his reconnoitre a few days earlier, but it now swung open. It was pitch black inside, and he hesitated until a voice from the darkness told him to come in and shut the door. A light then came on, which would have blinded him had he not anticipated this and put a hand up to shield his eyes. Stepping smartly to one side and outside the beam of light, he squinted into the blackness and made out the car driver, whom he now recognised by the scar on his face as Lennie Pearce.

'Have you got the stuff?'

'Let's see the colour of your money first,' came the reply, and Ter Braak held out the dollar bills. He had often wondered if these were forgeries, but they had satisfied Lloyd's Bank, so he was not surprised when they were accepted by Pearce, and the box pushed over towards him. He opened the lid and checked the contents. Everything he had asked for was there, so he picked up the container and made his way to the door. 'Nice doing business with you,' he said.

'You know where to find me if there's anything else you want,' replied the spiv.

Ter Braak was soon back on his bike with the goods safely stored in the saddlebag. He peddled as fast as he could through streets which were now familiar to him, praying that the bottles clinking in the saddlebag would not break. A quick glance over his shoulder confirmed what he had suspected, and expected - a car was following him at a discreet distance.

Putting into action the plan he had prepared, he waited until the road narrowed, and suddenly did a u-turn up onto the pavement and back the way he had come, past the car, which came to a halt, and started to turn. But Ter Braak was soon out of sight, and safely back to St Barnabas Road without being followed. Wheeling the bicycle down the narrow path which led to the back garden, he reached the safety of the garden shed, and emptied the saddlebag. Delighted that the bottles had not broken, he let himself in and managed to reach his room without being seen.

However, the tension of the evening was still not over as he faced another clandestine session with his radio. His batteries were now virtually exhausted, and he still had to get a reply.

29
LONDON

In St James's Street, Guy Liddell did not enjoy his meeting with Brigadier Harper, which was a tense affair. He was relieved to escape and update Tar.

'Jasper isn't a happy man. He's managed to persuade C to lend us an agent to operate in Cambridge, but it seems this chap has been poached by the Special Operations Executive to set up a course at their new training centre, down near Beaulieu, I believe. Like me, C is very much against this new upstart organisation, but as they have the personal support of Winston, and in fact were set up as his behest, they get what they want.'

Tar put his head in his hands. 'That's all very well, but when will we get this agent?'

'Not this side of Christmas.'

The resultant expletives echoed around the room for some time.

30
HAMBURG

'Yes Boeckel, what is it you want?'

'I'm sorry to trouble you major, but a rather disturbing rumour is doing the rounds.'

Ritter knew what was coming from his deputy, but decided to keep the discussion strictly formal. 'What have you heard, Hauptmann?'

'Word has it that the invasion has been postponed indefinitely. Is that true?'

'I've not received any orders to that effect, but the delay does seem ominous,' responded Ritter, who suspected that Hitler had now lost interest in invading England.

Boeckel looked worried. 'I had hoped that the lack of action was due to the weather, which has hardly been suitable for crossing the channel. I presume nothing will happen now until the Spring at the earliest.'

'That's one way to look at it, but you've no need to worry – your job's safe. Even if the invasion is cancelled, we'll still keep running the LENA spies who are still at large.'

'Delighted to hear that Herr Major. Does that include Fukken?'

Ritter frowned. 'I wish I knew.'

31
CAMBRIDGE

Coming down to breakfast the next morning, Ter Braak presented his hosts with a large joint of beef which took their breath away. 'Where ever did you get this from?' exclaimed Mrs Serrill.

'A friend of mine,' he replied, with a broad smile.

'I hope it's not one of those spivs,' chipped in Mr Serrill, but with a grin on his face that suggested he did not much care even if it was.

'I just hope on Christmas Day the gas will be enough to cook this,' mused Mrs Serrill, thinking of the drops in pressure she had experienced in the past and fearing everyone would be cooking something at the same time on the 25th.

'There was a good frost the other night,' announced Mr Serrill. 'I can pick the sprouts from the garden today, and we've already got enough spuds in the shed, so it looks as if we can have a proper Christmas after all. I told you old Adolf wouldn't beat us.'

After their lodger had left at his usual time of around ten o'clock the two sat staring at the piece of meat on the table. 'You know Elsie, he must've got this on the black market, but if we keep quiet about it, well, does it really matter?'

Mrs Serrill was not so sure, but as the woman of the house, and the one who did the shopping, queued for hours, juggled the rationing and struggled with recipes with ever disappearing ingredients, she shrugged her shoulders.

That satisfied her husband. 'Good, now we can't let Adolf spoil all our fun - I must try and get a tree from somewhere.' True to his word, Mr Serrill came back the next day wheeling his bike with a fir tree balanced on the saddle and handlebars. He had to admit it was only modest, but it had been all that was available.

Ter Braak gratefully accepted the invitation to help the Serrills decorate the tree which, when finished, looked very much the part, complete with asbestos powder as fake snow.

Christmas Day dawned, and the cold crisp morning saw Ter Braak return from the service at Our Lady and The English Martyrs. Mr and Mrs Serrill had a shorter walk back from St Barnabas Church at the end of their road.

Ter Braak went straight up to his room and came down with the last of his surprises. Mr Serrill was sitting in his chair studying the *Radio Times*, and nearly choked when he saw the bottle of malt whisky, a bottle of sherry and another drink which he did not recognise.

'This is for you,' announced Ter Braak, pushing the sherry across the table to an astonished Mrs Serrill. He then turned to Mr Serrill. 'And, this whisky is for you.'

'Thanks very much lad, but what's that other bottle?'

'This is Jenever from my country. My friends got this for me, but I'm not sure if it's jongue or oude, sorry, that's Dutch for young or old. Let's open it and find out.' He poured a glass and took a sip of the liquid which he rolled around in his mouth. 'This is old Jenever. You can tell by the malty flavour and its smoothness. The younger stuff is more neutral, a bit like vodka, but smelling of juniper. Here, try it yourself.'

Mr Serrill took a gulp and immediately started coughing. 'Jesus, lad, that's got a kick to it. Here, Elsie, you try it.' His wife nervously took a sip and blinked as she swallowed. 'Yes, lovely,' she said with a hoarse voice. 'Let's set the table, we can eat very soon.'

The three sat down to a meal of which Mrs Serrill was rightly proud. She had managed to roast the potatoes in their skins in the fat from the meat, and had swapped some of their home grown sprouts with a neighbour down the road who had a surplus of carrots from his allotment.

Pouring gravy over his plate, which was piled higher than he had seen it since the beginning of the war, Mr Serrill grinned. 'You know, Jim down the road told me that girls now paint their legs with this stuff, and then get their mates to draw a line down the back with a pencil or something, as they can't get stockings anymore.'

'They use an eyebrow pencil,' explained Mrs Serrill. 'I'd do the same if I still had legs worth looking at, and not all these varicose veins,' she added wistfully, looking towards her husband in the vain hope of some comforting remark.

After the meal, Mr Serrill sank into his chair with another glass of whisky, which he quickly drained. He was soon snoring. The lodger helped to clear the table, and felt obliged to pick up a tea towel and to the surprise and delight of Mrs Serrill, began drying the dishes. When everything had been cleared away, Ter Braak picked up the copy of the *Radio Times* which Mr Serrill had dropped on the floor. It was the Christmas issue with a caricature of Father Christmas on the front cover wearing a tin hat marked BBC, and saying, *Here is the Christmas News and this is Father Christmas reading it.* Ter Braak did not realise that genuine newsreaders announced their names before the bulletins to assure listeners they were not listening to a fake enemy transmission.

As he turned to the pages listing the various broadcasts, Ter Braak learnt that the Forces had their own programmes, and was amazed to see they were given the news in Dutch, French and even German.

At that point Mr Serrill woke up and saw what his lodger was reading. 'We're on the Home Service,' he advised. 'Not much on now that ITMA has finished, but there's Christmas Star Variety tonight at quarter past seven.'

'ITMA? Whatever's that?' asked Ter Braak.

'It's a really funny show and stands for *It's That Man Again* and goes back to something in the papers about Adolf. The last series finished earlier in the year, but I hope they'll do another soon. The sketches take the mickey out of officialdom. I like it where Tommy Handley plays the Minister of Aggravation and Mysteries in the Office of Twerps, with the power to confiscate, complicate and commandeer.'

'The best bit is Mrs Mopp. "Can I do you now Sir"?' joined in Mrs Serrill, imitating the office char played by Dorothy Summers.

'No, no, it's got to be Jack Train pretending to be a German spy,' argued Mr Serrill, picking up his empty glass and speaking into it. "This is Funk speaking".'

The genuine spy nearly had a heart attack, for a second thinking he had heard his own real name.

To Ter Braak's relief, the couple eventually ran out of catch phrases. Mrs Serrill then picked up the *Radio Times*, and began searching the pages. Her husband looked across at her.

'What is it you're looking for, Elsie?'

'I'm trying to find out when the king will be giving his speech, but I can't see it anywhere in here.'

'Ah, yes, my country also has a royal family, but they've been driven away by the invaders,' joined in Ter Braak, trying to sound as if he cared.

'Yes, and I wonder where our royal family will go if Hitler makes it over the Channel?' mused Mr Serrill. The spy shared his host's curiosity but felt unable to reply.

Mr Serrill did not seem to be expecting a response from him and turned to his wife. 'Sorry, Elsie, I don't know why, but His Royal Highness isn't doing one this year, but don't forget that talk by Princess Elizabeth back in October on Children's Hour.'

The day passed in an alcoholic haze, interrupted by a break for beef sandwiches and a jar of pickled onions that Mrs Serrill had squirreled away for a special occasion. The wireless was duly switched on for the Variety Show at seven fifteen, but off again when the next programme turned out to be a piano recital. The dart board then came into its own until the news at nine pm, followed by some frantic re-tuning of the set by Mr Serrill.

'What are you trying to find?' asked Ter Braak.

'Radio Hamburg of course. It's time for Lord Haw Haw,' and on cue, that voice rang out, 'Germany calling, Germany calling.'

Ter Braak realised he was listening to the one Englishman who had seen the light - the defector William Joyce. He was taken aback by the reaction of both Mr and Mrs Serrill, who treated his appeal to surrender with utter contempt, but it did seem they had some support for his prophesy of 'working men soon exercising a formidable opinion.'

The party was still in full swing at eleven o'clock when there was a hammering on the front door and a shout of, 'Put that light out.' Moving as fast he could, given the unsteady state of his legs, Mr Serrill rushed to the hall, and saw at once the reason for the rude interruption. The blackout curtain across the glass panel in the front door had fallen off. Opening the door, he was faced with a shifty looking man wearing an ARP helmet. 'Hello, Fred, Happy Christmas, sorry about this. I'll put it up straightaway,' he grovelled.

Fred was unmoved by the seasonal greeting. 'Just you do that, at once mind you.' He started to walk away, only to turn and stand with his hands on his hips waiting for his command to be obeyed.

Mr Serrill slammed the door shut, replaced the blackout curtain, and tottered back to the others. 'That was Fred, bloody conchie,' he slurred, as he slumped into his chair.

His wife had made quite a dent in her bottle of sherry but was still sufficiently aware to notice the quizzical look on Ter Braak's face and did her best to explain. 'A conchie means he's a conscientious objector. Fred claimed his religious beliefs didn't allow him to fight for King and Country. Went before a tribunal, but he belonged to some union, Peace Pledge I think, and they coached him on what to say. Managed to get himself graded as B. That kept him out of the army, but he had to do something, so ended up as an ARP Warden.'

This interruption brought the day to a close, with all three making their way slowly and somewhat unsteadily upstairs to bed. The spy decided this was not a night to bother with his transmitter.

'Only a few more days and I can see the professor again,' thought Ter Braak before falling asleep.

32
CAMBRIDGE

Major Dickie Dixon could have driven to work, but always preferred to walk to his office in Regent Street. Leaving his rented semi-detached house in Chesterton Road, he crossed the road, and made his way down De Freville Avenue. Turning right into Montague Road and past the allotments to his left, he glanced enviously at the three large detached houses on the other side of the road. He had always felt they were much more suited to a man of his station, but his masters had declined to meet the extra rental they commanded.

Turning left at the end of the road and into Ferry Path, he crossed the bridge over the River Cam. Shivering at the cold which rose from the gently flowing water, he hurried on to Midsummer Common, and soon reached Christ's Pieces. Glancing at the half finished structure, he wondered just when they would finish the air raid shelter.

Arriving at 83 Regent Street, which proudly announced *Art Needlework* over the window of the ground floor shop, he made his way up the narrow stairs to his office on the first floor. He was joined by his RSS colleague Jack Hester, who asked, 'Is today the day, major?'

'Yes, at long last. Once he's arrived I'm going to arrange for him to meet Bob Pearson.'

Hester looked surprised. 'The chief constable of the Borough Police himself? I'm impressed. I didn't think the police were going to be involved with this chap.'

'Officially they're not. Only Bob and his deputy, Superintendent Charles Wilson, are going to be in the know. Not even DCI Bone will be told. I'm going to have to watch what I say to Bone, as we worked together on the Schmidt case.'

'But they know we're looking for a missing parachutist, don't they?'

'Oh yes, but that dates back to the round robin issued when the 'chute was first found. Since then, we've relied on the fact that any foreigner coming into town will be reported to the aliens officer based in the police station. Superintendent Wilson heads that section, and he can be counted upon to let me know when any suspicious report crosses his desk.'

'What do you think this MI6 bloke will be like?'

'I don't really know. He comes with the best of references, and seems very experienced in the sort of cloak and dagger stuff that Six pride themselves in.'

'Who is he going to report to?'

'Me! At least I'll get to know what he's up to…'

Both Dixon and Hester looked up at the sound of a polite knock on the office door.

'Your visitor, Sir,' announced Nancy as she ushered in a man of medium build, with a nondescript face, looking nothing like a trained MI6 killer.

Dixon put out his hand. 'I'm Major Dixon, and this is Captain Jack Hester of the radio security service. And you are…?'

'They call me Nemo.'

'Ah, Latin for nobody. Most appropriate. Good to have you with us, Nemo. I take it you've been briefed on your target?'

'Yes, Sir. German spy who left his parachute at Haversham at the start of November. Thought to be operating somewhere in this town. No description, or any other details known at this stage. My orders are to find him, and prevent him affecting other current operations.'

'You have it in a nutshell. Now, I need to introduce you to the chief constable of the Borough Police, and his deputy, so that, if necessary, they can smooth over any problems you may encounter. Those two gentlemen, Captain Hester here, and myself, will be the only four people in Cambridge to know you are here and what your mission is. I take it Major Robertson confirmed you are to report to me alone?'

'Yes, Sir. How should I contact you?'

'I'll give you a number so you can telephone me at home. We can then meet somewhere if necessary. Where will you be staying while you're here?'

'Here and there. I don't plan to stay in one place too long. I find it pays to be mobile.'

Dixon smiled. 'Sounds like a good plan to me. Now, let's give Bob Pearson a ring.'

The resultant telephone conversation saw Nemo accompanying Major Dixon later that afternoon to the tall cast iron lamp post in the middle of Parker's Piece, where they met two gentlemen who, despite uniforms covered with heavy overcoats, still looked like policemen. Introductions were made, and it was agreed that Nemo would be left to his own devices, with discreet help provided if needed.

It was another cold day, with low clouds and occasional showers. No one was keen to stand around, and the policemen were the first to take their leave. Dixon turned to Nemo. 'Now, keep in regular contact, and also, of course, whenever there's any major development.'

They shook hands and the major turned to walk back to his office. He resisted the temptation to look over his shoulder for a few paces, but finally succumbed. To his amazement, Nemo was nowhere to be seen.

33

LONDON

Brigadier Harker was his usual grumpy self. Guy Liddell knew his boss had to answer to higher authority, and could appreciate the pressure he was under. However, he was only able to report the arrival of Nemo in Cambridge, his initial meeting with the regional security liaison officer, and his disappearance into the backstreets of the town in search of the missing man.

'The only people within the borough police force who know of the presence of Nemo are the chief and deputy chief constables. Cambridge was one of the towns we checked during the weeks after the parachute was found, and there were no registrations recorded then that couldn't be explained away as genuine refugees. Superintendent Wilson advises that the situation is still the same.'

The brigadier looked tired and harassed. 'What's Nemo doing now?'

'He's started on a trawl of all the pubs in Cambridge. This is one of the recognised ways of keeping an ear to the ground. Even if the spy himself hasn't been seen, quite often the regulars and especially those with some involvement in shady dealings seem to know what's going on, and who is new on the scene.'

'How many of these pubs are there?'

'That's the problem. There are over one hundred, so I believe. I hope this chap can hold his liquor.'

Harker sighed. 'Nemo needs to keeps his wits about him while he's getting drunk every night, and at our expense as well. Keep the pressure on, and let me know as soon as there's further news.'

As soon as he had left Harker's office, Liddell went to see Tar Robertson to update him. Tar voiced his fears. 'Won't Nemo become well known in Cambridge? You know what towns are like. Any stranger turning up in pub after pub is going to arouse suspicions, and word soon gets around.'

Liddell reassured him. 'No need to worry. Dixon reports that Nemo is a master of disguise, and can change his appearance at the drop of a hat. Well, actually, the donning of a hat. It seems that putting on, or taking off a hat or glasses, changing a coat, carrying an umbrella or a bag are all proven methods of altering your appearance.

Even a small pebble in one shoe will result in a limp and change of gait that will fool even the most clued-up observer. Added to that, Nemo can chat away in a range of accents from Cornish to Scottish. I agree with Dixon that we have the right bloke for this job.'

'What happens if he manages to catch this spy. Can he carry out the brigadier's orders to liquidate him?'

'Certainly. This man is a trained killer. Came top of his class at the commando school up in the Highlands.'

Tar looked at his boss and frowned. 'I hope he gets the chance to prove his ability sooner rather than later. I dread to think of the consequences of this missing man blowing our double agent set up.'

34
CAMBRIDGE

Returning from one of his now regular visits to Marge, Ter Braak noticed that bags of sand had been tied to lamp posts in residential areas for fire watchers to use. The cold weather had not abated, and Ter Braak turned up his collar, and thrust his hands deeper into his coat pockets as he trudged along. There were still patches of frozen snow here and there, which made it treacherous under foot. He could find his way about in the blackout, but the slippery pavements produced a further hazard, and he was glad to see he was now in St Barnabas Road with not far to go.

He carefully moved sideways to avoid the lamp post just ahead, and the next thing he knew, found himself flat on his face in the road. He lifted his head gingerly, and wondered what had happened. Sitting up, he looked about him, and could see nothing in the gloom. He groped about and discovered his glasses lying near him in the road. Putting them back on, he heard the sound of approaching footsteps, and out of the blackness a pair of helping hands pulled him to his feet. As he stood, his head spun, but the unknown helper propped him up and reassured him.

'Take it easy, old chap. You've had a nasty fall. I bet it was one of those sandbags which the kids have been playing with. They're now all over the place, and a proper hazard in the dark. But you don't need me to tell you that. Now where do you live?'

'With Mr and Mrs Serrill at number 258.'

'Good heavens, then we're neighbours. Are you their Dutch lodger?'

'Yes.'

'Let's get you indoors. Now take it easy old chap, lean on me. We'll soon have you home.'

The frantic banging on the front door brought Mrs Serrill limping as fast as her gammy leg would let her. 'Oh, my heavens, Jan, you have been in the wars,' she exclaimed and soon had him in a chair in the sitting room with a cup of tea in his hands. 'Now, just you drink that. I know you don't take it, but I've put a good spoonful of sugar in it - you need perking up.'

Ter Braak nodded his thanks, and sipped the steaming, sickly liquid. Squinting through his spectacles he then recognised his rescuer as the man who lived next door. 'Sir, thank you for your help. It was very kind of you.'

'No trouble, my friend. I've seen you out and about, but we've not been introduced. I'm Edwin Cross, and I live next door at number 260. Tell me, what brings you to this neck of the woods?' Ter Braak hadn't heard of woods having necks, and without thinking, trotted out his cover story, including the reference to Dunkirk. Before Mr Cross had the chance to say anything, Mrs Serrill butted in. 'Now don't go asking him about Dunkirk. It's a painful memory, isn't it, Jan?'

Ter Braak nodded, delighted to be off that particular hook. Mrs Serrill then bent over his face. 'You've a nasty cut on your forehead. Just you sit still my dear Jan, and I'll soon have that cleaned up for you.'

With that, the spy's rescuer decided to take his leave. 'I'll be off now, as I can see you're in safe hands. Mind how you go in the dark. Give my regards to Bert. I'll see myself out, TTFN.' With that, Edwin Cross was gone.

Sitting back in his chair, Ter Braak was grateful for a moments peace and quiet, only to have Mrs Serrill begin painting him with a nasty looking yellow liquid, which stung as she went over his cut. He recoiled and tried to get up. 'Whatever's that, what are you doing to me?' But she pushed him back. 'Don't panic. It's only tincture of iodine. It'll keep this nice and clean, and the yellow stain will wear off in a day or two.'

As he was wondering just how yellow he looked, Mr Serrill arrived home, banging the front door behind him. He came storming in, wearing his home guard uniform, sank into his usual chair, and sat in silence, glaring at the far wall. 'What's the matter with you?' said his wife.

'They've stopped the *Daily Worker*, they have. And I thought we were fighting this war to save democracy and free speech.'

'Why are you so upset? You've never taken that newspaper, well, not to my knowledge.'

'I know I haven't, but that's not the point. I don't agree with their views, they're even more left wing than me, but it's the principle of the thing. We have a right to a free press, don't you agree Jan? After all, you're with the Dutch Free Press, aren't you?'

Ter Braak played for time. 'I'm sorry Bert, this hurts. What was it you said?'

Mrs Serrill leapt to his defence. 'Leave the poor man alone. Can't you see he's had a nasty bump on the head. Fell over in the blackout, and was rescued by Edwin.'

Mr Serrill looked up and was mortified. 'Jan, I'm so sorry, I didn't realise. Are you all right?'

'Yes thank you Bert. Elsie has patched me up. Tell me, what does Edwin do? Shouldn't he have been called up by now?'

'He's a surveyor, works with the council. Deals with bomb damage repairs.'

'I've not seen too much of that since I've been here.'

Mr Serrill nodded. 'I suppose we've been lucky, but I do feel for those poor souls whose houses have been damaged. They don't get any insurance money or help from the government.'

Ter Braak had never given the matter any thought, but was surprised. 'They have to pay for the repairs themselves?'

'Yes, but Edwin said there's a scheme being put together by parliament that'll allow people to claim, but only at the end of the war, whenever that is. The amount they'll get will depend upon how much money we've got left. From what I read in the papers, that'll be sod all.'

'Perhaps Germany respects all your college buildings, and doesn't want to flatten them before they invade.'

'Invade us? I know what happened to your country, but that was a darn sight easier for Adolf. He didn't have to cross the English Channel.'

Ter Braak nodded. 'Yes, I agree that's quite a barrier, but given the might of the German forces...'

'Just let Adolf try. I hope he knows he's got us fellows in the home guard to contend with.'

'I'm sure he does. But if you'll excuse me, I'll just have a lie down and rest my head. It's still aching a bit. Thank you for cleaning me up.' With that Ter Braak struggled to his feet and made his way upstairs, chuckling to himself at the thought of the home guard taking on the might of the German army.

Reaching his bedroom with his head still aching he took the Browning automatic from his raincoat pocket and prepared to unload it. He now felt safe in the Serrill household at night. Without thinking, he picked up the pistol, pulled the slide to the rear and watched the round pop up. He let the slide move forward, and started to take up the pressure on the trigger. Then something told him to stop. He looked down, and to his horror, realised that he had not removed the magazine. He had therefore chambered a live round and was about to shoot himself in the leg. Sweating profusely, he gingerly released the pressure on the trigger, and with a shaking hand put the gun down on his bed and sat there shivering. It was some time before Ter Braak could focus and remove the magazine to make the pistol safe.

The spy forced himself to transmit his routine message to Hamburg. As usual, there was no reply and he crawled into bed only to lie there for hours reliving the moment when he almost brought his freedom to an abrupt end.

35
BERLIN

Major Ritter had been dreading the moment when he would be summoned to the Abwehr headquarters in Berlin. When the order arrived on 1st January 1941, he wondered how much of the coming year he would live to see. Arriving at Tirpitzufer 72, he was kept waiting for over half an hour by Admiral Canaris, and by the time Ritter was admitted to his office, he was fearing the worst.

'I understand you still haven't received any word from your man in Cambridge. Is that true?'

'Yes Herr Admiral. We've been listening out for him day and night since his departure, but so far, nothing. I've also checked with Madrid and there's been no letter from him.'

'Why not?'

'He could have been caught, but that seems unlikely, as there was more time to prepare him for his mission. I also ensured there was no advance notice of his arrival. His radio could be faulty, but they've proved to be reliable so far, at least for the agents who have managed to establish themselves.'

'So, major, you know the importance of this mission. What do you propose to do about it? I need to be able to report to the Fuhrer. When will that be?'

Ritter then wondered if Canaris had not mentioned the mission to Adolf so if it failed, he could just forget about it. On the other hand, perhaps he had told him in which case…The major had no doubts about the consequences of failure in those circumstances.

'If nothing's heard soon, we'll need a backup. I request, Herr Admiral, that you remove your veto on the use of *JOHNNY*. He's already active in England, and makes regular radio contact. He could be looking for Maud tomorrow.'

The admiral glared at Ritter. 'Certainly not. I don't wish to jeopardise that source, which I believe has potential for even greater success.'

'In that case, I have two good men, both of them already well through their training, and if I haven't heard from Fukken by the end of January, one of them will be dispatched.'

Canaris looked sternly over his half-rimmed glasses. 'Situation noted major. I'll await your further report. That will be all.'

36
HAMBURG

Ritter returned to his office knowing he had to find Maud one way or another. He still hoped Fukken would make contact, but his military training told him to plan for the worst. He decided he needed a meeting with Dr Praetorius.

The doctor's prime function was as an economic adviser, but he had gained the nickname of 'the Pied Piper', due to his record of tracking down suitable candidates from occupied countries, and persuading them to act as spies for the Abwehr. Invariably, they all had some shady past which was held against them, together with the threat of a one-way ticket to a concentration camp if they refused to co-operate.

Having completed his PhD at Southampton University in the early 1930s, Praetorius was fluent in English, but also an acknowledged expert on British ways. Accordingly, he had been Ritter's first choice to tutor Fukken to improve his chances, and ever since the Dutchman's departure the doctor had kept an ear open for news of his pupil. He was still annoyed at not being told anything of his mission, but realised that if it was so important, a follow up would be necessary. He came to the conference with Ritter well prepared.

'Herr Major, it's clear to me that if Fukken doesn't report back to us very soon, we'll need to send in another man. This conclusion is based on the fact that his mission, which I'm not deemed senior enough to know about, must be of such importance that it has to be completed regardless.'

'My dear doctor, I'd be only too delighted to tell you, but I'd be shot if I did. But you're right that it's important. Accordingly, I've set a deadline for the end of January and if we still haven't heard from him by then, we'll send another man.'

Praetorius nodded. 'Just as I thought. However, I think we need to look carefully at how Fukken was handled, to see if there's anything we can do to improve the odds of success, second time around. I've been giving the matter some thought, and if I may?'

'Please go on.'

'The first item is his radio and how it should be carried. Disguising it in a suitcase appears to be fine, but there's much debate about whether it should be strapped to the agent or put on a line from the main parachute harness. When strapped to the man, it does protect the more fragile components from damage upon impact, but on the other hand, it could well cause injury when the spy lands.'

'Yes, those are reasonable points. What's your recommendation?'

'If we look back at previous agents, the three who were dropped by parachute before Fukken all survived and made contact. It could be significant that all had their sets strapped to them. Fukken, on the other hand, had his on a rope tied to his harness. I accept that his apparent failure to report may have nothing to do with that approach, but as we know that sets tied to agents have survived, I propose the next man adopts that method.'

'Yes, under the circumstances, I'll arrange that. While we're on the subject of luggage, Fukken has been the only man so far to take a second suitcase with spare clothes in it. I believe he was issued with a *Revelation* case from the stores. Again, that may not be anything to do with his silence, but if you think about it, a man can be more mobile if he only has one case containing his radio, and wears extra underwear to keep him going until he has the chance to buy more.'

Praetorius was not convinced. 'What if he's stopped at a checkpoint, and searched. How does he explain away his extra layers?'

'A fair point assuming he's strip searched, which I think is unlikely, at least initially. A man with one suitcase would give the impression of a typical traveller, whereas with two...No, I think we should ban a second case for clothes.'

The doctor could not think of a convincing argument to support his doubts, so he conceded the point. On the next he was resolute. 'Now, coding. As instructed, I taught Fukken how to use one of our more complex book based codes. It's not for me to reason why, nor do I know which books you told him to use, but all I can say is that Fukken was never the best at coding, even with the more straightforward circular disc code he was taught as a LENA agent. None of the agents still under training are brilliant at coding. In fact they are worse than Fukken, and even he had to take a written copy of his coding instructions with him to make sure he got it right.'

Ritter was horrified. 'What happens if he's caught?'

'Hopefully he'll be able to destroy it before he's searched, but it was either that or risk receiving gobbledygook. So, my recommendation is to let the next man use the usual disc code.'

The major knew he had a problem. 'My decision to have Fukken use the book based method was so I could keep his messages confidential. But if we can't decode the message...' His voice trailed off. Ritter tapped the desk nervously then reached a decision. 'Advice accepted. Please arrange to issue the next man with a code disc.'

Praetorius smiled and then played his ace. 'Thank you Herr Major. I should just say that to maintain your illusion to Captain Boeckel that Fukken is still on the LENA payroll, I took disc eight, which he should have used and destroyed it. The next to be issued will therefore be number nine, so no-one except us will know about Fukken's different treatment.'

For once, Ritter was lost for words.

37
CAMBRIDGE

Ter Braak greeted the arrival of January and the New Year with mixed emotions. It was now some two months since his clandestine arrival. He had failed to receive a reply from Hamburg and to make matters worse Mrs Serrill had told him she would not be able to obtain any more temporary ration cards after the end of January. 'You must write to the office that issued your original card and ask them for a new one,' she insisted. To cap it all, his supply of cash was dwindling, and obviously would not last forever.

Finally, the day arrived when he was able to return to Clements Place. In front of the professor again, the spy launched into his concerns about his out of date ration book, failing radio batteries, inability to obtain a reply to his transmissions, and fears over diminishing funds.

The professor frowned. 'You certainly have a number of problems. The most pressing is clearly your ration book. I don't know anything about the regulations but I'll make some enquiries. I presume the one you have is forged?'

'Yes. Major Ritter told me they have a good man over here who'd sent him some originals to copy.'

'That's interesting. So my friend Nikolaus does have at least one other active agent over here. I wonder who it is?'

'Ritter didn't say. I wondered if it might be a civil servant who secretly supports Adolf.'

'That could be true. Someone who maintains a low profile and couldn't be used for your mission. I don't suppose we'll ever know.

Now, back to the batteries for your set. Not my field, you understand, and from what you say they may not be the cause of the problem. However, let's look on the bright side and assume it's not the set. If so, you won't stand a chance to get it to work without charged up batteries. From what I hear it's possible to get almost anything on the black market.' Realising Ter Braak might not know what that meant, the professor began to explain, only to be interrupted by the spy, who confessed to his dealings with the spiv Pearce, including short changing him on the exchange rate.

A look of alarm spread over the professor's face. 'I know you were trying to save money, but that was a very silly thing to do. There's every chance Pearce will find out what you've done, and will be after you. That sort of person is happy to cheat others, but won't take too kindly to being cheated himself.'

'I never thought of that,' said Ter Braak.

'Now, as for your cash. I would have thought that the amount you brought with you ought to have lasted quite a bit longer.'

Ter Braak looked at the floor. He had not had the nerve to own up to his regular visits and payments to Marge, not to mention his funding her move to somewhat better rooms. He had never enjoyed visiting the slum dwelling in Doric Street, and her new place in South Street, although still modest, was in a much better area.

The professor noticed this lack of response and while suspecting that Ter Braak had not mentioned everything, decided not to press the point. 'I may be able to lend you some cash, but you'll have to leave that one with me for the time being. You have sufficient money for the immediate future?'

Ter Braak nodded, hoping that he could at least still afford to see Marge. 'Yes, thank you professor, but before I go, how do you know Major Ritter? You seem to me to be a perfect example of English respectability and tradition.'

The professor gave Ter Braak a long stare and was some time before replying. 'Nikolaus Adolf Fritz Ritter...what a good old German name. I met Nick in America back in the 30s when I was at Princeton University on an exchange visit. He had graduated as a textile engineer from the Prussian Technical School and ended up running his own business in the States for a number of years. That's where he learned his fluent English. Moved in quite influential circles.

In fact, that's how I first met him, at an ambassadors' reception one night. I eventually worked out he was involved with the Abwehr. He didn't deny it and when I was leaving to return to the UK he told me about his alias, Dr Rantzau, and we agreed he would use that if he ever wanted to contact me again. He's got two children, Klaus and Katherine. Used to send them presents on their birthdays but not any longer. Oh, the good old days...'

Ter Braak noticed that the professor's usual brisk manner had disappeared when recounting memories of happier times. He paused for a moment, but was unable to restrain his curiosity further. 'I'm certainly not complaining but, why are you prepared to help me?'

'That's a good question. Why indeed?' The professor reflected for a moment. 'I suppose it's Nick Ritter's fault really. He introduced me to some of his countrymen, and even arranged for me to meet Adolf himself. I soon came to see Hitler as the saviour of Germany and indeed the whole world.'

As Ter Braak walked back to Montague Road, he reflected upon the professor's faith in Hitler. Before his departure from Holland, he had shared that view. However, his time in England had started to sow seeds of doubt. The words of Winston Churchill echoed around his mind. 'We shall never surrender.'

He knew he had to find the super weapon being developed by Maud.

38
HAMBURG

Major Nikolaus Ritter looked at the calendar on his office wall, and his heart sank. It was now the third week in January 1941 and, with still no contact from Fukken, it was clear there was no alternative but to send in another man, and pray he would be more successful. Summoning Dr Praetorius, the major announced, 'Time we had a look at who is to follow Fukken.'

'Certainly Herr Major. So, who's it to be?'

'If it was down to me, I'd just let *JOHNNY* take over, but Canaris has forbidden that. The only ones who stand any chance of finishing their training in time are Jakobs and Richter. What's your judgement of these two? Remind me of their backgrounds, please.'

The doctor opened the file he had brought with him, and flicked through the pages. 'The better educated of the two is Josef Jakobs. After the last war he qualified as a dentist and practised in Berlin for nine years. He's also a brave man, judging by the Iron Cross First Class he claims to have been awarded during his military service. Just as brave as you, if I may say so.'

The major smiled at the compliment. 'I seem to recall he's married with a young family.'

'Correct. Two sons and a daughter. He's forty-two, so he does have a degree of maturity'.

'Didn't he get involved in some shady dealings while he was drilling teeth?'

'Yes. He went to jail in Switzerland in '34 for selling adulterated gold for fillings. When he got out and came back to Germany he turned to procuring false passports for Jews and helping them transfer their funds out of the country, for a generous fee of course.'

Ritter raised his eyebrows. 'I presume he was banged up again, for that.'

'Yes, indeed. He served eighteen months in Oranienburg, but got himself out by volunteering for the Luftwaffe meteorological section. That's when I offered him the chance to join us.'

Again Ritter looked surprised. 'It sounds as if he's still a serving Luftwaffe officer. I don't suppose it makes a great deal of difference, but that means if he's caught, he'll be shot and not hanged.'

Praetorius shrugged his shoulders. 'A mere technicality if you ask me, and hopefully it won't come to that. Now, if we turn to Karel Richter, he's twenty-nine, single and a merchant seaman born in Sudetenland. Back in '39, he decided he didn't want anything to do with the war, so he deserted when his ship docked here in Hamburg, and hightailed it to Sweden. He was soon sent back where the Gestapo, in their inimitable way, branded him a traitor and packed him off to Fuhlsbuttel Konzentrationslager. If that wasn't bad enough, he was made to help defuse unexploded bombs.'

'He must have been a quick learner, or he wouldn't be one of our options today.'

'Or just lucky. Anyway, he didn't need to be asked twice to join us. However, he's not proved exactly the ideal student. Often late for lectures, has an abominably slow Morse rate, drinks like a fish, and to cap it all, has been involved in a number of fights.'

Ritter realised he now had to make a decision. Thinking aloud, he reviewed the facts. 'On the face of it, Jakobs is the more stable, with his family responsibilities, but I wonder if they might hold him back. There's obviously no such problem with Richter. However, is he too free-minded? There's no doubt both are rogues in their own way. On balance, I think a more mature approach is required...yes, it needs to be Jakobs.'

The doctor stood up, keen to close the meeting. 'So be it. I'll push him through the remainder of his training as quickly as possible. When do you want him to leave?'

'By the end of this month at the latest. But before you go, we need to decide on his cover details. As you know Jakobs' target will also be Cambridge. Let's have a look at those names and addresses *JOHNNY* sent us a few months back.' Ritter pulled out a file from his desk drawer, and thumbed through it. 'I reckon this one will do. It's not in Cambridge. It's a house at 33 Abbotsfield Gardens in somewhere called Woodford Green. The name to go with it is James Rymer.'

Preatorius thought back to his time in England. 'I remember Woodford Green, it's south of Cambridge, in Essex. But where do we get his passport and ration book from?'

'They'll come from Berlin. The Admiral has insisted his people handle the actual production, just as they did with the documents for Fukken. They're copying the ones *JOHNNY* provided, so they'll look the part. All I have to do is give them our choice of name and address. They'll enter those together with the remaining details and have the documents back to me within a day or so.'

Praetorius gathered together his papers. 'I'll tell Jakobs the good news and get him ready for the end of the month.'

39
CAMBRIDGE

Being paid to go on a pub crawl had sounded like the perfect job, but after only three weeks, Nemo was far from convinced. Having obtained a town street plan and a list of hostelries from the chief constable, he had plotted their positions on the map, and begun working his way through the one hundred or so pubs, keeping his eyes and ears open for any sign of the missing Abwehr agent.

It had seemed a thankless task until he reached the Blackamoors Head, a scruffy establishment in Victoria Street. As he entered the public bar, Nemo looked through the smoky haze, and judged he had dressed appropriately for this visit. Hearing an Irish voice, and not wishing to be caught out by a native, he dropped his plan to pose as a paddy.

As he walked towards the bar, all conversation stopped and heads turned to look at the middle-aged stranger, dressed in shabby clothing and wearing a cloth cap that had definitely seen better days. Nemo was encouraged by the silence his entrance had generated. Experience told him this was an establishment frequented by drinkers with a guilty conscience.

The cockney voice that ordered a pint convinced onlookers that here was a workman from London. Taking his drink to a seat away from the bar, Nemo sat quietly and was soon being ignored by the regulars. He listened to the chatter and quickly focused on a short stocky fellow, with a scar on his left cheek, holding court in the far corner. Suspecting that this character was likely to know what was going on, Nemo drained his glass and made his way back to the bar. 'Same again please. Who's the geezer with the scar?' he asked casually.

'That's Lennie Pearce.' The barman leaned forward and spoke in a whisper. 'Our Lennie is the king of the underworld in this town. Quite happy to take anyone on as you can tell by his face. He has a sister, Patsy, but don't be misled by her pretty face. She's as bad as her brother, although she tends to delegate the nasty stuff and just pick up the prize at the end. Definitely not a couple you want to cross, if you ask me. Why do you want to know?'

'I'm up 'ere from London for a few days, and it's always nice to know who's who.'

'Come off it, mate. You must have a reason for asking.'

It was Nemo's turn to lean forward and speak quietly. 'I've a foolproof way of dodging the call-up and I'm looking for some punters up 'ere.' Slipping a ten bob note across the counter, Nemo continued. 'Keep the change, but I'd be very obliged if you could put the word about for me.'

The barman nodded, and poured him his pint, which Nemo took back to his seat. He reckoned it took all of two minutes for the barman to call Scarface Pearce over, and a further minute for Lennie to swagger over to him and say in a very threatening tone, 'Hello my friend. I'm told you've a racket you want to run. I think you should know that this is my patch, and nothing happens here without my say so. Understand?'

Nemo looked suitably scared. 'Yes gov, but I've a friend who's got a dickey ticker, and 'e's 'appy to play the part of anyone who wants to dodge the line.'

'Ah, I see. He stands in at the medical. What's his price?'

'E'll do it for a brace of ponies, but there are many who don't want to get shot at and will willingly cough up to a ton to avoid the call-up. That's a good mark-up and plenty of room for both of us to take a cut.'

A brace of ponies was slang for fifty pounds and a ton, one hundred. The realisation there was a fifty pound profit to be made brought a smile to his face. With no intention of sharing anything he grinned. 'I think we might be able to do a deal. Where's this bloke hang out, then?'

'Down in the smoke.'

Lennie Pearce looked disappointed. His empire had expanded significantly since the start of the war, but not as far as London. 'Bugger it. Your mate sounded just what I need. I'm short of readies just now. I did a cash deal before Christmas. Some foreigner paid me in dollars, but not enough. When I find him I'll hang him up by his balls. Will this mate of yours travel up here?'

Nemo could hardly believe his ears and was about to say yes, when the door to the street opened and in walked a bobby.

'Soon be last orders, gentlemen' shouted the constable, as he looked intently at his watch.

A moan went up, but Nemo decided this was his passport to a quick exit and also some kudos in the eyes of Pearce.

'Don't you tell me when to stop drinking, you bloody bluebottle,' he yelled.

The policeman tried to calm the situation. 'Come on Sir, let's call it a day,' he urged, only to receive a punch for his troubles.

Nemo was promptly handcuffed and dragged out, to a chorus of jeers and catcalls.

Nemo's subsequent report made Major Dixon smile, and also caused much hilarity and admiration when it reached MI5 headquarters.

Tar was most impressed. 'This guy can certainly think on his feet. But does his report say if he had to reveal his identity to get himself released?'

Guy Liddell scanned the page. 'Apparently not. It seems Nemo spotted this chap Pearce slipping something into the bobby's pocket during the struggle to handcuff him. He thinks it could have been a bribe to get him off, or perhaps a regular sweetener, to look the other way on Pearce's activities. Anyway, he didn't dare take any risks, and continued to play up. Whatever the reason, he was released the next morning with just a caution.'

Tar's face lit up. 'A foreigner with dollars. That sounds like our man to me. Obviously Pearce is also searching for him. I wonder who'll get there first?'

40
CAMBRIDGE

Ter Braak woke with a start and found himself lying on his back. He forced himself to focus. At first, the ceiling looked like any other but then his eyes noticed the plaster cornice around the perimeter, and he knew at once where he was. Stretching out his left arm, he expected to find the comforting contours of Marge. His fingers searched in vain. The other half of the double bed was empty.

Surprised and not a little concerned, he raised himself onto one elbow and looked around. At the bottom of the bed he saw the usual chair, with his clothes hastily thrown onto it. Beyond that in the bay window was Marge wearing the bright pink silk dressing gown he had just bought her. She was sitting at the dressing table combing her hair, which was now a glowing blonde colour. The spy relaxed and lay down again.

Marge heard him stir, and turned. With a smile she rose, walked over to the bed and lay down next to him. Playfully ruffling his hair, she purred, 'You're awake at last my darling Jan.'

Ter Braak looked worried. 'How long... Did we?'

'You've been asleep for over an hour, and no, we didn't. You just couldn't relax, my darling. Tell me what's worrying you?'

'It's this war. I just can't see an end to it.'

'You're not alone in that, I can assure you, but tell me, Jan, who's Maud? Is that your wife? I thought you said you weren't married.'

Ter Braak felt faint, and was lost for words.

Marge prompted him. 'Come now Jan, I like to know that sort of thing.'

'Why do you ask?' he said, making a supreme effort to control his features.

'You were talking in your sleep. Something about...must find Maud. Come on, I'm curious. Who is she?'

'I can assure you she's not my wife, but just someone I need to find in connection with my work.'

'That's the paper for your countrymen who are still free, isn't it?'

Ter Braak breathed a sigh of relief. 'Yes. I'm told Maud lives somewhere in Cambridge, but I've not managed to trace her yet.'

'You'd better have a word with my other client...sorry, friend, Alan. He's always moaning about Maud.'

'Alan? Alan who? What does he do? Is he in the Forces?'

Marge looked sheepish. 'Sorry, I mustn't say any more. I have a rule not to discuss my clients with others. You wouldn't want me talking to them about you, would you?'

Ter Braak had to agree with her, but realised that this might just be the breakthrough he had been hoping for. 'Of course, my dear Marge, but don't you think you owe me? After all...' The spy looked around the room, reminding her that he had helped fund her move to this address.

Marge weighed up her conflicting emotions. He had certainly paid for the move to South Street which had transformed her life, but on the other hand she had a reputation for discretion.

'I'm very grateful to you, but...he's not in the Forces and never wears a uniform. That's all I can say.'

Making his way back to St Barnabas Road, Ter Braak wondered if this Alan's Maud was the Maud he himself desperately needed to trace. He realised there was only one way to find out. It only took a day or so watching Marge's address to learn when she would be out for a while.

After seeing Marge walk down the street, and making sure no one was watching, Ter Braak made his way to her door. His time in jail had been like a university of crime, and he had graduated with honours. As a result the lock on the door took seconds to pick, and he was soon inside. Careful to check that his shoes were free of mud or any other incriminating material, and wearing gloves, Ter Braak began a methodical search, making sure anything he picked up was replaced exactly as it had been left. He knew Marge always put his payments into a large ledger, and it did not take long to find the book, hidden under a pile of underwear.

Ter Braak sat on the floor and flicked through the pages. He gasped. Marge might as well have been an accountant, for listed on separate pages were details of her numerous clients, with details of her services listed below, together with a note of the payment received. He then noticed that against each person, Marge had written a few notes about the character concerned.

Unable to resist his curiosity, he quickly searched for his own entry. He read that she found him quiet but very generous. She also wondered what he was actually doing in the war, and speculated it might be something secret. Her last comment was that he was also a liar. He had said he was not married, but she was sure that Maud was more to him than he had admitted.

Then he heard a knock on the front door and Ter Braak dived behind the bed. Grasping his automatic, he flicked off the safety catch, and aimed it at the bedroom door.

Another knock made his heart race even more. He held his breath. Sweat tricked down his brow. After a few minutes he reckoned the visitor, whoever it had been, must have given up and left. Glancing at his watch, Ter Braak decided to allow himself no more than a further five minutes so he frantically turned the pages in search of the mysterious Alan. And there he was:, not as frequent a visitor as himself, but nevertheless still a regular customer. He scanned the scribbled comments to find out what he did and discovered she thought he was a scientist, who was troubled by someone called Maud. Marge wondered if she was a work colleague, but certainly one who seemed to be quite demanding.

Ter Braak's natural instinct was to get out before he was discovered, but frantic to find some other clue to help him track down Alan, he held his nerve and looked back over the diary entries. After a while he saw that Alan was a man of regular habits, with weekly visits each Friday at the same time, six pm, presumably on his way home. Quickly shutting the book, and replacing it under the pile of underwear, Ter Braak made a final check. Confident his visit would not be noticed, he made a rapid exit, knowing he would have to return and keep watch on Friday evening.

The spy cursed his training, or lack of it. He had been shown how to spot a tail, and take evasive measures, but no-one had bothered to tell him how to follow someone. He mulled over the problem and decided his only hope was if his target did not expect to be followed.

It seemed an age for Friday to arrive, and even longer for the clock to move round to the appointed time. Even allowing for single summer time, it was dark by then, and the blackout made Ter Braak's task of remaining in the shadows relatively simple. Just after six a tall young man in an expensive overcoat, with an intense frown on his face, arrived at Marge's front door, and was promptly admitted. Ter Braak looked enviously at the coat, and felt sure this must be the mysterious Alan. He wondered how long he would have to wait. It turned out to be about forty minutes. Ter Braak crossed the road and fell in behind his target as the man he believed to be Alan made his way cautiously in the blackout.

Keeping himself as far away as possible whilst still being able to spot the overcoat he coveted, Ter Braak lost count of the left and right turns he made. When Alan walked up a front pathway, he made a mental note of the house number and then walked to the end of the street and noted the name. As he made his way back to his digs, he wondered what time Alan would be leaving again for work but he knew it was not practical to loiter outside Alan's house in the morning. Alan could leave for work at any time, and Ter Braak would stand out like a sore thumb. What else could he do?

It was not until much later that a solution came to him. He would wait at the end of Alan's road in the evening blackout, and see from which direction he arrived. The next night he would be able to move closer to his starting point and, by that process, eventually reach Alan's office, or wherever he worked.

This system proved better in theory than in practice. After five nights, Ter Braak had progressed back less than half a mile along Alan's route home from work, and on two of those evenings, he had not made any progress at all, due to a darker than usual night and an inability to see where Alan came from. But on the sixth evening, fate smiled on him. Just as Alan came into view, he stopped and put his hands in his pockets, clearly searching for something. Not finding what he sought, he turned on his heels and set off to retrace his steps. This all happened in a matter of moments, and Ter Braak froze for a second. Realising that his quarry might now lead him directly back to his workplace, he took off, striding out as fast as he dared in the gloom.

Alan was walking quicker than usual, and it took the breathless spy some time to close the gap. Once in sight, Ter Braak eased back, to stay a few yards behind Alan, and eventually found himself in Free School Lane in the centre of town. Alan stopped in front of an ornate stone archway and rang the bell. After a moment or two, the heavy timber door creaked open and Alan was recognised and admitted, before the door closed again.

Ter Braak walked up to the archway, where a sign told him he was standing in front of the Cavendish Laboratory. Ter Braak wondered what they did there, presumably something scientific. He knew who would have to find out.

The spy could hardly wait to see the professor again. He finally admitted his involvement with Marge, but decided not to mention his continued payments to her. The professor just smiled and to Ter Braak's relief, agreed to make some further discreet enquiries.

'This is going to take a while, young man. It's involving a different college, and I just can't ring them up and ask a straight question. These are dangerous times, and I'm going to have to tread very carefully. In the meantime, I suggest you keep your head down. Remember there are some pretty desperate people looking for you.'

Josef Jakobs looked forward to his final briefing with Major Ritter. He had not met him before, but knew they were of a similar age and both well educated. He had also been told that Ritter was the holder of the Iron Cross First Class, and wondered if his own completely false claim to have the same award had reached his ears. Most importantly, he had a gut feeling that the forthcoming mission was of some importance to the major.

Entering Ritter's office, Jakobs made a point of staring directly at the Iron Cross pinned to the lower left side of Ritter's Luftwaffe uniform jacket, together with the ribbon confirming the previous Second Class award, on the right hand side. His own pinstriped three piece suit prevented him wearing any such medal, but he could tell by the look in Ritter's eyes that the major believed he was a fellow recipient of that decoration.

Bolstered by this illusion of equality, Jakobs relaxed as Ritter put his hand out. 'Good to see you, Josef. Do please take a seat.' The spy sat down and accepted the cigarette he was offered. When Ritter smiled, he revealed a glint of gold. *Upper right seven capped* thought the former dentist, at the same time wondering about the quality of the metal. He was brought back to reality when Ritter asked, 'Has Dr Praetorius explained to you the basic outline of your mission?'

Jakobs nodded. 'Yes, Sir. I'm to be dropped near Cambridge, to find out what has happened to the Dutchman, Engelbertus Fukken; although I knew him as Bertus.'

'Correct, but there's more to it than that, which I'll come to shortly. I believe you met Fukken before he left for England, so I take it you'll recognise him?'

'Indeed. Wears glasses, and had that silly little moustache. Sorry, I know it's none of my business what he looks like, but all the same! I found him very determined, and someone I wouldn't want to upset, but we got on well after I learnt he was also a Catholic. We did some parts of our training together. He was better at keying and helped me with my Morse, which I know is rather slow. That's until he was taken over by Doctor Praetorius for a mission that was obviously going to be a bit special, though poor old Captain Boeckel kept on insisting that Bertus was still on the LENA programme. I realised I must be going to do something similar when the doctor took over my tuition.'

'I take it he was of use to you?'

'Oh yes, especially the lessons on pounds, shillings and pence. I have to say, that I'm sure some of those who left earlier would have benefitted from this tuition as well.'

Ritter ignored the criticism. 'Now, I have to tell you that your mission is vital, and could well influence the outcome of the war.' This made Jakobs wonder what he was about to embark upon and made him think that the metrological office had not been too bad after all.

What he heard next made him wonder if returning to the concentration camp might not be a better option. 'I'm about to tell you something which mustn't, I repeat must not, be revealed to anyone else, on your oath to the Fuhrer.' Ritter took the stunned silence to be agreement. He looked Josef in the eyes, and went on. 'We've received information from a very reliable source that the English are developing a new weapon. No other details are known, other than the development work is being carried out in Cambridge, and someone called Maud is involved. Fukken was sent over at the beginning of November last year to base himself in Cambridge and quite simply, find Maud. So far he has failed to report, so it's now down to you to find Maud, and of course Fukken, if possible.'

Jakobs relaxed slightly. For a moment he had feared his mission might involve assassination. He had never seen himself as a killer, but finding someone, a woman called Maud, sounded more within his grasp. He then thought of poor Fukken. 'Do you have any idea what could have happened to Bertus?'

'No. He may be still searching for Maud, but hasn't been able to send us a message. You need to know he's not using his real name. He chose the cover name of Jan Willem Ter Braak, which I think had something to do with editors at newspapers he had worked for. Anyway, that's what's on his documents. His background story is that he came over at Dunkirk, and is with the Dutch Free Press in London. Now, talking about cover names, I have here two registration cards. They're just like the one being used by Fukken, and are based on genuine cards sent over to us from one of our men in

England. Admiral Canaris himself has overseen the production of these forgeries, so you don't need to worry about checkpoints. One is blank for you to use as a backup. The other is made out in the name of James Rymer of 33 Abbotsfield Gardens, in Woodford Green. We've chosen that address because it's some way away from Cambridge, and unlikely to be known by anyone living in the town.'

'If you have other men already in England, why can't one of them take over? In fact, why didn't one of them start the search for Maud in the first place?'

Ritter began to regret having such an intelligent and outspoken subordinate. He blustered. 'There are other factors which ruled out that approach.'

'You mean those men in England can't be trusted?'

Ritter was now convinced this spy was much too bright, but consoled himself that this in itself should ultimately pay dividends. He continued the charade. 'Certainly not. They're involved in other matters which need not concern you.'

'Alright, so I'm James Rymer. What's my reason for being in Cambridge?'

'I'll leave you to come up with a storyline that you're happy with.'

'I'll give it some thought. Now, what about cash? I'm going to have to support myself for some time.'

Ritter slid an envelope across his desk. 'Here's five hundred one pound notes. That's enough to keep you going, and also support Fukken if…no, when, you find him.'

Taking the money Jakobs looked thoughtful. 'So, let's assume I find Bertus, we solve the problem of this new super weapon and radio the details back to you. How do we get home again?'

The major knew the invasion had been postponed for the time being. Although no orders had yet been issued, he suspected its cancellation was permanent, and with it the chance of recovering any of his agents, in the short term. But he knew he had to give the impression that the mission to find Maud was not a one-way trip. Doing his best to sound as convincing as possible, he repeated what he had told Fukken. 'I have it on good authority that the invasion will be underway soon. The first wave of troops will be on the lookout for you. You have nothing to fear. We always look after our own.'

Jakobs had grave doubts about this but realised there was no point in raising them. He turned to his next concern. 'I presume I'll be dropped by parachute. When do I get a practice drop?'

Responding as he always did, Ritter confirmed that there would be no practice jump. He went on to give his usual advice. 'There's nothing to it. Just keep your legs together, knees slightly bent, and roll when you hit the ground.'

Jakobs said nothing, but gave Ritter a look that said, 'You've never jumped before, have you?'

The major knew he had been rumbled, and moved on as quickly as possible. 'Don't forget to arrange for the equipment department to issue you with a small spade so you can bury your 'chute after you've landed.'

'What, just like the one I found in Fukken's wardrobe after he'd left?' Jakobs asked, with a grin.

The colour drained from Ritter's face at this bombshell. Was that the shovel Fukken should have taken with him? If it was, he might have been unable to properly secrete his parachute, which could well have been found by now. Did that explain the silence? Ritter struggled to maintain his composure. 'That sounds like one of our standard issue. Now is there anything else?'

'What about a map?'

'Ah, yes. I'll make sure it's ready for you when you leave, which looks like being the last day of this month, the 31st. Good luck.'

The men shook hands, both praying that this mission would not be the death of them.

42
LONDON

Brigadier Harker seemed to be at the end of his tether. 'Please tell me you have some positive news. I don't think I'll be in this chair for much longer, as I'm sure Winston wants me out. I'd like to have this particular issue put to bed before I go.'

Liddell was not surprised by this. Gossip around the office had now reached fever pitch, and most were expecting another change at the top of MI5, with Colonel Sir David Petrie being the favourite to take over. Liddell tried to sound positive, while knowing there was still a long way to go. 'The good news is that the fracas in the pub the other week seems to have paid off, with Nemo now watching Scarface Pearce, as he uses all his underworld contacts to trace the elusive foreigner.'

'I hope Mr Pearce helps us get to this spy sooner rather than later. I dread to think what damage he may be doing while still at large. If he's sending messages with information which contradicts the stuff we're getting our double agents to transmit, friend Ritter is going to know all his men are blown.'

Liddell frowned. 'Yes, Sir, and with it our chance of influencing future events.'

43
CAMBRIDGE

Although he had promised the professor to see if he could obtain fresh batteries for his radio on the black market, Ter Braak did not relish the thought of contacting Scarface Pearce again, in case the spiv now knew the true exchange rate of dollars to pounds. Best leave that for the time being, Ter Braak decided. He was comforted by the knowledge that the professor was looking into the problem of his ration book. There were times when he had been unable to sleep for thinking about it. The spy normally slept like a log, but this could well be the undoing of him. The justice meted out at Pentonville Prison to at least three of his colleagues in December still haunted him.

Ter Braak's worries were well founded. Mrs Serrill had become increasingly concerned with the lack of a replacement ration book and the prospect of having to feed her lodger without the benefit of his share of the rations. Taking the bull by the horns, she visited the food office and brought home the necessary application form and placed it on the table in front of him, just as he was eating his morning toast.

'As I said before, the man at the food office, nice though he is, has told me again that he can't let you have any more temporary ration cards after the end of this month. Seems he was stretching the rules by giving you those cards up to Christmas, and he's already gone well beyond the proper limit. So you've got to fill in that form and apply for a new one, now.' She handed Ter Braak a pen, and stood over him in a surprisingly threatening manner.

Mr Serrill looked up from his paper. 'When she's got that look on her face, Jan, she'll not let you rest until you've signed on the dotted line, or whatever it is you need to do. So, if I were you...' He quickly looked down at his paper when his wife turned and glared at him.

Working on the basis that he would not need to post the form, Ter Braak did as he was told. Mrs Serrill smiled. 'There now, that wasn't too difficult, was it? This needs to go to the office that issued your original card, which was Feltham apparently. I've got an envelope with the correct address on it.' To his horror she grabbed the completed form, folded it, put it into the OHMS envelope, and made for the door, pulling on her coat as she went. 'I'll just pop down to the post box. I should be able to catch the morning collection if I'm quick.' With that she was gone.

Ter Braak looked on, open mouthed, and fearing the worst. His worries were confirmed at his next meeting with Professor Carpenter.

'Under no circumstances must you apply for another ration book. The one you have is, as we know, forged and may have a valid number, but certainly not against the name you're using. I've discovered, however, that the Dutch emergency committee in London could deal with this for you, assuming of course you were a genuine Dutch refugee.'

'Oh, God. Mrs Serrill made me complete a form asking for a new book only the other day. I didn't have the chance to destroy it before she put it in the post. What shall I do?'

'You must write again to the food office and tell them your application was a mistake, and that the Dutch committee has dealt with it for you. Which office did your application form go to?'

'Feltham, that was where my original card was issued.'

'I think that proves my point. I presume you've never been to Feltham?' Ter Braak shook his head.

'Ritter's 'good man' must have sent one from there for him to copy.'

'How am I going to eat in the meantime?'

'As I see it, there's only one way. You're going to have to find new accommodation, but on a bed and breakfast basis only. If you stick to tea and toast in the morning, your landlord won't need your ration book. You'll have to eat out for all other meals, but you've got enough cash for the time being, haven't you?'

Ter Braak did a rapid mental calculation. He had to be able to pay for his now regular visits to Marge, but could not bring himself to admit to this extra outlay. 'Yes, unless I have some unexpected expenses. Like black market batteries.'

'Ah, yes. I think you'll have to leave those for the present. You'd be better off spending your time and money on sorting out new digs.'

Realising he could kill two birds with one stone, Ter Braak made his way to Green Street and the office of Haslop and Co. Climbing the stairs to his rented room, he sat on the davenport, and penned the required letter to Mr H G Dodd, food executive officer at the Feltham food control office, explaining that the Free Dutch Committee had processed his new card. He apologised for his error, and confirmed he no longer required a new ration book from him. Sealing up the envelope ready to post, he turned his attention to locating new accommodation.

Walking back down the stairs, he turned left into the ground floor office of the letting agency. The receptionist behind the desk recognised him. 'Hello, Mr Ter Braak. We don't see you very often, but I'm glad you've come in. The rental for your office runs out at the end of this month. Do you want to continue beyond the 31st January?'

Ter Braak faced a quandary. He did not want to spend unnecessary money and compromise his ability to visit Marge but he felt the office might come in useful. He took the plunge. 'Yes, I'll keep it for the time being.' He opted to pay up to the end of February, and handed over the required two pounds, for which he received a handwritten receipt. At the receptionist's suggestion, he also left thirty bob with her to cover the same extra period of furniture rental, which she undertook to pass on to Coopers.

'Thank you, and as I'm here, perhaps you can help me. As you know, I'm at St Barnabas Road with Mr and Mrs Serrill. A delightful couple, but I do find the noise from the trains a bit disturbing. Do you have anywhere else a bit further away from the station, and on a bed and breakfast basis only? I'm going to be away a bit more now, and won't need any evening or weekend meals.'

The receptionist checked her filing cabinet. 'This might suit you. Miss Rosina Blackwood in Montague Road, number two hundred and eleven. That's quite some distance from the station and the railway line. Will that do? If so, I'll give her a call to let her know you're on your way.'

'Yes, It sounds just right. Thank you very much.' Setting off along Chesterton Road, passing Jesus Green and the river on his right, he soon found himself in Montague Road. Number two hundred and eleven turned out to be a neat, yellow brick semi-detached house, with a single storey bay window taking up much of the small front garden. He knocked on the door, which was opened by a smartly dressed woman, whom he judged to be in her late forties, or possibly early fifties. She had slightly greying hair tied back in a neat bun, and following the telephone call from the agent, was expecting him.

'Mr Ter Braak, nice to meet you. I'm Miss Blackwood. Do come in, and I'll show you the room.' He followed her upstairs into a small rear bedroom. He had made up his mind on his way over that the state of his batteries ruled out even thinking of using his transmitter.

'This will do just fine,' he confirmed with a smile. Polite negotiations took place over a cup of tea, and it was agreed he would pay ten shillings a week, inclusive of breakfast tea and toast, and that he would move in on 31st January.

Ter Braak realised he had to give the Serrills a plausible reason for leaving. The solution came when the reality of war struck home. A bomb was dropped on Mill Road Bridge and two residents were killed. This came not long after incendiaries had been dropped on Hills Road, in the Hyde Park Corner area, near to the junction with Regent Street.

On the day of his departure, he returned at lunch time and told the Serrills that a member of staff at his head office had been killed in an air raid. 'I'm so sorry, but I've been sent to London to replace him. I've ordered a taxi from the Market Hill cab rank to take me to the station to catch the ten past two train. It'll be here any minute.'

This upset the couple, who realised they had grown quite fond of their lodger. When the cab arrived Mr Serrill helped with the luggage, including the small brown case which, to his surprise, he found to be very heavy.

'That's my typewriter and other office bits and pieces,' volunteered Ter Braak in response to the questioning look from his landlord. Keeping his fingers crossed, and with some sadness, the spy waved goodbye as the cab drove away.

Shutting the front door, Mr Serrill sank into his chair, and thought back over the past three months they had shared with their lodger. The Christmas celebrations were undoubtedly his happiest memories. The problem was, the more he thought about it, the more he became certain that the drink and joint of beef Jan had produced could only have been bought on the black market. But who is to know? he reassured himself.

His reminiscences were rudely interrupted by Mrs Serrill. 'You got the front door key back, I hope?' she called from the kitchen. His heart sank. 'Bloody hell, I forgot all about it,' he said, as he jumped to his feet and grabbed his coat from the hook in the hall. 'I'll get my bike, and try to catch him at the station.'

The retired fireman was no athlete, and his initial burst of speed soon fell away, although his gasping continued as he pedalled as fast as he could, swinging left into Tenison Road, and left again at the end into the station yard. Leaning his bike against the fence, he ran past the ticket office onto the platform. Luckily, he was still well known to the staff, and no-one insisted that he buy a platform ticket.

The London train was just about to leave. The porter was closing the doors, and the guard had his green flag in his hand, ready to wave. Mr Serrill checked as many carriages as he could before the train pulled out, but could not see any sign of Jan. Riding back to St Barnabas Road, he wondered about the weight of his case, and the fact that he had not seen it before. He presumed it must have been locked in the wardrobe. And, why had he not seen their lodger at the station?

Those thoughts were put out of his mind when he arrived home to some abuse from Mrs Serrill. 'Now we're going to have to get another key cut, and I've checked his room and he's left some things behind.'

Meanwhile Ter Braak was settling into his new abode.

44
HAMBURG

Major Ritter had been present at the departure of every one of the eleven agents he had sent to England, and he had no intention of missing the take-off of Josef Jakobs. That was, until urgent demands from Admiral Canaris kept him at his desk in Hamburg, and he had been forced to delegate the task to Dr Praetorius.

By taking off late on Friday 31st January, the deadline set for the end of the month had only just been met. Sitting in his office the next day, the major waited anxiously to hear from the doctor. When Praetorius arrived quite late, Ritter knew not everything had gone to plan. Praetorius slumped into a chair, and it was some time before he spoke. 'Sorry for the delay, but I decided to wait until Gartenfeld had landed back at Schiphol airport, so I could report a satisfactory drop.'

The major felt frantic. 'And, wasn't it?'

'Unfortunately, no. It got off to a bad start when Jakobs couldn't get the canvas flying helmet on. The one brought for him was too small. So, we got him a metal helmet. Then there was nearly another problem with the flying suit. As instructed, Jakobs hadn't taken a second suitcase, and was wearing extra clothing. Getting the flying suit on was therefore hard work, but after a struggle we eventually got the zips done up.'

'If that's all that went wrong...'

'The take-off was okay, but when he got back, Gartenfeld reported that he was convinced poor old Jakobs hit the side of the plane as he jumped.'

'Did Gartenfeld think he was seriously injured?'

'Difficult to be certain, as his 'chute opened automatically on the static line, but yes, he felt sure he'd been badly hurt. In fact, he wondered if he was still alive.'

Ritter put his head in his hands. This news could be his own death sentence, and he struggled to stay calm as he thought over what he should do next. His first instinct was to send a message to *JOHNNY* and ask him to help. Then he thought of the orders from Canaris not to involve him.

He discussed his options with Praetorius, who responded instantly. 'My own view of Gartenfeld is that he's a cocky bugger, always claiming to drop our agents on the nail. The problem is we never get to know if that's the case or not. However, I do respect his experience as a pilot, and if he thinks Jakobs was badly hurt when he jumped, then he's probably correct. We have to bear in mind that any such injury would almost certainly be aggravated by the landing, and could then prove fatal.'

Ritter sat in silence. His conscience told him he should get *JOHNNY* to help his man, but he also knew the consequences of disobeying an order. It was some time before he stood up, and told the doctor what he planned to do.

45
CAMBRIDGE

Nancy Cox felt quite excited as she put down the phone. Knocking politely, she entered Major Dixon's office. She was aware of his concern regarding the still missing parachutist who had landed not far away from Hanslope and Bletchley Park, and had the hint of a smile on her face as she walked in. 'Excuse me, Sir, but I've just taken a call from a DS Mills of special branch. Another enemy agent's parachute has been found near a village called Ramsey, north of Huntingdon.'

'Not another missing spy! The country will be crawling with them before much longer,' exclaimed the major.

Nancy could not keep a straight face any longer and burst out laughing. 'Sorry Sir. I should have added that this time the man was still attached to his 'chute. He's been taken into custody, and is now in a cell at Ramsey police station. I've told them you'll be on your way as soon as possible.'

Dixon realised Nancy had caught him out. 'I'll have you arrested for misleading His Majesty's security services,' he said with a grin, as he stood up, pulling his coat on as he did so. 'Where did you say Ramsey was?'

The efficient Nancy had already sorted out the relevant one inch to the mile Ordnance Survey map, which she opened up on his desk. 'The shortest route looks like being out through Girton, past your golf club, on to Earith, then through Somersham and on to Warboys. Then it's only five miles or so to Ramsey. I'm not sure where the police station is, but it's only a small village, so I reckon you'll find it without too much difficulty.'

Dixon thanked her, grabbed the map, and ran from the office. In fact, he ran all the way home. As usual he had walked to the office and today cursed his habit of leaving the car on his drive. However, it was only a matter of minutes before he was making his way out of the town. Following the route plotted by Nancy he eventually reached Warboys where he turned onto the road to Ramsey. Looking around him, all he could see were hedges and fields. As he drove along the quiet country lane he reflected on the problem faced by the spy he was on his way to meet. The man would have needed somewhere well off the beaten track for a landing, but not so isolated that a stranger would stand out like a sore thumb.

The realisation that the man whose parachute had been found close to Bletchley Park had managed to overcome these difficulties nearly made Dixon drift into a ditch. Focusing intently for the remainder of the journey, he arrived at Ramsey just before noon, and as predicted by the ever-efficient Nancy, had no problem in finding the police station. Greeted by the experienced special branch officer, Dixon followed him to one of the cells, where he squinted through the small viewing window at a tall slender man with a sallow emaciated face and unkempt brown hair tinged with grey. Dressed in a dark suit and lying on the bunk with one of his ankles heavily bandaged, the spy was clearly downcast and obviously in some pain from his injury.

'That's him,' confirmed Mills, who then guided Dixon into the small interview office at the end of the corridor, where he shut the door, sat down and opened his pocketbook. 'Our man was carrying forged papers in the name of James Rymer, and is supposedly living in Woodford Green He now admits his real name is Josef Jakobs. He claims to have parachuted down late last night. As you can see by the bandages, he's injured. He hurt his ankle when he baled out, and the landing made it worse. The local GP, Doctor Hertzog, has seen him and confirms the ankle is broken but he's strapped it up and says it's okay for him to travel.'

'Good man. The quicker we get him to London, the better. Who found him?' asked Dixon.

'A couple of chaps from near Warboys were walking to work here in the village at about eight thirty this morning, when they heard a couple of gun shots. They presumed it was a poacher, but when more shots rang out, they decided to investigate. They found our man in a potato field on Dovehouse Farm, clearly hurt, and sheltering beneath his parachute. Much to their relief, he'd only fired his gun to attract attention, and he threw it away as soon as they approached. One of the locals, Charles Baldock, stayed with Jakobs, while the other, Harry Coulston, ran to get help. He decided to go to Wistow Fen Farm, where the owner, Harry Godfrey's a leading light in the Ramsey Home Guard.'

'Oh, no, not the home guard! That'll mean the whole county will know about this by tomorrow. They just can't keep their mouths shut.'

DS Mills nodded. 'Yes, I'm afraid so, but standing orders are to involve them in this sort of thing. A Captain Newton and a Lieutenant Curedale arrived on the scene and searched our man. It was obvious he was a spy when they found his wireless set partially buried and what we think is a coding disc torn up and scattered about amongst the numerous cigarette butts. Looks as if he had been in agony during the night and smoked all his fags to deaden the pain from his leg.'

'What else did they find on him?'

'A torch, two ID cards, one of which was blank, a ration book, a German-English Dictionary, some tablets, a touring map of England, and, would you believe it, virtually five hundred pounds in one pound notes. His Mauser pistol was nearby, where he had thrown it. Everything's been parcelled up for you to take.'

'Well done, Sergeant. How did you get him here from the field?'

'Harry Godfrey got his horse-drawn hay cart and Jakobs was bundled onto it, and brought here. There wasn't much sympathy for him, and from what I've been told, the cart just happened to find every pothole and bump in the road. It must have been a nightmare of a journey for him. When he arrived, Sergeant Jaikins, who's our Acting Inspector here, arranged for the doctor to check him over, and then he called me.'

Major Dixon smiled. 'You've all done a grand job. Pity about the home guard, but that can't be helped. I'll have a word with Jakobs now, if that is indeed his real name, and then get him off to London. I think it best if we use my car. I'll drive - are you free to come with me to cover him? I take it you're armed?'

Mills tapped his jacket where it bulged slightly over his revolver. 'Certainly Sir. Ready when you are.'

The journey to London was not without its difficulties. The major had the problem of finding his way south on roads devoid of signposts. Jakobs, wedged sideways in the back with his bandaged foot up on the seat, tried desperately to avoid his injured leg from being jarred as the car was thrown around corners. DS Mills, forced to sit in the front passenger seat with his revolver on his lap, began to get a stiff neck from constantly looking behind him to check on his prisoner.

To the relief of all concerned, the Wolsey saloon reached London's Cannon Row police station at just after four pm, to be greeted by Tar Robertson, anxious to get his hands on the latest Abwehr visitor.

46
LONDON

Josef Jakobs tried to sit up, but the pain from his shattered ankle made him cry out and forced him to lie back on his pillow. The soldier at the foot of his bed, the latest in the rota who had been guarding him continually since his arrival the previous evening, glanced across in complete disinterest.

Turning his gaze to the windows on the far side of the ward, Jakobs could see it was still daylight. Wondering what time it was, he looked down at his watch only to be reminded by the striped pyjamas and bare wrist that he had been stripped of all his meagre belongings and was now in the hospital wing of Brixton Prison.

The spy thought back over the past few days. He winced at the memory of the discomfort he had felt during his journey to London and his growing suspicion that throwing the car around all those corners was merely the beginning of some further and harsher Gestapo-style treatment. To his surprise, and relief, he had been seen by a doctor who had examined his leg and had insisted he be transferred to hospital. At least that had resulted in a reasonable night's sleep.

Jakobs recalled the police station interview before his transfer to hospital by a major from MI5. At least he had stuck to the story of being sent to transmit back weather details, but had he been believed?

His musings were interrupted by the arrival of two burly orderlies, who proceeded to lift him onto a stretcher. His first reaction was that he was being moved to the operating theatre for the vital surgery on his shattered ankle. The continued presence of the armed guard made him think again, and his doubts were confirmed when he was loaded into an ambulance which promptly set off across London.

'Where am I going?' asked Jakobs.

The soldier looked at him with distain. 'You'll find out soon enough. All I can say is it looks as if somebody very important wants a word with you.'

That very important person turned out to be Lieutenant Colonel Robin Stephens. Nicknamed 'Tin Eye' for the monocle he always wore in his right eye, he ruled the interrogation centre at Latchmere House, Ham Common with a rod of iron. Although denouncing physical torture, the self-confessed xenophobe had no qualms about applying the most extreme mental pressure.

After arriving at the former World War I hospital for shell-shocked officers, Jakobs was taken from the ambulance and, in accordance with Camp 020 standard procedure, carried into what he judged was a doctor's surgery. The spy's fears that he was about to be tortured abated when the genial face of Dr Deardon appeared, and began what he explained was a routine medical examination. The former dentist found it ironic that his next examiner was another dentist. He assumed this would be a futile check for any suicide capsule, but Lt Winn was also looking for secret ink hidden in hollow teeth, something admitted by previous spies.

Jakobs knew he was facing his toughest grilling yet when he was carried into a timber panelled room with heavy curtains drawn across the windows and his stretcher placed on the floor. Sitting behind his desk, Stephens glared down at his latest customer. Annoyed that he was unable to adopt his usual approach of leaving the victim standing to attention for at least an hour before starting the interview, he was still determined to show the prisoner that he was at his mercy.

Walking to the side of the stretcher, Tin-Eye squinted down through his monocle at the spy for several minutes before speaking. Using information gathered from previous agents, he asked in a quiet voice, 'Tell me, how is Major Nikolaus Ritter? Still pretending to be an expert at parachute jumps?'

This shook Jakobs. How did they know about Ritter? he wondered.

The silence was exactly what Stephens had hoped for. He increased the pressure. 'Is Dr Praetorius still recruiting all and sundry to serve the Fuhrer?'

Jakobs was by now truly speechless.

Stephens bent down and jabbed a forefinger at Jakobs. 'You see we know all about the Abwehr, so don't try to mislead us.'

The spy managed a weak 'Yes, Sir.'

'Name?' barked Stephens.

'Josef Jakobs, Sir.'

'Date of birth?'

'June 30th 1898, Sir.'

'Where?'

'Luxemburg, Sir. May I have a glass of water please?'

'No. What is your nationality?'

'German. Sir.'

'Are you married?'

'Yes, Sir, to Margaret.'

'Living where?'

'Berlin, Sir. Please may I have drink?'

Stephens yelled, 'I'm the one who asks the questions. Now, do you have a family?'

Jakobs paused. Deciding that there could be no harm in telling the truth, he nodded. 'Yes, Sir, two sons and a daughter, all living in Berlin.'

This seemed to please the Lieutenant Colonel, who continued. 'What did you do before the war?'

'I trained as a dentist and practised until 1933.'

'Why did you give up dentistry?'

'The economic situation in Germany got very bad, and people couldn't, or wouldn't, pay for their teeth. I had no choice but to stop. I then did a number of jobs, but eventually got involved with helping emigrant Jews and in October 1938 ended up in Sachsenhausen Konzentrationslager'

'Is that where you became involved with the Abwehr?'

'When I was released in March 1940, I was called up for military service and sent to the meteorological information section of the air force. It was then I was 'invited' to join the Abwehr by Dr Praetorius, but you know about him.'

'What mission did Major Ritter give you?'

Jakobs stared resolutely at his interviewer, and spoke as firmly as he could. 'He said I was to send back weather records.'

Leaning down so that his face was close to the spy, Stephens growled, 'and just how were you going to report on the weather without a thermometer or barometer?'

Not flinching, Jakobs responded, 'I was to buy them, Sir'

'Ah yes, that brings us to funds. Why did you have so much money? I have here the five hundred pounds which you had with you when you landed.'

'I was recruited as part of Operation LENA, to provide support for the invasion. I was told it will take place some time this summer. I needed that amount to keep me going until then.'

'How were you to send your weather records?'

'I was to transmit on the set I brought with me.'

Stephens picked up the manila envelope from his desk, and tipped out the contents, which Jakobs recognised as his coding disc that he had tried to tear up. 'With your messages coded on this?'

The spy nodded.

'What is your call sign?'

Jakobs hesitated. What should he tell him?

The delay annoyed Lieutenant Colonel Stephens, who banged his desk and shouted. 'I don't want to have to ask you again, now what is your call sign?'

The spy decided to say nothing, a decision he was to regret.

Stephens reverted to his quiet but threatening tone. 'Let me spell it out for you. This camp is not on any Red Cross list and so far as they are concerned, you do not exist. We will not torture you, but be under no doubt, you're at our mercy. If you don't co-operate, we'll liquidate your family in Berlin. Don't for one moment think that we can't. Now shall we start again?'

Jakobs felt faint. If he co-operated even to a small degree, and this news got back to Berlin, his family would suffer. If he did not, they were still in danger.

He struggled with his emotions. 'Sir, I'll help you in whatever way I can, but please don't let Berlin know. My family are not fighting in this war.'

After the interview had concluded, and with the stretcher and its patient loaded back into the ambulance for the return journey to Brixton, Stephens put a call through to Tar Robertson.

'Jakobs is now on his way back. I couldn't hold him any longer. In fact, I'm surprised the hospital let him go in the first place. They have this misguided notion that even enemy patients need to be treated. Anyway, Jakobs knows where he stands, and he's agreed to co-operate. He's under the impression that we're able to reach his family in Berlin.'

'Do you think we'll be able to use him as a double agent?' asked Tar.

'The man is clearly a rogue, but I think he could well be useful to you, if properly handled. However, there's the usual question over any publicity his capture may have generated. I'll have to leave that one with you.'

Tar thought back to the involvement of the home guard and wondered if wagging tongues would be the death of this latest spy.

47
CAMBRIDGE

Life at 258 St Barnabas Road seemed much quieter now the lodger had left. This worried Mr Serrill. 'We really ought to chase up the agency for someone else, before they lumber us with an evacuee. And we're going to miss Jan's thirty bob, not to mention his sugar allowance.'

Mrs Serrill sighed. 'I don't suppose we'll ever see him again, but I'd better keep those things he left behind just in case. I've also found a pair of his socks in the wash. I've left them all upstairs.'

On the other side of town in Montague Road, Ter Braak was grateful not to have been questioned about his background, and especially about Dunkirk. He was somewhat taken aback to discover another lodger in the house, a Mr Sam Harrison, who worked for Lloyds Bank. At least he will be able to change some more of my dollar bills, reflected the spy.

For her part, Miss Blackwood thought her new guest nice enough, but so different from Mr Harrison. She put this down to Sam being English whereas Mr Ter Braak was foreign and had been forced to leave his homeland and family.

At their next meeting, the professor was in a positive mood. 'I'm glad you've changed lodgings. That deals with the problem of your out of date ration book. We can now move on to your radio. From the appearance of that detector van, it's clear there's a system for listening in to radio transmissions, so you'll have to be careful when you start sending again.'

Ter Braak shook his head. 'No chance of any further messages without some fresh batteries.'

'Ah yes, new batteries. After your dealings with Pearce we're going to have to look further afield. Can you manage a trip to London?'

'I've told Miss Blackwood that I have to go there once a week to visit my office, but of course I've never been, but if it'll get me some fresh batteries...You'll have to give me some directions.'

'It's quite straightforward. You take a train to Liverpool Street Station, then catch a number eleven bus to Ludgate Circus. London buses are red, and the one you want is a double decker.'

'How will I know when to get off?'

'The conductress will come round to take your money and give you your ticket, which I think will be probably tuppence. Stay on the bottom deck and ask her to tell you when you're there.'

'Where do I go then?'

'Turn left down New Bridge Street and take the first on the left into Pilgrim Street. There's a shop on one corner called Hancocks. Look for number twenty-two. Knock on the door three times, and ask for Frankie 'Fingers' Broomfield.'

Ter Braak looked puzzled. 'Why is he called Fingers?'

'Because he can get his hands on almost anything, with no questions asked.'

'So, how much are these batteries going to cost me?'

'I've managed to get the price down to a fiver.'

'That'll take quite a bit of my remaining English money.'

The professor grinned. 'I know, which is why I've arranged for you to pay in dollars, but don't for heavens sake try to fiddle Frankie on the exchange rate.'

'I won't. I'll hand over twenty dollars. How did you set all this up?'

'You don't need to know. Let's just say that Frankie is a friend of a friend.'

Ter Braak realised there was more to the professor than met the eye, but knew it would be pointless to enquire further. 'When can I go?'

'Tuesday next week. Best of luck, and don't forget to keep your wits about you.'

As soon as Professor Carpenter opened the front door, it was obvious by the look on Ter Braak's face that the London trip had not gone well. 'So, how did you get on?'

Ter Braak sighed. 'I had no trouble getting on a number eleven bus from Liverpool Street station, and the conductress made sure I got off at Ludgate Circus. But there's not much of Pilgrim Street left. It was hit by a bomb a few days ago. There's also a pile of rubble in New Bridge Street, so it must have been a heavy raid.'

Professor Carpenter looked horrified. 'How badly damaged was number twenty-two? Was there anyone living there?'

'The building was still standing, but all of the windows had been blown out and there was a large hole in the roof. There was certainly no-one staying there. I asked some of the workmen who were clearing up rubble from the road if they knew where Mr Broomfield was, but they didn't. It didn't seem safe to ask a policeman, so I made my way back here.'

'I'm glad you didn't, but that's going to make it almost impossible to get you your batteries. Frankie Broomfield was the only person doing such deals who I felt we could trust. What did you think of London?

'It's certainly been hit quite hard. I noticed lots of bomb craters when I was on the bus, but life seems to be going on as normal.'

'As a nation we're famous for our stiff upper lip,' said the professor.

Ter Braak looked worried. 'Should I have another go at getting the materials for secret ink?'

'Certainly not. I'm glad you've not been able to use your secret ink, because if I were in charge, I'd arrange to open all overseas mail, coming in and going out, and test it for any such thing. They've taken all the graduate scientists from here, and they must be doing something.'

'When I was training in Hamburg, Herr Boeckel mentioned a system called poste restante, where letters are sent to another address and you collect them from there.'

'Yes, and if I were MI5, I'd open anything coming into the country marked poste restante as a matter of routine. Remember, you're supposed to put a return address on the back of the envelope, which automatically signposts where it's come from. If there's no such address, then it's obvious the sender doesn't want to be identified. No, we need to steer clear of all those methods.'

Professor Carpenter poured them both a drink, and paced the room deep in thought. 'I just can't get that maths joke out of my mind, the one by that RAF bloke, when you were on the train from Bletchley and changing at Bedford. You said one of them wished there was an easier way to get from X to Y. Have you remembered where they were going?'

'No, but I've brought along the map that Dr Praetorius gave me. I don't know how I'd have found my way to Cambridge from Haversham without it.' The professor glanced at the blue cover with its red lettering and recognised it as sheet twenty of Bartholomew's half inch series, covering not only the whole of Cambridgeshire, but part of Buckinghamshire also.

Ter Braak unfolded the map and laid it on the cluttered desk. 'Now where is it, ah yes, Bedford,' he said, locating the town with his forefinger. Tracing the railway lines, he continued. 'If they went north, they'd be heading for...damn, there's a branch line off to the left, and that goes to...Northampton. If they'd continued north, it would've taken them to Wellingborough. No, I'm sure it wasn't one of those. If they went south, they're heading for Hitchin, and the first stop is Cardington. Now, I'm sure I've heard that name before.'

'Probably in connection with the R101 Airship,' said the professor, knowingly. 'It was built in one of those enormous hangers, and I think that after that terrible crash in October 1930, they scrapped all work on airships, took the R100 apart, and shut the place down. Those hangers are still there I believe, and it might be worth having a look to see if they're back in use.'

Looking at the map again, Ter Braak muttered, 'The next stop is Southill. No it wasn't that. Then there's Shefford. Now that sounds familiar. You know, I'm sure that's where they said they were off to. Now what's around there? A few villages, Clifton, and Old Warden to the north. But what's this? Chicksands Priory on the road to a place called Clophill. I wouldn't think that the abbot and his monks could be involved in war work, but I could go and have a look.' Ter Braak then looked worried. 'My only concern is bumping into that family who helped me that night in Bedford.'

The professor stood up. 'Yes, I take your point. Perhaps a bit of dressing up may be called for. I'll see what I can find to help you.'

Ter Braak stood up to leave, but decided he just had to ask. 'Have you managed to find out anything about Alan and his work at the Cavendish Laboratory?'

'Unfortunately, no. It's almost certain he's involved in something very secret, as even the college rumour mill is quiet. Don't worry, I'm keeping my eyes open and I'll let you know just as soon as there's any news. Best of luck with your trip, my friend. I'll see you again next week. Take care.'

Any plans Ter Braak had to revisit Bedford were put on hold the next day. He was walking into town for his usual cup of tea at Dorothy's Café, when a voice from behind him sent a shiver down his spine.

'Hello Jan, I thought you'd gone to London.'

Turning round, he came face to face with Mrs Serrill. He thought quickly. 'Hello Elsie. Yes, I'm back for a day or so, staying at the Station Hotel.'

'I'm glad I've seen you again. You took our front door key with you!'

'Good heavens, the key. I forgot I still had it. Can I at least buy you a cup of tea, by way of an apology?'

Unsure if he was glad she had said yes, Ter Braak found himself sitting in his usual seat in Dorothy's, making frantic excuses for his reappearance. His concerns increased when Mrs Serrill remembered the items he had left behind. 'I've got a shirt and vest, and also a pair of your socks that were in the wash when you upped and left. I've kept them together, but I'd be obliged if you could come and pick them up.'

'Certainly, I'll pop over tomorrow to drop in the key, and I'll take them then. Do give my regards to Bert.' With that they parted, with Ter Braak's blood pressure now sky high.

Ter Braak called the next day to return the key and collect his forgotten items, and after he had left, Mr Serrill looked at his wife. 'You know, I like the lad, but there's something not quite right about the way he left us all of a sudden. And, there's that brown case which he kept locked away. Said it was his typewriter, but I think it was too heavy even for one of those. I think I'll go and see the police about him, just to be on the safe side.'

The assistant aliens officer was having another bad day. He had just had an ear bashing from a college don who was convinced that the number of empty Craven A and Players Weights cigarette packets and discarded bus tickets strewn around the street were not evidence of a slovenly society, but rather trails to guide the expected invaders. 'And university people think they're intelligent,' mused the policeman.

When Mr Serrill walked in, the officer recalled the face, but couldn't quite place it. As soon as he heard the story of the Dutchman, he remembered; he had run out of forms, and not logged the earlier report. 'I see Mr Serrill, he's back again, after saying he was off to London. And he's got a suspiciously heavy suitcase. Leave this with me. Thank you very much for reporting again.'

Fearing that putting this report in the system would bring to light his earlier failure, the officer screwed up the paper upon which he had jotted his notes, and filed it in the waste paper bin.

Unaware of his second reprieve, Ter Braak set out to discover what was at Shefford. His train journey to Bedford was uneventful, and after a quick visit to the gents, he emerged wearing a dog collar provided by the professor. He was sure he looked like a vicar, and as hoped, the disguise allowed him to relax.

Managing to get a window seat on the London train, he looked out as they drew into Cardington Station. The two enormous aircraft hangers were clearly visible, and the site was obviously in use again but, with no runways, he doubted it was being used as an aerodrome.

As he turned these thoughts over in his mind, the train pulled away again. It seemed to take ages to reach the next stop, Southill Station, and even longer to arrive at Shefford, where Ter Braak got off. To his relief, he discovered a small tea room tucked in among the other shops in the wide High Street. Emboldened by his disguise, he went in, sat down and ordered tea. The waitress soon returned with a tray complete with teapot, cup and saucer. 'Sorry, Father, but we've run out of sugar again. They base our allowance on trade before the war, and now we're so much busier, we just can't make it last,' she said with a smile.

'Busier, in this out of the way place?' queried the vicar.

'Well, Father, it's the priory. It used to be owned by Sir Algernon, but he sold it to the government in '36. Some sailors moved in at the start of the war, but now it's the RAF, although there aren't any planes, only some tall masts. They're often in here for a quick cuppa. But, I shouldn't be gossiping like this, but then you're a priest, so I suppose it's all right.'

'Of course it is. Bless you my dear,' Ter Braak replied, trying to sound and look as religious as possible.

The return journey was just as fruitful. The stop at Cardington gave him a chance for a second look, and he was able to see what appeared to be a barrage balloon being tested next to one of the hangers. Feeling a little uneasy as a cleric, it was with some relief he reached Bedford and unfrocked before changing trains en-route to Cambridge.

48
LONDON

Jasper Harker was not a man known to smile, but rumour had it that he had been seen not to frown when told that an enemy parachute had been found, this time complete with its user. Guy Liddell had responded to Harker's summons to provide a progress report.

'Dixon brought the man down from the landing site, which was some twenty miles north west of Cambridge. He was injured in the jump, but the local doctor patched him up for the journey. They arrived at Cannon Row at about four in the afternoon. Tar held a preliminary interview before the man was transferred to the hospital wing of Brixton Prison for the night.'

Harker butted in. 'And where is Tar?'

'It's the scheduled time for radio contact with SNOW. Tar attends in case there is a need for a quick response by us. He'll make it later, if there's no crisis.'

'Good. Now, where were we?'

'Our man claims his real name is Josef Jakobs, and that he used to be a dentist. He's admitted his documents are all forged, as if we didn't know. Ritter chose the identity of James Rymer and the Woodford Green address that we sent over via SNOW in August last year, but for some reason, they didn't use the registration number we gave them, ARAJ/301/29, which was, in fact, one of the few correct pieces of information. They substituted the letter prefix by numbers, 656, which would have been spotted by even the most dozy of country coppers.'

Harker looked thoughtful. 'I'm tempted to think that they wanted this man to be caught.'

'I tend to agree, Sir, but I don't suppose we'll ever find out.'

'So, are we happy that Jakobs is his real name and not another bluff?'

Liddell nodded. 'Yes Sir, my feeling is that he's telling the truth.'

'What about being a dentist? That's the best one we've heard so far.'

'It does seem to fit. He also claims to have been in a concentration camp and admitted he'd got himself involved in selling adulterated gold for dental work.'

'What was his mission?' asked Harker.

'On that he was surprisingly definite. He says he was to send back weather reports, notes on troop movements, and also airfield details, the squadrons flying from them, that sort of thing. However he then claimed he wasn't going to do any of that and was planning to go to

America where his aunt lives. He may have had that as a fall back plan, but his actions after landing suggest he wasn't going to help us on a voluntary basis. He tore up his cardboard code disc. Relating to that, Tar has made a worrying discovery. When he put together the bits from the disc, which I'm pleased to say were all retrieved by the local police, Tar noticed that it was numbered nine. The identical discs recovered from SUMMER, TATE and our last but short-lived double agent, were five, six and seven respectively, which poses the question, where is eight?'

Harker banged his fist on the table. 'It must be with our missing parachutist who landed near to Bletchley Park.'

'Precisely, Sir.'

'What's the latest on our man, Nemo?'

Liddell slid the report across the desk towards Harker. 'Here's the latest update from Dixon on Nemo. It raises an interesting question Sir, and I'd welcome your view.'

Harker scanned the papers. 'Deciding to follow this guy Pearce has certainly turned up some interesting information, although I'm not sure it moves us forward in our search for the missing spy.'

'Not at present Sir, but it's clear that both Pearce and his sister, who seems to be as big a villain as her brother, have a fearsome reputation in the criminal fraternity. From what the report says, the whole of the underworld in the town is now on the lookout for this foreigner.'

Harker continued reading and suddenly became red in the face. 'What's this about a stash of contraband in a warehouse and, good God, Nemo must have broken in to have been able to do such a detailed stock-take.'

'Yes Sir. That does seem to be the case. It prompted me to make some discreet enquiries, and it seems this new special operations executive establishment at Beaulieu, where Nemo comes from, teaches arson, sabotage, robbery, safe-breaking, key making, lock picking and of course, murder.'

'Whoever designed such a syllabus?' Harker asked.

'Some chap called Kim Philby. The funny thing is, nobody seemed to know how he got to know so much about such dodgy topics. But, that's not our problem. As you so rightly point out, Nemo did indeed break in to these premises, and strictly speaking, we should now let the local police know all about it.' Liddell leaned forward to emphasise his point. 'Sir, you will, of course, appreciate that such action would lead them to Pearce, and we'd lose all the help he's unwittingly giving us. Accordingly I propose we keep this little secret to ourselves for the time being. Perhaps when we've found our man we could mention it?'

Harker deliberated for a moment, as he weighed up his options. 'On balance, I agree. Do we know what Pearce is up to at the moment?'

Liddle shook his head. 'No, Sir. I spoke to Dixon yesterday for an update. He says Nemo carried out his break-in when he saw Pearce heading towards Addenbrooke's Hospital, which is on the other side of town, and he hasn't seen him since.'

'Do you think this latest arrival, Jakobs, may have something to do with the missing man? After all, he was dropped in the same area.'

'Nothing obvious to connect them, Sir, but then we don't know anything about the other agent. The amount of money Jakobs had with him is significantly more than we've found on previous agents. Those earlier spies were clearly expecting the invasion to take place shortly afterwards, when the need to pay their way would no longer apply. Jakobs claimed that the greater amount was to see him out until the invasion, which presumably isn't due until the weather improves later this year. On the other hand, some of that cash might have been en route to the Haversham parachutist.'

'If anyone can get to the truth it's Tin Eye. How's he getting on with his interrogation of Jakobs?'

'Unfortunately, he's not. After his first night in the hospital at Brixton, Stephens managed to get him to Camp 020, but was unable to keep him for long and he was soon back at Brixton. The medics then insisted that Jakobs needed urgent treatment so, on 3rd February he was transferred to Dulwich Hospital. He's still there, under guard of course, and to avoid any adverse publicity, he's been listed as injured Luftwaffe aircrew, although that nearly backfired on us.'

'Tell me, how come?'

'The staff at Dulwich included Jakobs on one of their routine reports to the PWIB, that's the prisoner of war information bureau. As usual, the PWIB responded by asking for his date of birth, next of kin, unit etc., which the hospital duly provided. The bureau were just on the point of forwarding this information to the Red Cross when I got wind of it.'

Harker blanched. 'My God, if that news had reached the Red Cross, they'd have made sure we treated him as a normal prisoner of war and...' His voice trailed off at the thought of this near disaster.

'Yes Sir, we'd have had to transfer him to a POW camp, where he could have passed on details of his interrogation to fellow inmates who might well be subsequently repatriated to Germany. As you know Sir, there is a regular exchange of injured prisoners from both sides who are deemed no longer fit to fight. However, I'm sure I've managed to nip this one in the bud.'

'Good man. Now, when can we get him back to Tin Eye? The Lieutenant Colonel must be tearing his hair out by now.'

'Not yet. The doctors are still treating him. I think we'll have to wait some weeks.'

Harker was just about to announce his opinion of the medical profession when the door opened and his secretary announced the arrival of Major Robertson. In strode Tar, resplendent as usual in his tartan trews. The major sat down and in response to the questioning looks on the two other faces around the table, addressed the director general. 'Sir, apologies for my absence, but I've been monitoring SNOW's latest link with Hamburg. I'm glad I was there, because Ritter sent a very interesting message. As usual, we had no difficulty in decoding it, and we discovered Ritter was telling SNOW they'd dropped an agent on 31st of last month. He said the man had parachuted down not far from Peterborough, but the pilot realised he'd been hurt as he left the plane and may even have been killed. SNOW was asked to advise if he discovered anything.' The two listeners looked at each other. They knew they had this man in hospital already badly injured, but still very much alive.

Liddell laughed. 'Good of him to tell us this. The question is, what do we say to him?'

'We need to think about this,' agreed Tar. 'I authorised a reply which acknowledged receipt and confirmed that he, SNOW, would keep his eyes and ears open and report accordingly.'

Liddell nodded his approval. 'That'll give us some breathing space, but I have a feeling this issue could well resolve itself. There's already some question over the suitability of Jakobs as a double cross candidate. His arrival was seen by quite a few people, including unfortunately some from the home guard, and we all know they can't keep their mouths shut. So even though Jakobs has said he'll co-operate with us, he's unlikely to meet the criteria for a double agent and will end keeping an appointment with the hangman.'

Harker checked the notes in front of him. 'I see he's a serving Luftwaffe officer, and if so, he'll be shot, following of course, an appropriate court martial. Anyway, gentlemen, we need to get him to Tin Eye as soon as possible. Please maintain the pressure on those medics, and keep me advised.'

The wider significance of Ritter's message to SNOW was not apparent to MI5. However, to his Abwehr colleagues in Hamburg, it showed that in spite of his gruff manner and the inevitable consequences for his career, the major had not been prepared to abandon one of his agents.

To Admiral Canaris in Berlin it confirmed that Ritter had disobeyed a direct order not to involve *JOHNNY* in his efforts to find Maud and, if only for the sake of the admiral's reputation, there had to be consequences.

49
CAMBRIDGE

Ter Braak had been unable to continue his daily persual of the local newspaper at his new home as Miss Blackwood saw no point in paying for something she could get for free on the wireless. When asked her how she found out about local news she replied, 'Gossip at the WI,' adding in response to his puzzled look, 'Women's institute – we meet regularly for a cuppa and a natter, and of course a chorus of *Jerusalem*. Oh, and we also make jam – there was a glut of plums last year, so we were knee deep in it. Used all mine up, though. Wish I'd kept a bit back, as it would have been nice to have in the morning.'

Sitting at the breakfast table finishing his tea and toast but without any jam, plum or otherwise, or even a paper to hide behind, Ter Braak was obliged to talk to Sam Harrison, his fellow lodger. They discussed the weather, and how cold it had been so far that year. And then they came round to the bombing raid of the night before last.

'Two people were killed, you know,' said the banker with a sigh. 'And at least four injured, including one of our customers. Poor old Elsie Serrill was nearly buried under that WVS mobile kitchen of hers. She's now in Addenbrooke's, and not very well, so I believe.'

The colour drained from Ter Braak's face and he dropped his cup, breaking the saucer, and spilling tea all over the tablecloth. His landlady came bustling in, just as he stood up, muttered an apology and rushed out. 'I wasn't going to shout at you, accidents do happen,' said Miss Blackwood to his disappearing back.

Ter Braak ran all the way to Addenbrooke's Hospital. Unlike his last visit to the engineers' store, this time he aimed for Trumpington Street and the main entrance to the wards. Racing up the front steps, he stopped at the enquiry desk, and paused to get his breath back. 'I understand you're treating the people who were injured in the bombing of a couple of days ago?'

The receptionist looked up with a kindly smile on her face. 'Ah yes Sir, the Cherry Hinton raid. Unfortunately, there were four of them. Who was it you wanted?'

'I'm looking for a Mrs Serrill.'

Checking the papers in front of her, the receptionist replied, 'Yes, she's up on the third floor, in Musgrove Ward, Women's Surgical, but she's too ill to see anyone at the moment other than family. Are you a relation? I know her husband's been here most of the night but he left a little time ago to get some sleep.'

'No, just a friend. I'll come back later.'

Making his way to Dorothy's Café for his usual mid morning tea, Ter Braak mulled over what to do next. Perhaps his rush to the hospital had been foolish. After all, he was supposed to be in London, and he had assured Elsie when he had collected the belongings he had left behind, that he was on his way back there the very next day. But he was fond of Elsie - she had been kind to him in a motherly sort of way, and he had to make sure she was all right. He decided to call again to check on her condition, but not to go up to the ward and risk being faced with awkward questions.

Ter Braak took to calling in at the hospital each day after supper at Dorothy's, on his walk back to his digs. Although he had been told that Mrs Serrill was holding her own, she still was unable to receive visitors, other than her husband. The spy had been forced to hide behind a pillar on one visit, when Mr Serrill left, looking exhausted and with a blank look on his face.

A week later Ter Braak was walking down the road from the hospital after his latest visit. The receptionist had been more upbeat this time, to the point that she was sure he would be allowed up to the ward in a day or two. Satisfied that his former landlady was now well on the road to recovery, he thanked the woman, told her he had to be away for some time and that he would visit Mrs Serrill when she was back at home.

For the first time for many days he left with a spring in his step. Ter Braak felt at peace with the world once again, and was sure the nights were getting lighter. The spy hated the winter evenings and of course the blackout made matters worse. Not yet being quite as familiar with the roads to his new lodgings, he was still smarting from the bruise he received when he walked into a telegraph post the previous evening. He missed Elsie's yellow tincture.

Suddenly Ter Braak felt something sharp dig into his back. 'I've found you at long last, you bastard,' came a voice he recognised – that of Lennie Scarface Pearce. Ter Braak paused, but was forced to go on, by what he now realised was the blade of a knife pressed up against him. 'Keep walking, and when we come to the next road, turn left, and head for the store. You'll no doubt remember it from our last meeting.'

Ter Braak did as he was told, and soon found himself opening the door to the engineer's store. Pearce switched on the light and pushed him inside and away from the door, which he shut and locked with one hand, while keeping his eyes on his captive. He held the knife in front of him, menacingly.

The spiv was so angry he had difficulty speaking, but Pearce soon spat out his demand. 'I've been looking for you for some time, you thieving bastard. You swindled me with those dollars of yours. I only got five bob each for them, which means you now owe me...lots. I'll be generous this time and call it a round one hundred dollars. And, I want to know who you really are. Dr Rantzau my arse! You could even be a Jerry spy.' With that, he moved forward, the blade of his knife glinting in the light from the un-shaded bulb overhead.

Ter Braak backed away. He had often imagined being cornered by the police or the military, but never by a crazy criminal. 'I'd no idea what a dollar was worth,' he lied. 'But I've got some cash on me. I'll pay whatever you want.' He moved his hand towards his inside coat pocket.

'Stop right there and keep your hands out of your pockets! Do you think I'm daft?' yelled Lennie Pearce, edging forward. Ter Braak obediently dropped his hand down, and backed further away to maintain the space between them. Putting his left hand behind him, the spy realised he could go no further, he was up against a workbench. His probing fingers touched something metallic, which he quickly realised was a large spanner. Without stopping to think, Ter Braak threw the tool at Pearce, with all his strength. Being right handed, his left handed throw missed and the missile clattered harmlessly against the opposite wall.

Seeing the spanner coming towards him, Lennie Pearce ducked quickly to avoid the missile. 'Good try' he said sarcastically, only to look up and find himself staring down the barrel of a Browning automatic.

'Drop your knife, and move back to the door,' ordered Ter Braak but Lennie Pearce, his face still contorted with rage, lunged forward. Ter Braak stepped sideways, bringing the pistol down hard on Pearce's head. The spiv grunted and sank to the floor, the knife dropping from his grasp. Ter Braak kicked it into a corner, and studied the body lying in front of him. His mind raced. What should he do? His first thought was to run. The key was in the door, and he could soon be well away. But he could not see this petty crook forgetting about him. Ter Braak had cheated him over the exchange rate, and now humiliated him as well. Pearce would still be out for revenge.

His thoughts were interrupted by the sounds of Pearce regaining consciousness, and struggling to his knees. The spy knew he had no option. The look of hate on Pearce's face turned to surprise as the bullet hit him. He clutched his stomach and watched in horror as blood trickled out between his fingers. Ter Braak stood frozen to the spot as Pearce quietly crumpled in front of the spy, twitching for some time on the dusty floor, in a slow and painful death.

The sound of the shot echoed around the store for what seemed to Ter Braak to be ages, but eventually silence returned. The killer sank to the floor convinced that someone would have heard the noise. He held his breath, but nobody came and a strange calm came over him as he recalled the advice he had been given in prison. Carefully putting the gun back in his pocket and pulling on the leather gloves from his raincoat pocket, he dragged the body to the back of the store, took the wallet from the inside jacket pocket, removed the wad of notes inside, and tossed it back on top of the body. He pocketed the cash to make it look like a robbery. Taking out a handkerchief from his pocket, the spy picked up the spanner and wiped it clean before replacing it on the bench, which he also cleaned for fingerprints from when he had touched it. After a final look around to ensure there was nothing further to incriminate him, the spy opened the door, wiped the handles clean, and quietly let himself out, locking the door behind him.

Walking away unobserved into the blackout, Ter Braak took a roundabout route back to his lodgings, dropping the store key into a drain along the way. When he finally reached the sanctity of his bedroom, he collapsed onto his bed, the realisation that he had killed a man finally sinking in.

50
CAMBRIDGE

Professor Carpenter's eyes opened wide. 'You've done what?'

'I've shot someone,' repeated Ter Braak, and then went on to relate the demise of the late Lennie Pearce.

'My God, I bet that made for an interesting confession. I take it you do go to confession?'

'Of course. On my first trip to Peterborough I went into St Peters and All Saints and during my confession, admitted to being a German agent. The death of Pearce has been worrying me, so I went back to St Peters and confessed to his shooting.'

'How did the priest react?' asked the professor.

'He asked me if it was in self-defence. I said, yes, so he told me my action wasn't a sin.'

'I bet that was a load off your mind.'

'At first, yes. But I keep asking myself if it really was self-defence. After all, I only shot him because of my worry about what would happen to me in the future,' Ter Braak admitted.

'Aren't you afraid that the priest could report you?'

'He doesn't know who I am, and in any event, he's bound by the seal of the sacrament and can't reveal anything heard in confession, even under penalty of death.'

'From what you've told me, the man you killed was a rogue, and there's a good chance the police will be glad to see the back of him and won't lose too much sleep over his death. Whether the same applies to any of Pearce's cronies, I'm not sure. There could well be someone who'll want to even the score.'

Ter Braak looked resolute. 'Don't worry, I'll keep my eyes open'.

'Good. Now, about your mission. I've been a bit cheeky and kept this to the end. I think I've found the Maud you're looking for.'

Ter Braak opened his mouth in amazement. 'How did you...who is she? Please tell me.'

'It was a bit of luck really. I had to go over to the university financial board offices. A silly problem about my superannuation. Saw the treasurer, Thomas Knox-Shaw. While he was looking for my file, I happened to see some papers on his desk. Many years ago, I taught myself to read writing upside down. It's been invaluable on numerous occasions. Anyway, I could see that Tom had what looked like a draft invoice on his desk, with details of expenditure for the previous month. It listed things like salaries, wages, materials, overheads and even travelling expenses.'

'Did it mention Maud?'

'Patience, my dear friend, patience. The name at the top of the list for salaries was a Dr Hans von Halban. I'm sure I've heard that name before, but I can't remember where. However, what upset me was that, based on the amount being claimed for him, he's being paid a darn sight more than me.'

'Where does Maud fit into this?'

'I'm coming to that. When Thomas saw me looking, he hurriedly put the invoice away in a folder labelled *Maud Committee* on the front. So now we know that Maud isn't a person, but a group of people.'

'What does Maud stand for then?'

'It could be the name of the committee chairman, or it might be an acronym, that is M, A, U and D are the first letters of a title. It's any one's guess what that might be.'

Ter Braak looked disappointed. 'It seems we're not much further forward. Any news on the mysterious Alan who's also involved with Maud?'

'Not yet. I have to track him down together with our foreign friend mentioned on that Maud invoice, Dr Hans von Halban.'

'Well, I never,' said Sergeant Halsey, as the woman walked out of the police station. 'That's got to be the highlight of my twenty-five years service.' He ran up the stairs, two at a time.

Detective Chief Inspector Bone heard the footsteps and thought perhaps he had a murder on his hands. When the sergeant came in he gave him a second to get his breath back. 'What's the panic then?'

'Guv, you'll never guess who's just been in to report a missing person. Patsy Pearce, you know, sister of that scumbag Lennie we've been trying to nail for years!'

The chief inspector sat up, looking hopeful. 'She's as bad as he is. Perhaps her brother's done one shady deal too many and his victim has at last fought back. I presume it's Lennie who's missing?'

'Yes. She says she hasn't seen him for nearly a week. She wasn't worried at first as he's often out of circulation for days, especially since the start of the war. He's got his grubby little fingers into an ever increasing number of pies – my words, not hers.'

'It's tempting to do nothing, but we'd better list him as missing.'

Inside the engineers' store the corpse of the late Lennie Pearce was beginning to smell. Fred Butler, the hospital engineer, was in Tipperary ward up on the third floor recovering from a hernia. His assistant, Billy McKay, was busy keeping the boilers going in the cold weather, and had no need of the store. In any event, his boss had not entrusted him with a key.

Miss Clare Alexander SRN, was on her rounds. Always immaculate, highly efficient, and proud to be the youngest matron in the country, she had endeared herself to the staff by being prepared to roll up her sleeves and help out when staff shortages dictated. Sweeping into women's surgical, she checked that all the wheels of the beds were pointing to the front. It was only a small point, and one for which some could see no reason. 'Discipline!' she would thunder in response to anyone who had the nerve to ask.

'Good afternoon, Sister, how are things today?'

'Just fine Matron,' responded Sister Megan, also a nurse of the old school and one who shared the standards set by her superior. Walking down the Nightingale ward, with its line of beds on both sides, all separated by neatly folded screens, Matron nodded to those patients who were awake, and acknowledged by name the long term residents she had come to know. She was followed at a discreet distance by Sister Megan.

Reaching the bed of an older woman, with bandages around her head, and one leg in plaster, she paused and lifted the clipboard from the end of the bed and glanced at the notes. 'How are we today, Mrs Serrill? Feeling better after your fight with that bomb?'

'Much better, thank you Matron. My headaches aren't so bad now.'

'Good, that was a nasty bang on the head. Had us all worried for a bit, but keep your chin up, and we'll soon have you home again.' With that, she continued down the ward.

Arriving back at her office after an inspection which even she considered quite satisfactory, Matron reached for the paperwork which had filled her in-tray that morning. There was a nervous knock on her door. 'Enter,' she boomed, and the door swung slowly open, and a very timid Billy McKay shuffled in, cap in hand. 'What can I do for you Billy?' she asked, smiling in an effort to put her visitor at ease.

'It's the store, Matron. Something's gone off in there, and I haven't got a key.'

'Didn't Fred leave you one?' asked Matron incredulously.

Billy shook his head.

'We'll soon see about that. Follow me,' and she strode into the corridor, with a breathless Billy running to keep up. They soon reached men's surgical.

'Sorry to butt in, Sister, but may I see Fred, please? I need a word with him.'

'Certainly Matron, follow me.' When Fred saw Sister and Matron marching towards him, he slid down in the bed, trying desperately to hide under his blankets, but to no avail.

'Hello Fred, Billy here has a problem, and we need your key to the store. Where is it?'

Fred meekly took the key ring from his locker and handed it over. 'It's the big one on the end, Matron.'

'Thank you Fred, we'll get these back to you in due course. By the way, don't leave Billy without a spare key in future. Good day.' And with that she was off, leaving Fred quivering in her wake.

Handing the keys to a still nervous Billy, Matron had a sudden thought. She had not seen inside Fred's store for some time. 'Lead the way, Billy, I'll come with you. Let's make sure everything's tickety boo in Fred's hideaway.'

DCI Bone reckoned he could have hidden behind the pile of paper that had built up on his desk. He had always said that the Emergency Powers (Defence) Bill, passed in August 1939, would be a nightmare for the police service, and he had been proved correct. Ministers and government departments seemed to be revelling in their new power to issue regulations as orders in council, all of which had the full force of the law. That left him with the never-ending task of keeping up to date, let alone the problem of enforcing the new regulations.

The first file he picked up covered the suspected black market operations of stallholders in the market. The DCI reckoned that Lennie Pearce would be involved to some degree, and smiled at the prospect of an interesting interview with him.

And then the telephone on his desk rang. Picking up the receiver, he heard the familiar tones of his regular bridge partner. 'Hello Clare, calling to apologise for the other night? I don't know – leaving me in four diamonds, and you without an opening hand... You what? A body in the engineers store? Okay, I'm on my way.'

The drive to the hospital in the black Wolseley area car only took a matter of minutes, and the DCI accompanied by his sergeant were soon inspecting the corpse with handkerchiefs over their faces to mask the odour.

'I think we now know where Lennie Pearce is. Look at that scar on the left cheek,' muttered DCI Bone.

The sergeant peered down. 'I reckon you're right, Guv. I'll secure the scene and call Donald Camarch. He's the doctor on call this week. I'll also get some pictures taken, and arrange for fingerprints when we've got the body to the mortuary, but I'll bet my pension on it being old Scarface. It looks as if we're now minus one major villain.'

'Good man. Sergeant, I'll leave that with you while I go and see Matron and get her side of the story.'

It wasn't long before the DCI was sitting at the bedside of a very shifty looking Fred Butler, who soon admitted to hiring out the store to Lennie for emergency storage facilities in exchange for a weekly bribe. The DCI pondered for a moment, and concluded that the engineer had not broken any laws. 'This is a matter for Matron,' he said.

From the look on Fred's face, it was obvious he would have preferred to have been arrested and thrown in jail.

The typed report of the incident was soon on the DCI's desk, and leaning back in his chair, he lit his pipe and puffed out grey smoke, while mulling over the next step. Summoning his sergeant, he invited his views.

'Well, Guv, my pension's safe. The fingerprints confirmed it was indeed Lennie Pearce. Seems he's been dead for some time. Anyway, we've got the bullet. All we need now is the gun. How many men do you want me to put on this case? I'm sure I don't need to remind you, Guv, we've got an awful lot on at the moment.'

The DCI looked keenly at his sergeant, and took the hint. 'I agree, I don't think we can tie up too many resources on this. Someone out there's done us a great favour.' With that, he tossed the report into his filing tray. 'By the way, how's that sister of his taking it?'

'She's hopping mad. Swears she'll find out who did this, and sort him.'

'That would be a neat ending, wouldn't it? She tops the gunman, and hangs for murder. Better keep an eye on her.'

Someone else keeping an eye on Patsy Pearce was the man from MI6. Nemo had kept his ear to the ground following the disappearance of Scarface Pearce, and soon heard that he had been topped by someone, and that his sister was out for revenge. It had been a simple decision to transfer his attentions to her.

51
CAMBRIDGE

Patsy Pearce was feeling frustrated. She was also angry and thirsty. Reconciled to having to live with her feelings, she thought she would at least quench her thirst and as she was in that part of town, she decided to drop in to the Blackamoors Head. Walking into the bar, she heard a voice that she was convinced was Lennie. She turned to greet her brother, only to realise it was not him because he was still dead and buried, his grave marked by a simple granite headstone that had fallen off the back of a lorry.

Walking up to the bar, she sank onto a stool and ordered a pint, and a whisky chaser. The barman recognised her and offered his sympathies for her loss. She gave him a weak smile. 'Thanks Barney, but I wish I could get my hands on the bastard that did it. I'd swing for him, truly I would.'

'Haven't the rozzers got any idea?'

'Nope, and I'm not convinced they're bothered, if you ask me. Only natural, I suppose. Our Lennie must have been a real pain in their arses.'

'Don't you have anything to go on? After all, you were quite close, and I'm sure he must have told you something.'

'Lennie kept his cards very close to his chest. Told me, what I didn't know, I wouldn't be able to worry about.'

'What was he up to when he disappeared?'

'No idea, he didn't say. The only thing I can remember is that in the weeks before he popped his clogs, he was going on about some dollars he'd got and how he'd been diddled over the exchange rate. Our Lennie didn't like to be cheated.' Patsy drained her pint. 'Where do you think he might have got them?'

Barney scratched his balding head. 'Certainly none of the regulars, they wouldn't have ripped him off. They value their good looks too much. No, it must have been a stranger, someone who...I know, we did have a foreign geezer in here before Christmas, after some under the counter stuff. I put him in touch with Lennie, and that's the last I heard. The bloke never came back here, at least, not when I was behind the bar.'

'What did he look like?'

'I'll have to think, but he gave me a name...Dr Rooting...Dr Ranting, something like that.'

'Thanks Barney, I'd very much appreciate it if you could remember what he looked like. There's a drink in it for you when you do.' With that she finished off the whisky chaser, slid off the stool and walked towards the door. Turning, she wagged a finger at the now petrified Barney. 'I'll be back in again tomorrow, so get thinking, I don't want to have to help you remember.'

The barman took this for the threat it was intended to be and began sweating. He racked his brains in an effort to recall the man with the foreign accent, but without success. For the rest of the day, he found it hard to concentrate, and made a number of uncharacteristic mistakes when serving. He was relieved to reach closing time, and hardly slept a wink that night, but woke with a start and realised he must have dropped off at some point.

'That's it,' he shouted. 'Brian was in the bar when that foreigner came in. He's an artist and ought to have a good memory for faces. I'll ask him.' With that, he fell into the peaceful slumber of a man reprieved.

When Patsy opened the door to the bar the following evening, she knew at once that Barney's face would not need to be re-arranged. 'Come on Barney, I can tell you've remembered. What was he like?'

Barney slapped a piece of paper onto the bar. 'Last night I remembered that Brian, you know, that hairy artist, was in the bar and he remembered this guy because of his funny foreign accent. He's done this picture for you. Looks like him, as far as I can remember.'

She looked down at the pencil sketch. 'Black hair, glasses and a funny Hitler type moustache. How tall was he?'

Barney had no idea, and looked blank.

'Okay, this'll do. Put the word out, will you, I want this man - alive. If he's the one that did for Lennie I want to make sure he dies slowly, and very painfully.' As she left, Barney did not have the nerve to remind her she had said there would be a drink in it for him, even though he had stood Brian a double for his pains.

It was not very long before Patsy Pearce was feeling much happier. News that she was looking for a foreigner had spread quickly through the criminal fraternity, many of whom were grateful for the chance to get in her good books. The breakthrough had come when Alice, a waitress in Dorothy's Café happened to mention to her brother the foreign gentleman who had become a regular. 'I'll miss his tips if he ever leaves. Only a few coppers, mind you, but on my wage, that's more than welcome.'

Her brother, who was also a regular at the Blackamoors Head, had heard on the grapevine about the elusive foreigner, and thought it prudent to mention his sister's tale to Barney. The next day a furtive Patsy Pearce was sipping tea in Dorothy's Café, when she spotted her prey. A tall man, with dark hair and a small moustache and wearing glasses. 'He's just like the sketch. It's got to be him,' she muttered under her breath, and followed him at a discreet distance when he left.

She soon realised this was a man who did not want to be followed. At first, she took the stops to look in windows as merely an interest in the goods on display, but soon noticed that he was staring in shops which had become victim to the ever increasing shortages, with virtually nothing on sale. She concluded he was looking at the reflection in the window to check on anyone behind him. When she lost the man, after he made several sudden changes in direction, she became convinced that this was indeed her quarry. Deciding she needed some fresh faces to keep tabs on him, she called in a few favours.

Alice only remembered customers who left her a tip. That way she could ensure she served them on their next visit. Patsy did not pay expenses, and so the rota of strange faces that began to appear in Dorothy's and did not leave a tip went unnoticed by her, if not by Ter Braak.

At his next meeting with Professor Carpenter, he reported his fears. 'There's no doubt about it, I'm being followed. Quite a few people seem to be involved, but they're all pretty hopeless, and I've managed to lose them.'

The professor looked worried. 'I hope they didn't follow you here.'

'I can assure you they did not. I used a very roundabout route and every trick in the book. But who do you think they're working for?'

'I reckon they must be pals of that spiv you shot. I can't imagine the security service would use such amateurs. Of course, there could well be an MI5 man following them, but he's going to be an expert, and I doubt even you would spot him.'

Ter Braak grimaced. 'I think it's time I took care of this.'

'I agree we need to do something, but let me think...We need to dictate the time and place. This is what you must do.'

Ter Braak listened carefully, and after a long pause, nodded. 'Okay, but what happens afterwards?'

'You must take a holiday. I inherited a small cottage, even smaller than this, up north. It's away from everywhere. You could lie low there for a bit and let the dust settle.'

'Sounds perfect to me, but how do I get there?'

'Can you ride a motorbike?'

'Yes,' said Ter Braak.

'Good. The gardener at college has one for sale, and he's also got a few cans of petrol stashed away. He managed to persuade the area petroleum officer that we needed some agricultural fuel to keep the college lawns looking smart. If we strap a few cans to the back of the bike, it should get you there. You certainly won't be able to buy any en-route without the necessary ration book.'

'When will I be able to leave?'

'I can get the bike and the fuel by the end of the month - ten days time. There's one problem though, the money for the bike. I have the funds but they're tied up at the moment, and it'll be difficult to get at them in time. You could lend me some of your cash.'

Ter Braak nodded. 'No problem. I've got quite a bit after emptying Pearce's wallet. If I let you have my dollars as well, can you get those changed?'

'Yes, I'll organise that for you. Just keep enough to see you through to the end of the month. Now back to basics. I suggest you warn your landlady you'll be leaving, so she's not suspicious about a sudden departure. It's going to be a long journey, so you'll need to put on as many clothes as you can.'

'How much luggage can I take with me?'

'The petrol has to be your first priority, so I doubt there'll be room for anything else. Certainly not that heavy radio of yours.

Anyway, I don't know why you hang on to it, after all, it's no use to you now, and I'm sure Nick Ritter won't want it back.'

'Difficult to throw away, and certainly confirmation of a spy in town.'

The professor grudgingly conceded the point. 'Agreed. Where can you leave it?'

'I was told in Hamburg that a good place to hide such things is the left luggage at a railway station.'

'Perfect. Take both of your cases there and let me have the ticket. I'll collect them later, and bring them up to you when I come. I can't get away until the next vacation. It's quite late this year, Easter Sunday isn't until the 13th April.'

'Where do I pick up the motorbike?'

'We need somewhere quiet. I'm thinking about that air raid shelter they're building on Christ's Pieces. It should have been finished months ago, but work had to stop when they found those old bones. They've had archaeologists, and God knows who else, down there ever since. You'd think at times like this, finishing off an air raid shelter would be more important than preserving a few old relics. When I walked past the other day, I could see it's nearly finished, but it's not yet open to the public. We can get inside and sort things out before you leave. I'll meet you there on the evening of the 29th, which is a Saturday. You can then get away in the early hours of Sunday morning, when it should be quiet.'

Meanwhile Patsy Pearce was closing in on her victim. After weeks of being unable to follow their quarry, her rota of observers suddenly found that Ter Braak had become careless, and soon established that he was staying in Montague Road, but was rarely out late at night.

'Let me know if you see him after dark,' she briefed her team.

Ter Braak began to prepare for his departure. He warned Miss Blackwood that he had to move to London, and then took his final confession at St Josephs Church in St Neots, as he could no longer face the journey to Peterborough. On the appointed Saturday morning, he had breakfast and waited until his landlady returned from the butcher's, carrying her meagre meat allowance.

'If you think this isn't much, just imagine what it'll be like next week, when the ration goes down again,' she moaned, before wishing him a safe journey to London.

Ter Braak then realised that he had handed over too much money to the professor, and had not allowed for his last week's board and lodging. He left as quickly as possible before Miss Blackwood remembered that he still owed her for that week's board.

Leaving his two suitcases at the railway station left luggage, Ter Braak passed the day in town, wandering around the streets that had become familiar to him. It was a long day and as it started to get dark, he knew the time had come for his final cup of tea.

Alerted to his location, Patsy Pearce loitered outside Dorothy's Café in Sidney Street, and after a short wait, followed her target at a discreet distance as he walked towards Christ's Pieces.

Behind her was a real professional.

52
CAMBRIDGE

'Sparks' Spencer was annoyed. He had expected to install the wiring for the lighting in the new air raid shelter some time ago, but then there had been the stupid delay following the discovery of old bones. Work had come to a grinding halt, and the site had been crawling with archaeologists for what had seemed ages.

At last, he had finally made it to Christ's Pieces. He realised it was 1st April, and hoped this was not an April Fool's joke. He breathed a sigh of relief when he found the shelter ready for his cables. Descending the main entrance steps into the darkness, his torch picked out an oil lamp on the central bench. It was unlit, and the soot stains around the glass told him it had run out of fuel. Someone had been there. Were they still there?

With some trepidation, he swung his torch round, and relaxed when the room seemed to be empty. Then he caught sight of a man lying on the floor, which at first seemed to explain the reason for the lamp, a drunk sleeping off a heavy night. When his torch picked out a pool of blood and a gun lying on the floor, Sparks Spencer realised that this was no drunk, but a body, and a lifeless one at that.

Responding to the frantic telephone call, DCI Bone and PC Vasey soon reached Christ's Pieces. They found the dazed electrician slumped against the main entrance of the underground shelter. He greeted them and gestured down the steps. 'He's in there. Take my torch.' With that, he turned away and was violently sick.

'Constable, make sure he's okay, and get a statement from him as soon as you can. I'll take a look below,' ordered the DCI as he descended the short flight of stairs. The beam of the borrowed torch illuminated bench seats against the outside walls, and another down the centre of the shelter. The torch then picked out the body of the man dressed in a raincoat over a blue pinstriped suit. He was lying on his right side with his head slightly under the right hand bench, just before the emergency exit ladder at the far end. A trilby hat was on the floor nearby and close to the body a hand gun lay in a large pool of congealed blood. Three newspapers were on the floor under the middle bench.

The DCI had seen a great number of corpses during his years in the force, but even with all his experience, he still had to make a supreme effort to bend down and feel for a pulse. The icy cold skin made him shiver, and it was immediately obvious that there were no signs of life. He stood up again and joined his subordinate outside, who was by now taking a statement from the electrician, who was struggling to put what he had been through into words.

'Bloody hell, that gave me a real turn. I thought it was a tramp at first, but then I saw the gun,' he gasped, adding that he had not disturbed anything before rushing to the phone.

The DCI gestured to PC Vasey for a word in private. 'Okay Constable, you stay here, and keep the place secure. You can let him go when you've got his statement, but make a note of where he'll be, in case we need to speak to him again. I think we'd better keep this quiet for the time being, so tell him to keep his mouth shut. I'll get the doctor, a photographer, and some back-up.'

Very soon, it was obvious to any passer-by that something was going on at Christ's Pieces, and a small crowd had gathered, kept back by two burly bobbies, who told anyone who asked that a tramp had died as a result of the cold weather. Down inside the shelter, the doctor was examining the body, and the photographer was setting up his equipment, and it was not long before the corpse had been taken by hearse to the mortuary in Mill Road, accompanied by Constable Vasey.

After his further search of the now empty shelter, the DCI caught up with his colleague, whose ambition was to become a detective. The young man saw this as a chance to shine, and he was ready with his notes of the items found on the body. He reported enthusiastically to his boss. 'Guv, there was a Dutch passport in the raincoat pocket, in the name of Jan Willem Ter Braak. It says he was born in 1914, which makes him 27. I'm not an expert in passports, Guv, but I can't see any police stamp, or anything to show his port of entry. And there's something else which doesn't add up. His registration card has his Christian name before the surname, and it also shows his address as 'Cambridge, 7 Oxford Street'. I don't know there's any Oxford Street in the town, and the street name should be written before the name of the town, not afterwards. As if that wasn't enough, the card is dated after 20th May last year, when the issuing process changed, leaving the address to be filled in by the holder. It's clearly all in the same handwriting.'

'Well done Vasey. You certainly know your stuff. So, the chances are that both the registration card and passport are forgeries and not very good ones at that. Given the gun as well, we might have ourselves a Jerry spy.'

'My thoughts as well, Guv. Another odd thing was that he was wrapped up in several layers of underclothes.' Bursting with pride the young PC continued. 'The suit he was wearing had a label inside, from Fifty Shilling Tailors. They're in Petty Cury. With your permission, Guv, I'll have a word with them in the hope that they remember him.'

'Off you go, and report back as soon as you can. In the meantime, I'll let MI5 know we may well have someone else they might be interested in.'

'Someone else, Guv ?'

'Yes, in September last year, the home guard picked up a man who was acting suspiciously near Willingham, that's a small village north of here, between St Ives and Haddenham. He was Dutch too, name of Schmidt. Well, that's what he said it was. They quickly shipped him over to us. The chief constable then called in Major Dixon, MI5's regional security liaison officer, who interviewed Schmidt, then carted him off to London. No idea what happened to him after that. Anyway, I got to know Dixon quite well on that case.

I'll call on him at his office in Regent Street. Now, off you go, and get back to the station when you've been to Petty Cury.'

The RSLO was pleased to see the DCI again, and lost no time in accompanying him back to the station. After inspecting the passport and registration card, the major called his office in London, and re-joined the DCI just as the doctor was leaving.

DCI Bone brought him up to date. 'Dr Camarch popped in to tell me that the body was in an advanced state of rigor mortis, and reckons he's been dead for at least thirty-six hours. Says the cause of death is the bullet wound to the head.'

'So who does he think shot him?' asked the major.

'Dr Camarch isn't one for off the record comments, but he's of the opinion that the poor chap shot himself.'

'At least that would be a nice neat ending to what's been a troubling and worrying episode. I've had a word with Major Robertson, and he's confirmed that the card details leave us in no doubt that this man was a German agent. We think he's probably the parachutist who arrived near Wolverton in early November last year.'

'Ah yes, I remember the All Forces alert that went out about that. If it is him, I wonder what he's been up to since then?' mused the DCI, as a breathless Constable Vasey ran into the office.

'Where the hell have you been?' said Bone. 'This is Major Dixon, and we've been waiting for you for over two hours.'

Vasey acknowledged the major politely, apologised for the delay, and opened his pocket book. 'I saw the manager at Fifty Shilling Tailors, and luckily he remembered our man. He knew he was Dutch, and also where he lived. Seems the waistcoat of the suit he bought needed some alterations. He had recorded his address as 258 St Barnabas Road, so I nipped round there and spoke to the landlady, a Mrs Serrill. She's in the WVS and hadn't long been released from hospital. Got caught in that bad air raid on Cherry Hinton, back in February. Lucky to be alive by all accounts. Anyway, she knew Ter Braak. Confirmed he arrived on Monday 4th November last year, having been referred to her by Haslops, the agents in Green Street. Seems he left all of a sudden at the end of January. She was devastated to learn he was dead as she obviously quite liked him. I then had a word with Haslops, who confirmed that in addition to seeking a room, he came back a few days later and rented their spare office on the first floor. They also said he hardly ever used it. However, before Ter Braak left Mrs Serrill, he went back to Haslops claiming he had to leave due to the noise from the railway. They put him onto a Miss Blackwood in Montague Road. I've spoken to her and she confirmed Ter Braak was with her from the beginning of February to the end of March, when he left to go to London.'

The DCI beamed. 'Well done Vasey, you've certainly been busy. We'll have to take formal statements from Mrs Serrill and Miss Blackwood, but I think, Major, you have a more pressing problem on your hands?'

'Thank you Chief Inspector. Yes, this man is certainly a German agent, and my problem is that, given the violent nature of his death, there will have to be an inquest. We don't want news of this to be reported in the press. You know what they're like, they love a good spy story. It's vital that the hearing is *in camera*. Any idea who'll be holding this one?'

'It'll be the borough coroner himself. Walter Wallis, of Wootten and Wallis in St Andrews Street. You'd better have a word with him. Your people will have more clout than us.'

'Thanks, you can leave that with me. I'll see you at the inquest no doubt, but in the meantime, can you find out if this man had a radio? If he's the same as his predecessors, who've all been notably incompetent, he'll have one in a brown case, which will weigh a ton. It might be at his last address, but if not, try left luggage at the station. These men appear to be briefed that that's a good place to hide things.'

53
CAMBRIDGE

As senior partner of Wootten and Wallis, solicitors and commissioners for oaths, Walter Wallis naturally had the benefit of the largest room on the first floor suite of offices they occupied at 5, St Andrews Street. Sitting at his desk, he was grateful for that extra space on what he knew was going to be an interesting day.

DCI Bone, Major Dixon and Dr Camarch all sat expectantly in front of him. As borough coroner, he had summoned them to give evidence at the inquest on the body found on 1st April in the air raid shelter on Christ's Pieces.

'Gentlemen, thank you for coming today. I'm sure you all appreciate why I've chosen my office rather than the guildhall for this hearing, which is being held *in camera*. I'd just like to formally record that my decision to do so was based on the information provided by Major Dixon, which convinced me that this case has a bearing on national security, at a time when we must all be vigilant. Needless to say, you're not to discuss what you hear today with anyone not authorised to hear it. Now, as you know I'm charged with establishing the identity of the deceased, and how, when and where he died. Let's deal with the identity first. Detective Chief Inspector Bone, the floor is yours. Please tell us who this man was, and the reasons for your conclusion. But first, kindly take the oath. You know the form.'

The DCI took the Bible from the coroner's desk and rattled off the oath he had uttered many times. 'Thank you, Sir. The deceased had on him what purports to be a Netherlands passport, number 696672, in the name of Jan Willem Ter Braak. It has an issue date of 25th July 1939, and expires on 24th July this year. I can confirm that the passport had no police or official stamp to show any port of landing. We also found on the body a national registration card number BFAB 318-1. It had been made out in the same name, Jan Willem Ter Braak, and bore a signature which agrees with that on the passport. However, as you will know, the surname should precede the forenames. There's also the address, which is shown as *Cambridge, 7 Oxford Street*. For the record, Oxford Street doesn't exist, and of course, it's not normal to find the name of the town written before the street. Also, the address should have been entered by the user of the card and not the issuer, as in this case.'

The coroner took the proffered documents, and opened the passport at the photograph. 'I take it this is a picture of the deceased?'

'Unfortunately, the bullet made a bit of a mess of his face, but as far as we could tell, and bearing in mind the problem with the likenesses of passport photos, they are one and the same. Now, Sir, I believe that Major Dixon would like to comment on both of these documents.'

After taking the oath, Dixon took a moment to gather his thoughts. 'The chief inspector has already drawn attention to the errors on the passport. Turning to the national registration card, the details on it relate to a card issued originally from the Feltham office, to a William John Withers, a civil servant employed by the prison commissioners. I'm not authorised to explain how, but I can say that these details, and some of the errors evident on the passport, were all fed to German intelligence for the precise purpose for which they have been used. Therefore, I can confirm that the deceased was indeed a German agent.'

The coroner looked surprised. 'Thank you major. That's a very definite statement, and I'm grateful to you for being so positive. For my part, I agree there's no such location as Oxford Street within the borough, and in the light of all the evidence now before me, I accept that this man was an enemy agent. But I have to ask, as the passport and identity card are forgeries, was this man actually Ter Braak, or someone else?'

The major frowned. 'There's no way of knowing, Sir. In our experience, enemy agents rarely use their real names, and our view is that Ter Braak is almost certainly an alias, but I trust that won't prevent you issuing the necessary paperwork to the registrar.'

'No, I'm happy to use the name Ter Braak. In any event, that could be changed if the next of kin ever came forward to request it, and were able prove an error had been made. So gentlemen, subject to that proviso, I'm satisfied that we've established an identity for the deceased. Now, the death certificate will also require details of an occupation.' With a smile, he continued. 'In the light of what you've told me Major, it seems I should describe Mr Ter Braak as a German spy.'

Major Dixon looked aghast, and spluttered, 'No, no, I must protest...' but relaxed when he saw the grin on the face of the coroner.

Walter Wallis held up his hands. 'Objection noted, Major. Just my little joke. I'll record him as "of no fixed abode and rank or profession unknown." Now, the next question is the cause of death.' He looked across at the doctor, and handed him the Bible.

The medic cleared his throat, and rattled off the oath. Taking out a small notebook from his jacket pocket, he read from his notes. 'I observed a small triangular wound on the left temple, one and a half inches above and to the left of the left ear. On the right temple, there was a cruciform wound about one inch by half an inch just below the right ear. In my professional opinion, these injuries were the result of a gunshot which caused haemorrhage and laceration of the brain.'

The coroner addressed the three men in front of him. 'Are we all agreed that the cause of death was a shot, presumably from the gun lying near the body?' They all nodded.

The DCI turned a page of the file in front of him. 'For the record, I can confirm it was a Browning automatic revolver, number 406225. There were ten rounds in the magazine, with one in the breach. A spent cartridge case was found on the floor of the shelter. The odd thing is that, assuming he started out with a magazine with the full thirteen bullets in it, the gun would seem to have been fired twice. However, there was no evidence of a second shot within the air raid shelter.'

The doctor looked up sharply over his half-rimmed glasses. 'I know it might not be relevant to these proceedings, but my recollection is that the gunshot wounds of the late Mr Pearce could well have come from this calibre of weapon.'

'Ah yes, the late Lennie Pearce, former villain of this parish. We've sent the gun away for testing to confirm that it was indeed used in this case, but I consider that to be a formality. We have the cartridge case from the Pearce incident, and we will of course check to see if the same gun was used then. If it was, that would certainly raise a number of further questions, but that's another matter entirely.'

The coroner was silent for a moment as he carefully completed his notes. With a thoughtful look on his face, he continued. 'Thank you Chief Inspector. We'll need to come back to the question of just how Mr Ter Braak died, but before we do, I'd like to get the two remaining questions I'm required to answer out of the way, that is, where and when? As for where, are you able to confirm that it was in the air raid shelter on Christ's Pieces?'

'Yes, Sir. That's where the body was discovered by the electrician sent to install the wiring. The place wasn't yet open to the public and Mr Spencer was adamant he hadn't disturbed anything. There was no evidence to suggest the body had been moved after the shot, so the air raid shelter it must be.'

'Thanks for that,' continued the coroner. 'The next question is when?' He looked expectantly at the doctor, who peered over his glasses as he replied.

'It was clear to me that the body was in an advanced state of rigor mortis, and my view is that death occurred at least thirty-six hours earlier. I saw the body on the 1st, so this poor chap expired late on the 29th, or perhaps during the early hours of the 30th March. I'm sorry, but I can't be more specific.'

Walter Wallis nodded. 'Thank you doctor. I think under the circumstances, I'll assume he died on the 29th. Now, we're all agreed he was shot, but we now have to determine "how the deceased came by his death", which as you will appreciate is not the same question as "how did he die?" It seems we have two options to consider. The first is that he took his own life, requiring me to return a verdict of suicide. The alternative is that he was killed by a person or persons unknown, leading to a verdict of unlawful killing. I'd now like to invite each of you in turn to give me your views, and to explain why you've reached such a conclusion. Doctor, you can open the batting.'

'The injuries I saw were entirely consistent with the gun having been held to his head, and in a location that could have been self-inflicted. Beyond that, I'm not prepared to go.'

'Thank you doctor, now Chief Inspector, what's your view?'

'I agree with you, doctor, the wounds were just as I've seen with other such cases, where there's been no doubt that it was a suicide. That said, as a policeman, I'm still unwilling to completely rule out the involvement of someone else.'

'Thank you for your thoughts, Chief Inspector. Now Major, may we have the benefit of your view?'

Major Dixon realised he had a critical job to do. Their failure to catch this spy as soon as he had landed had caused his department some considerable anxiety, not to mention some high level criticism. It was essential to the security services that this case was brought to a close as quickly and as neatly, as possible. Knowing that he had taken the oath he chose his words very carefully.

'Sir, we have here the body of someone who was, without doubt, a German agent. Again I'm not authorised to explain how I know, but I can say that this man was most probably intended as the advance guard of a German invasion, which, thank the Lord, hasn't yet taken place. He'll have arrived here with generous, but nevertheless finite funds, on the basis that the invading troops would soon take over and remove the need for him to pay his way. Thanks to the DCI's further enquiries, we now have our hands on the radio set he had with him, and while this is still to be examined in detail, it does seem to have been used extensively, judging by the state of the batteries, which are dead. There's also the important fact that there was only one shilling and ninepence in change on the body, and we've not found any more cash in the belongings he left at his digs. Bear in mind also that his last landlady has confirmed he left owing a week's rent of ten shillings. So, that suggests he had sufficient funds to keep him going provided the invasion took place shortly after he arrived. When that failed to materialise, he transmitted messages asking for more money, and when the cash also failed to arrive, he must have realised he had no way of maintaining his front. I would add that his forged ration book had expired, and without that, or the cash to eat in a restaurant, he'd be unable to feed himself. Obviously, any attempt to renew his ration book would bring him into contact with the authorities, and certain exposure. It should be remembered that although the number was genuine, it would have shown up as relating to someone else.'

There was silence in the room until the doctor spoke. 'In the light of what I've just heard, I think I'd say it was a case of suicide.'

The DCI shook his head. 'I'm still not sure, but I accept I don't have any concrete evidence to back up my doubts. But, Major, why was he dressed with so many layers of underclothes?'

'It seems to me that he put all those clothes on, and also had some newspapers to add to the layers, because he was planning to spend a night out in the open, or at least somewhere without any proper heating, possibly even the air raid shelter itself.'

The DCI stroked his chin as he turned the matter over in his mind. 'You said he'd probably asked for some more cash. Are you suggesting that this was to be delivered to him by another spy who presumably parachuted down a couple of nights ago? How do we know this man didn't shoot Ter Braak and scarper with the money?'

The major thought quickly and addressed the coroner. 'Sir, am I obliged to respond? I know this hearing is in camera, and I've been as candid as I can, but I do feel we are now straying into operational matters that I'm not at liberty to discuss.'

The coroner deliberated for a moment, before responding. 'No, Major, I see no need to pursue what is essentially only speculation. Now, Chief Inspector, your misgivings are noted, and I have a great deal of respect for your opinion. However, as you say, there's nothing specific to back up what I can therefore only describe as a hunch. On the other hand, everything points to the deceased having run out of money and with it, the ability to survive undetected within the community.'

Walter Wallis paused for a few seconds, as he gathered his thoughts, then he delivered his verdict. 'Gentlemen, in the light of the evidence before me, I'm satisfied, beyond reasonable doubt, that this man killed himself, and I'll therefore return a verdict of suicide. I will issue the required paperwork to Arthur Leverington, the registrar, to allow the body to be buried. In view of the deceased's lack of funds, it would seem that the cost of the interment will fall upon the borough.'

At this point, a relieved Major Dixon announced that it might be possible for his department to meet those costs. 'We're very keen to tie up the loose ends as soon as possible. Perhaps we could talk about it?'

The coroner smiled. 'That would be very good of your people, Major. Please stay behind afterwards, and let's see what we can sort out. Now, I think this brings these proceeding to a close. Thank you everyone for your contribution, and again I'd remind you of the need for absolute secrecy.'

The DCI and the doctor both departed, with the policeman still convinced that this was not the end of the matter.

54
DULWICH, LONDON

Staff Nurse Jones had the knack of getting on with anyone, and this, coupled with her nursing skills, made her a favourite on ward C2, men's medical at Dulwich Hospital, a former workhouse infirmary, located at the bottom of Denmark Hill in south west London. She even managed to maintain her smile after the loss of her brother, killed when his Spitfire was shot down during the Battle of Britain.

The arrival on ward C2 of an injured German airman tested the young staff nurse to her limit. She was told that, unlike her brother who had been trapped in his burning fighter, the German airman had managed to bail out of his stricken aircraft and survive, suffering only a broken ankle. Nurse Jones did her best to banish any thoughts that this man, Josef Jakobs, might have been the one who had earlier shot down her brother, and concentrated upon nursing him with the same dedication given to the other patients on her ward.

When first admitted, Jakobs had been sullen and, not surprisingly, suspicious of the motives of the medical staff. However, as the days went by, he grudgingly accepted that his treatment was beyond reproach and his attitude to the enemy softened somewhat. He gradually became more talkative. From the odd remark, it became clear to those attending him that he had some medical knowledge, and certainly enough to realise that the damage to his tibia and fibula was a Pott's fracture.

In spite of his care, Jakobs encountered a number of setbacks. First, he developed a fever with his temperature rocketing to over one hundred and two degrees Fahrenheit. The medical team were then faced with sepsis of the wound, followed by broncho-pneumonia. Luckily, the recent availability of the new and revolutionary, sulphur drugs allowed them to cure what had been, until not long before, a potentially fatal condition.

To the surprise of the ward staff, Jakob's recovery did nothing to cheer him up. In fact as he improved, his mood darkened and he retreated even more into his shell.

Staff Nurse Jones was, as always, optimistic. 'Here's a nice cup of tea for you, Mr Jakobs. That'll cheer you up.'

'Thank you Nurse,' grunted the spy, wondering why the English always considered tea to be the cure for everything. Putting the cup on his bedside locker, Jakobs lay back and sank even deeper into his mood of doom and despondency. Cheer up? How could he when he was stuck in a hospital bed with a broken ankle? And when it was mended, he would be carted back off to the interrogation centre.

'What's the date today, Alf?' asked Jakobs, looking at the soldier sitting on a chair at the foot of his bed. Jakobs was guarded twenty-four hours a day, seven days a week, and this deployment had soon become known as a cushy number - indoors, in the warm, food available, and with only an injured German flier to look after. Not surprisingly, the same names appeared regularly on the rota, and in spite of the order that no fraternisation should take place it was only natural that over time a degree of mutual understanding would grow up between the guards and the guarded.

Today was the turn of 7347271, Private A. Porter, who turned and grinned. 'What's the date? Now Josef, you know I'm not supposed to give you that sort of information. But have you seen the headlines today? Another beating for your air force. Here, have a look,' and Alf tossed that day's edition of the Daily Mirror across to him.

Jakobs scanned the page, wondering just how true the claim for the number of Luftwaffe planes brought down might be, when he realised what Alf had done. He looked at the top of the front page and saw it was Monday 7th April 1941. He knew he had arrived at Dulwich Hospital on 3rd February, and a quick mental calculation shocked him. *'That's virtually nine weeks!'* He handed back the soldier's paper.

'Thanks, Alf, but I don't want to read your propaganda.' He was just about to enquire who was on duty that night, when his guard stood up, snapped to attention and saluted. Jakobs knew this meant the arrival of an officer, and lo and behold, Tar Robertson appeared around the curtain which shielded Jakob's bed from the rest of the ward.

Tar returned the soldiers salute. 'Morning Porter. I need a word. Leave us alone for a moment, please.'

'Yes Sir, I'll wait by the door,' replied the private, who then made his way down the ward, his progress followed by all those awake in other beds.

Tar picked up the guard's chair, moved it to the side of the bed, and sat down. He disliked hospitals and their ever present smell of disinfectant but this was a visit he had to make. 'Hello, Josef. How are you today? Is that ankle of yours still giving you gyp?' Jakobs was just about to say that it still hurt like hell, when Tar took a passport out of his tunic pocket, opened it at the photograph page and held it up. 'Ever seen this man before?'

Jakobs squinted at the picture and although he did not think it was a very good likeness, he knew instantly it was Engelbertus Fukken, the man he had been sent to find. He played for time. 'Let me put my glasses on, so I can take a closer look.'

He put on his spectacles as slowly as he dared. Fukken must have been caught but what had happened to him before that? Had he found Maud? Had he managed to send a message to Hamburg while he, Josef had been trapped in hospital? If not, finding Maud and this new super weapon was still down to him, but what could he do in captivity and with this broken leg?

Taking the passport from Tar Robertson, Jakobs read the signature below the picture. After a pause, and when he felt able to control his voice, he replied, 'I have no idea who this is. Who is J. W. Ter Braak?'

'I was hoping you could tell me that. Are you sure he's not a friend of yours? He has a standard issue radio, so we know where he came from. He was found shot in an air raid shelter in Cambridge a few days ago. Seems he committed suicide when he ran out of money.' Looking at his watch Tar added, 'He's being buried today, as we speak.'

'No, I'm sure I've not seen him before. When did he arrive?'

The amount of detail to be given out to Jakobs had been the subject of heated debate between Tar, Liddell and Harker. Eventually it had been agreed that there was no need to hold anything back, as all three no longer saw Jakobs as a candidate for turning and using as a double cross agent. Not only had it been over two months without contact with his radio, his arrival had also been seen by too many people, and a firing squad was now almost a certainty. Tar had no need to be circumspect. 'We think he landed at the beginning of November last year. A parachute and harness were found rolled up in a ditch.'

Already knowing the answer to his question, Jakobs asked, 'I wonder why he didn't bury his 'chute?' Enjoying himself for the first time since his arrival, he went on. 'Are you telling me that this man has been at large for, what is it, five months?'

Tar felt obliged to give the impression of some success. 'It's not always our policy to arrest agents immediately, but to give them some rope to see who else they contact. What do you think his mission was?'

Jakobs relaxed. He took that question as evidence MI5 had not traced Fukken until they found his body, and had no idea what he had been sent over to do. He kept up the pretext. 'I imagine it was the same as me. Weather reports, troop movements, that sort of thing.'

'What was his code? Was it the same as your coding grid, you know, the one you tried to destroy after you'd landed.'

'I've no idea. Individual codes weren't talked about. With mine, I tore it up in desperation. I knew I was going to be captured, and I thought that having that sort of stuff with me could mean I'd be shot out of hand.'

'Is that why you tried to bury your radio too?'

'I was in great pain, and I'll admit it, scared stiff. I wasn't thinking clearly, but please remember, I only used my gun to get help, and not to kill anyone.'

'I hear what you say,' Tar said, standing up, and so confirming that the interview was at an end. 'Sister tells me you should be fit to leave in another week or so. Then you'll be off to the centre you went to at first. Lieutenant Colonel Stephens will want another word with you.'

After Tar had left, Private Porter returned to his post. 'Interesting chat with the Major?'

'Not really, Alf. However, it seems that your holiday, and mine for that matter, will be over soon. Sister thinks I'll be okay to leave in a week or so.'

Neither the spy nor the soldier looked forward to that.

55
LONDON

The train from Cambridge had arrived at Liverpool Street station on time, and Major Dixon stood patiently in the queue for a taxi. When it came to his turn, he heaved his two suitcases into the back of the cab, and in order to maintain the anonymity of his office, told the driver to, 'take me to St James' Street and drop me by the building with the To Let sign outside.'

'Oh, you want MI5 then,' said the cabbie with a grin, as he pulled out into the busy traffic.

'Good of you to come down so quickly,' smiled Tar Robertson, as the RSLO struggled into his office with his luggage.

'I've got the police report on Ter Braak, and I was right about his radio,' replied the major, gesturing towards the small brown case. 'He had left it at the railway station left luggage office. I wonder when the Abwehr will realise that's the first place we'll look?'

'Yes, sometimes, the way they go about things, you'd think they want us to win this war. Has Jack Hester seen it?'

'I showed it to him briefly, but he didn't want to do a detailed examination. He felt it should be looked at by B3(b) Branch, so I'm going to hand it over to them for a full report. Jack did volunteer to take a look at Ter Braak's lodgings to see if he could work out how the set might have performed. As you know, he's been very critical of the aerials on the earlier sets we've recovered.'

'Good man. I'll be interested to see his report. Now, what else have the police turned up?'

The major referred to his notes. 'Dealing with the body first, there was the blue pin striped suit he bought from Fifty Shilling Tailors. That's what led the police to the Serrills, in St Barnabas Road. But I'll come back to them later. Under his suit, he was wearing a pullover, shirt and four vests, plus two pairs of long-johns. Everything he had on was virtually new and had been bought over here, except for his shoes. They were British, but had been mended recently. He either came over in them and had them re-soled, or somehow got hold of a second-hand pair after he'd arrived.'

'Either way, it's good to know the Abwehr are spending their funds on our craftsmen. What did he have in his pockets?'

'The usual. An empty wallet, a pipe with tobacco in it and ready to smoke, a tobacco pouch with more tobacco, a comb, fountain pen, and a catholic charm. No notes, not even ten bob in the wallet, and he only had one shilling and ninepence in loose change in his pockets. Nothing else, so it looks as if he was just about broke.'

'Unless he had a stash of cash somewhere else. What about the other suitcase? It's a *Revelation* isn't it?' Tar said, looking at the larger of the two cases.

'Yes, but again nothing out of the ordinary. Just another suit, some shirts, even more vests and long pants, ties, socks, a torch, razor blades, and a couple of penguin Books, *Europe in Chains* and *The Press*. Which reminds me. The three newspapers which had been left under the seat in the shelter have been checked, and there's nothing written on them. No marks or anything. Seems as if they were only there for extra insulation.'

'What, in addition to the four vests?' queried Tar. 'How odd.'

'It seems our Mr Ter Braak was a forgetful chap as he left a few things behind at Montague Road.'

'Anything interesting?'

'Not really. Just a pair of shoes, a pair of boots and two packets of typing paper. No sign of a typewriter, and the police didn't find one at the office he was renting. He also left some belongings at St Barnabas Road, but Mrs Serrill saw him in town after he was supposed to have gone to London, and got him to collect them.'

'Didn't his reappearance in Cambridge make her suspicious?'

'Yes. She claims to have got her husband to go to see the assistant aliens officer at the borough police, but she thinks he did nothing again.'

Tar raised his eyebrows. 'Again?'

'Apparently so. I've asked the DCI to look into that as a matter of urgency. In the meantime we've found a number of bus tickets in the pockets of his suit. These show he'd been travelling around the area. Seemed to be especially fond of Peterborough, but he also went to London at least once.'

'I presume we're getting the Cambridge police to follow up these leads?'

'Actually, no. I've told them not to make any enquiries outside their own area, as that will involve other forces, and I was concerned about maintaining secrecy.'

'Upon reflection, that's a good move,' Tar conceded. 'We don't want too many people to be in on this. There's more than enough public awareness of the fifth column threat already. But we must find out what this man was up to in his five months at large, and why the system didn't pick him up. I'll get some copies of his picture to issue to relevant RSLOs. What does the chap look like?'

'Here's his passport, and the registration card which I phoned you about when he was first found.'

Tar picked up the two documents. 'You know I just couldn't believe it when you read out those entries, and they matched the details we'd fed to the other side via SNOW. But it seems we needn't have bothered, as they've included quite a few mistakes of their own that should have highlighted the document as a forgery. The fact that he wasn't picked up suggests that no-one with sufficient knowledge saw any of his documents.'

'Yes, he seems to have been a lucky chap in that respect.'

'Any news about the gun?' asked Tar.

'The police still have that. They've sent it for ballistic examination, but the DCI considers that to be a formality. I presume their file will be closed in the light of the suicide verdict at the inquest, but the DCI was interested to see if the same gun had been used to kill someone else. Some villain, I gather and one the police seem quite happy to see the back of.'

'Perhaps our spy has done the Cambridge police a favour, then. But, that's none of our business. I'm glad the hearing went well. I presume you didn't have any problem getting them to hold it in camera?'

'No, the coroner was only too pleased to have an excuse to keep the public and press out.'

'Splendid. I'm also delighted that the verdict was suicide. It helps to tie things up. I take it you passed on the DG's offer to meet the burial expenses?'

Dixon nodded. 'Yes. I tried to make it conditional on Ter Braak being buried under another name so he'd disappear completely.'

'I can't imagine that went down well?'

'No, it didn't. The coroner was in a quandary. He admitted the borough was finding things difficult, now that they're getting air raid damage and casualties, and the town obviously needs the money. I stressed the point regarding national security, but Mr Wallis was clearly wondering what further damage a dead spy could do. In the end, we reached a compromise. As coroner, Wallis was under a legal obligation to record the true findings of the court, but he had a quiet word with the registrar, and it seems there must have been a slip up when conveying the relevant details, as the Great Shelford cemetery records now show that a Lyam Willenson Braak died on 2nd April. At least he's in an unmarked plot.

'I suppose that's as much as we could expect. Did you attend?'

'Yes. The burial was last Monday, on the 7th and I thought I should see the process through to the bitter end. Bitter describes it very well. The wind was icy and the land girls working in the surrounding fields looked as if they were frozen to the core.' Dixon shivered at the memory. 'There was no formal service at the graveside and even though he's the enemy, I must admit to having some grudging admiration for the chap. After all, it must have taken some guts to go through what he did. Anyway, everything went off without any fuss, and the press seem to have swallowed the story of a tramp dying in the cold weather.'

Tar looked delighted. 'That's good news. Well done. I'll tell the DG his offer to meet the funeral costs did benefit us. Let me know when you get a further report from the police.'

Dixon was about to take his leave when he paused. 'Do we have any information on Ter Braak's mission?'

'No. I interviewed Jakobs last Monday, and he said he didn't know, but assumed it would've been the same as him, weather conditions and troop movements.'

'Do you believe that?'

Tar hesitated. 'Jakobs is clearly a cut above the previous agents sent over. As for Ter Braak, well, the fact that he survived undetected for some five months speaks for itself. So, on balance, no. I reckon they were both tasked with something more than weather conditions and troop movements. The question is, what?'

56
CAMBRIDGE

DCI Clive Bone had been obliged to accept that the coroner's verdict of suicide appeared to fit the facts, and there was no doubt that his friend, the RSLO, was delighted. But when the ballistics report on the gun found next to the corpse came in, the DCI cheered out loud.

Upon his recommendation, PC David Vasey had been transferred from uniform duties to plain clothes CID, as a reward for his smart work in tracking down the Serrills and Miss Blackwood. Bone handed Vasey the report. 'I told you I wasn't entirely happy about the suicide verdict, and I think this opens up a new line of enquiry. It certainly gives someone a good motive.'

Detective Constable Vasey scanned the page. 'This is the same gun that was used to kill Lennie Pearce!' he exclaimed. ' It doesn't take a genius to work out who might have wanted to get their own back.'

'Yes, his sister Patsy. Let's get her in, and see what she has to say for herself.'

The DCI was looking forward to grilling Patsy. When DC Vasey returned to the station and reported she was not at home, and nowhere to be found, he was not best pleased. His mood worsened when it became clear that she had dropped out of sight and no-one knew, or was brave enough to say, where she was hiding.

'I'm convinced she's implicated. She must turn up eventually,' grunted the DCI.

'Yes, Guv, she's involved in too many deals to be absent for long.'

The DCI nodded. 'I agree. Better let the county constabulary know, just in case. Now, let's give some thought to the link this gun gives us. If, as it seems, Ter Braak shot the late Mr Pearce, we have to ask ourselves, why?'

'Knowing Pearce, I'd say it was probably something to do with the black market. If I was looking for anything like that, Guv, I'd have turned to him first.'

'Okay, so Ter Braak wanted some under the counter stuff. But what, and who for?'

'We know he was staying with the Serrills at the time, and that would have included the Christmas period. Perhaps he wanted to treat them. Shall I have a word?'

'Yes, and of course, keep your eyes open for our friend Patsy.'

Mr and Mrs Serrill were surprised to see DC Vasey on their doorstep again, but showed him into the front parlour. He sat down, and tried to soften the blow that was coming.

'How are you now Mrs Serrill? Last time I saw you, you were still suffering from that nasty bang on the head.'

'Much better, thank you Constable. But, I see you're not in uniform?'

'No, I've transferred to plain clothes. I'm a detective now. Look, I'm sorry to have to bother you, but I've a few more questions about Mr Ter Braak.'

'Ah, Jan, such a nice lad,' joined in Mr Serrill. 'We did have some laughs together, especially over Christmas.'

'It was Christmas I wanted to ask you about. We've now obtained some evidence that suggests he must have been involved in the black market. Did you ever see anything that could have come from such a source, you know, things that were beyond the usual ration limits?'

There was a short silence, and then Mrs Serrill burst into tears. 'I knew we shouldn't have had anything to do with those things he got.'

Mr Serrill put his arm around his wife. 'It's my fault, officer. I persuaded her we should take them.'

'What did he get?'

'A lovely piece of beef. Said it was from a friend of his and it was so tasty,' said Mr Serrill, wistfully.

'Anything else?' asked DC Vasey, notebook and pencil in hand.

'He came down on Christmas Day with three bottles, scotch for my Bert, sherry for me, and some odd stuff from his own country. It was too strong for me,' Mrs Serrill added, tears still running down her face.

DC Vasey stood up. 'Thanks for being so honest with me. You know, of course, it's against the law to accept goods obtained in such a way. I'm going to have to report this, but I do appreciate how helpful you've been in this business. It'll not be my final decision, but I'll put in a good word for you. I'll see myself out.'

As he left, he looked back to see the couple hugging each other, both in tears, and convinced that their world had just come to an abrupt end. He walked back to the police station with a heavy heart.

'Thanks for coming to London again' said Tar Robertson to a tired Major Dixon, who'd been stuck on the train from Cambridge for several hours due to an unexploded bomb.

'Those UXBs cause almost more havoc that those that go off,' the major moaned. 'Anyway, I've had an update from the police.' He sat down with a bulging file in front of him.

'Why did Ter Braak slip through the net? I'm being hounded by Jasper Harker,' asked a desperate Tar. 'If we're not careful, we'll have Winston on our backs as well.'

'The Serrills are telling the truth. Mr Serrill did go to see the assistant aliens officer at the borough police shortly after Ter Braak arrived. Then he went again after his wife had met Ter Braak in town, after he'd said he was off to London. In both cases the officer did nothing. On the first occasion he even said he was sure the man would pop along and report himself.'

Tar banged the table with his fist. 'Of course he didn't pop along and report himself. Spies don't hand themselves in. I don't know, we put all these systems in place and then some silly sod goes and mucks up the system because he's too lazy to do his job. I trust this man is being suitably dealt with?'

'He's being hauled up in front of the chief constable,' replied the RSLO with a smile, 'Knowing Bob Pearson as I do, he'll wish he'd never been born.'

'I suppose it's a comfort that the system should have picked up Ter Braak if it had been operating as it was supposed to. Anything else to report?'

'I said that DC Vasey is a bright lad, well, he's excelled himself again. He remembered Mrs Serrill telling him that Ter Braak only got their room because he was a non-smoker. However, there was a filled pipe and a tobacco pouch on the body.'

'OK, so he used to nip out for a crafty smoke,' said Tar with a laugh.

'I doubt it, as he'd have set fire to his code. Vasey had a closer look at the pipe, emptied out the tobacco, and found this hidden underneath.'

Tar took the piece of flimsy typewriter paper handed to him. 'These are instructions on how to prepare his code. And there was us looking for coding disc number eight. Well I never. Those Penguin books weren't for reading after all. Give that man a medal. I'll get this off to Bletchley, together with the books. That should keep them happy.'

'Any news on the radio?' asked the RSLO.

'Yes, I've had a full report.' Tar read from the file on the desk in front of him. 'Ter Braak's set is a transmitter and receiver. There's no way of determining the incoming frequency but there were two crystals for transmitting, on frequencies of 4508.5 kc/s and 5435.3 kc/s. The higher one's for daytime , the lower for night. Sounds daft, but the length of the aerial was only suitable for daytime. The LT battery was dead, and the HT down from 270 to 195 volts, so there's no doubt the set's had considerable usage. The night-time frequency matches that which the young VI picked up, the weak transmission, that led us to your part of the world.'

The major smiled ruefully. 'That's interesting. I've now heard from Jack Hester, following his visit to St Barnabas Road, where the Serrills showed him the room at the back which Ter Braak used. The report from DCI Bone recorded the fact that he used to keep his bedroom window open in all weathers. Ter Braak told Mrs Serrill it was for the fresh air. Jack reckons it could have been so he could drop his aerial out, but if he did, it wouldn't have given him the best result.'

Tar pointed to the report on his desk. 'This confirms that the length of the wire was for the daytime frequency yet all the evidence points to Ter Braak transmitting only in the evening.'

'Yes, and it gets worse for our poor old spy. Jack put his mind to where he could have obtained a suitable connection to earth, which he assures me is vital for the proper operation of any transmitter and receiver. He searched the room, and found some faint scratch marks on the left hand gas lamp bracket that could have been the result of twisting a bare wire around it.'

'Did you say he used a gas pipe? Surely he could have blown himself and the house to smithereens if there'd been a spark?'

'Yes, in theory.'

'What do you mean?'

'Mr Serrill wouldn't leave Jack on his own during his visit. He followed him around like a pet dog, and was always asking him questions. At first Jack did his best to ignore him, but eventually he gave up, and explained he was looking for a suitable earth connection. When he suggested the gas pipe, Mr Serrill roared with laughter, and took him downstairs, and showed him where the redundant gas pipes had been cut off. It seems the previous tenant, who was kicked out for smoking, had complained of a smell of gas. Mr Serrill was sure he'd imagined it, but to stop him moaning, he had the pipes going up to the first floor cut off and capped.'

'So, there was no connection down to the ground. I presume that affected his signal strength?'

'Yes. Jack says it would be down substantially, in addition to any further loss due to the inadequate aerial. But at least there was no risk of an explosion.'

'Then he won't have been able to make contact with Germany from the Cambridge area and probably didn't receive any incoming messages either,' exclaimed Tar with a grin.

'No. He must have been trying night after night without success. I reckon the only person to have picked up any of his transmissions was that young VI.'

'Luckily for us. How does Ter Braak's set compare to others we've recovered?'

Tar turned to the back of the report he was reading. 'This addendum compares all the ones we've recovered from incoming agents, and the set's identical to those we recovered from Pons and Waldberg. The sets from Caroli and Schmidt are also technically comparable.'

The RSLO looked thoughtful. 'I suppose Waldberg could make contact as he was virtually on the coast, and well within range of any listening post on the continent.'

'Yes. He admitted to getting a couple of messages off before we caught him. I guess those transmissions were effectively his death sentence. Once he'd sent them, he was no longer suitable for turning.'

'Yes, you need to know what's been said, and have as few people as possible know about it.'

'Precisely. The fact that we were able to get to Caroli and Schmidt very quickly made all the difference.'

The RSLO laughed. 'Yes, and there's the Abwehr thinking the sets they give to their agents are up to the job, when in fact they only work because we've gingered them up to make sure we get through.'

58
CAMBRIDGE

The DCI was a worried man as he made his way to the office of the chief constable. What did he want this time? The Watch Committee probably had another bee in its bonnet. The previous month he had been told to crack down on cyclists riding without lights, and before that, it was drivers not having their car bumpers painted white, as required by the blackout regulations. However, he could appreciate his chief's position. The Watch Committee, made up of the great and the good of the town, had the power to sack him or anyone else in the force for that matter.

When he got back, it was obvious things had gone well. 'You look happy Guv. What did the chief have to say this time?' asked DC Vasey.

'You'll be pleased to know he's approved your recommendation not to charge the Serrills. He accepts they wouldn't have got themselves involved in the black market if the assistant aliens officer had done his job properly. He's had that chap up in front of him and torn a strip off him. The man's now been transferred to some humdrum job, where he can do no further damage. However, the main reason for the summons was something else entirely. I told him about our new line of enquiry, and of course, he wasn't too happy about us losing track of Patsy Pearce. Anyway, he's given me this address to watch. Get yourself down there right away, and let me know when she leaves.'

'But, how did the chief get this?' asked an incredulous DC Vasey, staring at the piece of paper.

'He didn't say, but remember, he started as a constable, pounding the beat, just like us. Although he's now in his ivory tower, fielding all the political balls that come his way, it's obvious he still has his contacts. Once a copper, always a copper. Now off you go, and keep in touch.'

Turning to his in-tray, the DCI was soon immersed in files on crimes thrown up by the many new regulations churned out by the various government departments. The recent reduction in the level of the meat ration had been overlooked by at least one butcher. 'Lucky customers' muttered the DCI, before arranging to visit the errant trader.

It was several hours later and he had just picked up the file on the case of an Eastern Counties bus driver who had driven into a column of soldiers, when his sergeant came in looking puzzled. 'Guv, I've just taken a very strange message from the station master. It seems young Vasey ran into the station, and asked him to tell you that she's taking the train to Bristol, and he's following.'

The DCI sat back in his chair. 'It does look as if the chief was right, after all,' and he went on to explain the discussions he had had with his boss. 'We're going to have to trust young Vasey not to lose her'.

DC Vasey was determined to stick close to his quarry, and was glad he had been promoted to plain clothes, as his former uniform would have stuck out like a sore thumb. After the train arrived at Bristol's Temple Meads station, he watched from a distance as she had waited for a taxi. He then upset the remainder of the queue by pushing his way to the front and, waving his warrant card, commandeered the next vehicle. As he climbed into the taxi, he smiled at the realisation that he had just achieved one of his lifetime ambitions with his instructions to, 'Follow that cab.'

This was a part of the country that was new to him, but he soon realised they were travelling south, although only for a few miles, as before long they arrived at an airfield surrounded by tall, barbed-wire fencing. To his surprise, it appeared to be handling non-military aircraft with a Douglas DC3 with British civil markings being prepared for take-off.

The taxi in front stopped at the air ministry checkpoint, and after an inspection of what looked like a ticket and passport, was waved through. Their taxi followed, and Vasey was soon on the phone in the guard's hut to the commanding officer. He explained his mission, and was directed to the main office block. The young constable thrust a ten shilling note into the hand of the driver and to the cabbie's delight, then ran off without waiting for his change. Vasey made his way as fast as he could to the COs office, where he was greeted by a flight sergeant. 'Please wait here. We're just checking out your story.'

'We've got to stop that plane,' shouted the now desperate detective, pointing to the DC3 which, as he watched, was being loaded with passengers and luggage. He paced the floor for what seemed like an age, then the CO's door opened and a group captain emerged, smiling and holding out his hand. 'Detective Constable Vasey, I presume. Welcome to RAF Whitchurch. I've managed to check out your story. Luckily, I got through to Cambridge without any delay, and your boss was very pleased to hear from me. They were getting worried about you. Anyway, I've told the control tower to hold the plane. If you care to follow me, I'll get you on board, and you can do the necessary.'

The travellers were all strapped in ready for their flight to Lisbon, but for some reason the passenger door remained open with the access steps still in place. The man next to a port-side window reckoned he knew the reason for the delay. 'There's an RAF staff car racing up to us. I reckon some bigwig is late for the flight.'

All eyes were on the group captain as he entered, followed by a civilian. The passengers strained to hear what was being said to the air hostess, who then pointed to a woman sitting in one of the seats. Walking up to the third row, DC Vasey paused. 'Professor Carpenter? Professor Audrey Carpenter?'

The woman looked as white as a sheet, but nodded her head. To the utter amazement of the passengers and crew, DC Vasey then said 'I'm arresting you for the murder of Jan Willem Ter Braak. You do not have to say anything, but anything you do say will be taken down and may be given in evidence. Please come with me.'

The professor undid her seat belt, and turned to the passenger in the aisle seat next to her. 'I'm so sorry to trouble you, but it seems there's been a mistake. If you'll excuse me, I'll sort it out.' The neighbour stood up to let her out and Carpenter followed the group captain and detective constable down the steps onto the runway. To her horror, she was put in handcuffs by a military policeman, who ushered her into the staff car, just as her suitcase, which had been retrieved from the aircraft hold, was put in the boot.

The steps to the aircraft were wheeled away, and within seconds of the passenger door being slammed shut, the engines spluttered into life, and the plane taxied to the runway. It climbed into the sky, its passengers wondering why a professor should have killed someone, and who the man called Ter Braak was?

The drive back to Cambridge was completed very swiftly, thanks to the help of two RAF outriders on their motorbikes. Sitting in the interview room, Audrey Carpenter stared defiantly at her inquisitor.

DCI Bone was an old hand, and he sat quietly for some time, turning over the pages of his file. Eventually he spoke.

'Professor Carpenter, why did you kill Ter Braak?'

She replied with a stony face. 'I didn't and I demand to be freed at once. I intend to make sure the chief constable knows all about the abominable treatment I've had. He's a friend of mine, I'll have you know. I'll get you sacked if it's the last thing I do.'

Unmoved by the threat, the DCI continued. 'Come now professor, let's not waste time. It was Chief Constable Pearson who put me on to you. He's received very reliable information that you were in the air raid shelter on the evening of Saturday 29th March. He's as sure of your guilt as I am.'

'I don't know where that information came from, but I can assure you it's not reliable, and I insist you say what proof you've got to back up your allegation.' The professor sat back with a smirk on her face, leaving the DCI slightly concerned, when the interview room suddenly swung open and DC Vasey came in holding some sheets of paper. He whispered in the DCI's ear, and having been directed to take a seat next to his boss, he began to speak.

'Professor, I've found these notes in the false bottom of your suitcase. They appear to be about listening posts, decoding at Bletchley Park, and the apparent use of machines to assist in decoding Enigma messages.'

The smile fell from the professor's face.

59
CAMBRIDGE

When the figure in front of him visibly sagged, the DCI knew he had got his 'man'. 'Would you care to tell us about your involvement in all of this?' he asked a downcast Professor Carpenter.

Deciding to protect his family in Holland, she claimed she only knew Engelbertus Fukken as Jan Willem Ter Braak, and described how he had first made contact, her initial rebuttal and his further efforts to find her. She went on to explain how pleased she had been to have been given a second chance to help him, and the thrill she had felt from harbouring a real life German spy, while at the same time maintaining her mask of academia. 'It was all going so well until he killed that spiv. I told him he shouldn't have got involved with such a person, and as for cheating him over the dollar exchange rate, well, how stupid can you get? He thought shooting the man would put an end to the problem, but he didn't bank on his associates taking over.'

'When did he find out someone was after him?' asked DC Vasey.

'He realised quite quickly that he was being trailed. His basic training in Germany left a lot to be desired, but anti-surveillance measures seem to have been well taught.'

'So what happened that night in the air raid shelter?' prompted Bone.

'We agreed it would be best if he left Cambridge for a bit. I have a holiday cottage up north, and I managed to get hold of a motorbike and some petrol so he could ride up there. We were going to meet in the air raid shelter for the handover. However, when I wheeled the machine out of its garage at the college, the bloody thing wouldn't start, so I had to leave it and walk over to Christ's Pieces. When I went down the main steps of the shelter I saw him lying on the floor in a pool of blood.'

Vasey pounced. 'How could you see him? There were no lights in the shelter.'

The professor gave Vasey a withering look. 'My dear detective, I'd thought of that, and had given Jan an oil lamp to take with him. He had lit it and it was still alight on one of the benches.'

DCI Bone stared intently at the professor. 'I put it to you that he wasn't dead when you arrived, as you say, but that instead you killed him to prevent him exposing you for the traitor you are.'

'No, that's wrong. I didn't shoot him, but someone else most certainly did. I'm hopeless at the sight of blood and couldn't get too close to the body as the bullet had made a mess of the face. But, I knew it was him because I recognised his suit and raincoat and his wire rimmed glasses...' Tears trickled down the professor's face. DCI Bone gave her time to recover before going on. 'Come now, Professor, you're an intelligent woman. You must have realised that Ter Braak was likely to be caught, and would almost certainly implicate you. So, instead, you shot him, and with his own gun, to make it look like suicide.'

Audrey Carpenter paused, debating. The two policemen waited expectantly. 'I didn't shoot Jan, but as I know I'm going to be hanged, I might as well admit the truth. I did all I could to help him. As well as offering him sanctuary in my cottage up north, I told him I'd use my contacts to get him out of the country, eventually.'

'Assuming you didn't shoot Ter Braak, who did?'

'Come on Chief Inspector, it's obvious. It's got to be one of the spiv's associates, or more probably, someone from the security services. They must have been moving heaven and earth to track him down since his arrival, five months ago. All I know is it wasn't me.'

Bone shook his head, doubtful. 'But how could a stranger get close enough to Ter Braak to shoot him in the head, in a way that would look like suicide? He was obviously a determined character and not someone who'd give himself up. But he would have trusted you.'

Professor Carpenter was quiet for a moment before speaking softly, with some emotion. 'Jan was a very brave man. He realised he had to throw MI5 and the underworld off the scent. We decided that he should make sure he was followed to the shelter, where he planned to take them on. He was then going to hide up north, for a time. He knew he might not be able to win against an MI5 professional, but if that was the case, his sacrifice would allow me to take over the mission. I think you'll agree we very nearly pulled it off.'

DC Vasey picked up the papers from the suitcase. 'These notes deal with listening stations, and code breaking. Who were you going to give them to in Lisbon?'

'I didn't have a specific contact. I was just going to take them to the German Embassy for them to pass them on to Hamburg, where Jan's controller was based.'

'How on earth did you get all this?' the DCI asked.

The professor sat with her hands in her lap, fully intent on saying nothing. But, vanity got the better of her. She knew the evidence could only lead to the hangman's noose, but she would show them how clever she had been, how she had figured out what was going on from fragments of information, and put all the fragments together, just like a in jigsaw puzzle!

'It was quite easy,' she replied, smiling. She then described Ter Braak's travels which had led to the discovery of the listening posts at Hanslope Park and Chicksands. 'The key was the RAF chap on the train joking about him and his mate travelling from X to Y. We soon worked out that 'Y' was a play on the word wireless, and the presence of complicated aerials had to mean listening posts.'

Warming to her task, and still keen to show her brilliance, she continued. 'It was the reference to X which floored me, at least to start with. Jan was sure the RAF chap had got on the train with him at Bletchley, so that seemed to point to where X was located. But what went on there took a bit longer to work out. I knew a chap called Gordon Welshman. Not in my college, but we met some time ago at a social do. I got on quite well with him, even though he was a mathematician, with no sense of humour. As soon as war was declared, Welshman disappeared. I asked about him, and discovered it was common knowledge amongst maths graduates in their final year that he'd taken a couple of his own chaps off to Room 40. I'm sure I don't need to tell you that Room 40 was where they broke German codes in the last war, so it was obvious to me we were talking about cryptography. The two RAF men were travelling from X to Y that day, though of course the enemy transmissions intercepted by the Y stations would always go in the opposite direction, to X, for decoding.'

'But how did you work out that 'Room 40' was definitely at Bletchley?' asked an annoyingly impressed DCI.

'The porter at Bletchley Station was unwittingly very helpful by talking about Bletchley Park, and the fact that many of the passengers getting off there all looked like boffins. One of the missing maths graduates also gave me a clue. He had to come back for something, clean socks if he's anything like the students I deal with, and he told a friend he'd only had to travel an hour and a half or so on the Varsity line. As you know, that's the railway line that runs between here and Oxford and goes through Bletchley. I've checked the timetables, and it takes about an hour and a half or so to get here on the train from Bletchley. Then Jan told me about a friend of his landlady, whose daughter was transferred there because she spoke German.'

'You're also suggesting we're using machines to crack enemy codes. How did you come to that conclusion?' asked Vasey.

'When I was at Princeton University in America, on an exchange visit some years before the start of the war, I met this rather eccentric Englishman. He'd been a Fellow of Kings College and a bit of a genius, who was working on his PhD. Name of Turing. He was a mathematician who was convinced machines could solve the most complex of problems. I think his thesis was on that sort of possibility, but I know for certain he also studied cryptology. Not sure when he returned to England, but I do know he was back here again by 1939, with some calculating gadget built on a bread board. He and Gordon Welshman were like twins that year, always together, talking, but stopping when you came up to them. He disappeared at about the same time as Welshman, and I'm positive he's also at Bletchley. I did wonder why a machine was needed, but then I remembered Jan telling me that the Germans would have liked him to encode his messages with an Enigma machine, whatever that is, but they're too big for agents to lug around. However, it seems logical to me to use one machine against another.'

DC Vasey nodded, in grudging admiration at this conclusion. He looked down at Carpenter's notes and scanned the last few pages. Reading the handwritten details, he paused, horrified, and slid the documents across to his boss, who then looked like he'd seen a ghost.

'My God... the development of an atomic bomb,' muttered Bone. With all the self-control he could muster, the DCI asked in a quiet but firm voice, 'I see that you believe we're building an atomic bomb here in Cambridge. Would you care to elaborate, Professor?'

Audrey Carpenter smiled. This had been a difficult nut to crack. Again she would show them how clever she had been. 'Jan's mission was to find Maud and the new super weapon being developed in Cambridge. All the other stuff we discovered about decoding and the like was just a bonus.'

'Some bonus for German intelligence,' muttered the detective constable.

The professor nodded. ' Yes. Considering how much effort the government have put into telling us to *keep it under your hat*, it's surprising how careless people can be. The first clue that helped us track down Maud was some pillow talk from a friend of Jan's. I've never met the woman, and I won't tell you her name, but it seems she told him that another of her clients had mentioned Maud. Jan traced this man, Alan, back to the Cavendish Laboratory. I then managed to establish he was Alan Nunn-May, a physicist working in the old lab. But what he did was a closely guarded secret.'

The DCI and DC both waited expectantly for the next revelation. The professor, who was by now in her element, paused for dramatic effect, as if giving a lecture to her undergraduates. She then went on to relate her chance discovery of the invoice on the treasurer's desk. 'What made me concentrate on it was the amount being claimed for the first name on the Salaries list, a Dr Hans von Halban.'

'Very interesting, but how did that lead you to Maud?' asked Bone.

'When the treasurer saw me looking at the invoice, he hurriedly picked it up and put it in a folder marked *Work for Maud Committee*. I couldn't discover what 'M.A.U.D' stood for, nor why that committee was formed, so I turned my attention to finding out what Nunn-May and the doctor were working on. I had no luck with Nunn-May, but I knew I'd seen the name of von Halban somewhere before.. I was tidying my study and came across a back issue of the magazine *Nature* when it came to me, he'd had an article published before the start of the war. As you know, I'm not a scientist, but I am a keen amateur astronomer. My hobby put me in touch with other enthusiasts, and as a result I got to know Sir Richard Gregory, the Professor of Astronomy at Queens College. He's always keen to help amateurs. Until war was declared, Richard was also the editor of *Nature* and I became a regular reader. Once I knew what I was looking for, it didn't take me long to find the article by Hans von Halban. It was in a 1939 pre-war issue and titled the, *Liberation of Neutrons in the Nuclear Explosion of Uranium*. It was then I thought that M.A.U.D probably stood for *making a uranium detonation*. I'd love to know if that's right, but I don't suppose I'll ever find out.'

The two policemen shook their heads.

60
LONDON

When Guy Liddell shut his office door and poured them both a Scotch whisky, Tar Robertson knew his boss had some delicate matters to discuss. He was not disappointed. 'I've just got back from a meeting with the Cambridge Borough Police Chief Constable, Bob Pearson. You'll be pleased to know they've solved the mystery of Patsy Pearce's disappearance after Ter Braak's shooting. Bob correctly guessed that it was Nemo who put the frighteners on her, and told her to get out of Cambridge, but nobody knows where she's gone.'

Sipping his drink, Tar smiled. 'Patsy Pearce isn't the type to retire so young. She must be up to her usual antics somewhere.'

'Yes, I'm sure she's still in business, but that's not our problem, thank goodness.'

'Any news on Nemo?' asked Tar.

'I'm told that he's now engaged on another task, but it seems the official debrief on his visit to Cambridge merely confirmed that he'd completed his mission.'

'Which as far as we're concerned is correct, but I'd still like to know exactly what went on in the air raid shelter that night.'

Liddell nodded. 'So would I, but we need to keep our eye on the ball. The main reason for my meeting with Bob was to make sure the borough police had accepted the suicide verdict at the inquest. I didn't want them pursuing the question of who might have shot Ter Braak. I'm pleased to say that Bob Pearson now takes the view that there's a war on and it doesn't really matter. He's ordered their file to be closed.'

'That's good news. When I last spoke to DCI Bone, he was still convinced the Dutchman didn't top himself,' Tar replied.

'Yes, DCI Bone is a wily old copper. I suspect our tip-off might have had something to do with his subsequent change of heart.'

'You mean us giving them the location of Lennie Pearce's stash of black market stuff?'

'No, I was thinking of my later message to the chief constable confirming the involvement of Professor Carpenter and giving him her address.'

Tar smiled. 'Yes, we do have to thank Nemo for not just concentrating on Ter Braak but keeping his eyes open to see if he was involved with anyone else.'

Liddell picked up a file from his desk. 'Talking of Audrey Carpenter, Bob Pearson gave me this. It's a copy of her formal statement. She certainly had a good memory and seems to have passed on everything Ter Braak told her.'

'Why do you think she did that? She was obviously a Nazi supporter and could have taken it all with her to the scaffold,' Tar asked.

'I think she couldn't resist showing how clever she'd been, but then again, she was British born and might have had a conscience after all.' Liddell flicked through the document. 'Not surprisingly, she mentions our friend Major Nikolaus Ritter, and the incompetent Hauptmann Boeckel at the Klopstok spy school in Hamburg. Which brings us neatly onto the first arrivals on the south coast on 3rd September last year.

Tar nodded. 'Yes, what a hopeless bunch. One of the four didn't speak English, and even if they hadn't managed to send those two transmissions, I doubt they would have been suitable for turning due to the number of people who were party to their capture.'

'It seems Ter Braak read about the execution of Waldberg, Kieboom and Meier, which certainly hit the headlines. But he didn't know about the acquittal of Pons.'

'No, and I'm not surprised the censor blue-pencilled all press reports about it. The general public would never have understood why the jury swallowed Pons' story that he'd never intended to spy and was on the point of giving himself up. But I suppose it demonstrates the sort of society we're fighting for, and at least he was re-arrested as an illegal immigrant, and interned for the duration.'

Liddell turned to the next page of the statement. 'The professor now mentions Gosta Caroli, who passed through the Klopstok while Ter Braak was in training.'

'Ah yes, SUMMER. Ironically, Ter Braak didn't know he wasn't that far away from him when Caroli was under house arrest at the Home for Incurables at Hinxton, just south of Cambridge.'

Liddell burst out laughing. 'Or about Caroli's failed escape on that motorbike.'

Tar joined in the mirth. 'It was a good job he pinched a government machine that hadn't been properly serviced, and duly broke down.'

'Didn't he have a canoe strapped to the pillion?'

'Yes, it seems he intended to use it to paddle across the Channel, but it kept falling off so he threw it over a hedge. I suppose he then realised he was trapped over here and duly gave himself up.' The two chuckled as they imagined the farce that had unfolded back in January.

Liddell turned to the next page of Professor Carpenter's statement. 'Now we come to Wulf Schmidt, or TATE as you christened him.'

Tar grinned. 'A very promising man, in my opinion. He's proving to be a vital replacement for SNOW.'

'Ah yes, our friend Owens. I wonder if Ritter believed our story that he'd lost his nerve and had to give up his spying.'

'There's no doubt in my mind that if we'd not shut him down and locked him up in Dartmoor Prison, he'd have blown our whole double agent scheme apart.'

Liddell nodded. Reading on, he looked up in surprise. 'Would you believe it? Ter Braak got to know Jakobs quite well, and even helped him with his Morse keying during their training.'

Tar sat quietly for a moment before he spoke. 'You know, I feel a bit guilty about Jakobs. I interviewed him when he was first delivered to London by Dixon. As usual, I told him that it was in his interests to co-operate, and while I didn't make any specific promises, I think his subsequent behaviour, especially his help in breaking Richter when he arrived, was probably aimed at self-preservation.'

'He was always *a gonner* in my mind. Don't forget the home guard were involved in his capture, and their inability to keep their mouths shut would have ruled him out as a double agent.'

'Yes, I suppose you're right. At least we didn't have the risk of another trial. His standing as a serving Luftwaffe officer did give us the benefit of a court martial and the virtual guarantee of a guilty verdict. But I do wonder if Jakobs' real mission wasn't to do with weather reports but as a follow up to find Maud. After all, there seems to be little doubt that Ter Braak failed to make radio contact, and I can imagine the panic in Hamburg. If I'd been in Ritter's shoes, I'd have sent in another man.'

'So would I, but whatever his mission, I have to admit Jakobs was a brave man right to the end. I'm told his last words to the firing squad at the Tower of London were, 'Shoot straight, Tommies.'

Tar looked impressed. 'Yes indeed. By the way, have you managed to discover any more about this mysterious Maud Committee?'

Liddell leaned forward and lowered his voice. 'Yes but this information is so secret that not even Winston Churchill is privy to it all. I know I can trust you to keep it to yourself.'

'Naturally.'

'It seems that although earlier research had verified the principle of nuclear fission, nobody knew how to construct a bomb light enough to be delivered by any current bombers. However, early in 1940, two immigrant scientists working in Birmingham, Otto Frisch and Rudi Peierls, came up with a scheme to build a viable atomic device that would be small enough to be dropped from a plane. They wrote a memorandum which, for once, galvanised the government into action, and a committee was set up to progress the matter. Much of the development work was passed to the Cavendish Laboratory in Cambridge.'

'Where did the name Maud come from?' Tar asked.

'The original title was 'the atomic bomb sub-committee,' but that was thought to be too much of a security risk, and alternatives were sought. The story goes that a member of the committee happened to mention his governess, Maud. When it was realised that this could also stand for 'military application of uranium detonation,' the name stuck.'

'How did the Germans get wind of this?'

'As soon as Ter Braak's mission was discovered, everyone who knew about the Maud Committee was subjected to a further security check, and the leak traced back to a civil servant with previously undetected Nazi sympathies. In view of the sensitivity of the matter the trial was held in camera, and even the hanging was hushed up.'

Tar shuddered. 'Just think what would have happened if Ter Braak or the professor had managed to get their findings to Berlin.'

61
BERLIN

Admiral Canaris stared at the package that had just been delivered to his office by special messenger. Marked *For the attention of Admiral Canaris only*, he broke the seal and with more than a little interest, tipped out the contents. A buff envelope, addressed in stylish handwriting to Major Nikolaus Ritter, Hamburg and endorsed *Confidential*, fell onto his desk together with a typed note that recorded the journey the envelope had made to Berlin.

He picked up the envelope and turned it over, noting that the gummed flap was still intact. After issuing instructions that he was not to be disturbed, Canaris lit another cigarette, opened the letter, and sat back to read it.

Dear Nikolaus, or should I say Dr Rantzau?

It's been a long time since we were last in touch, but I trust you are well and holding your own in this war. You'll be pleased to know I'm still a supporter of your Fuhrer and was therefore only too pleased to help your agent, Engelbertus Fukken aka Jan Willem Ter Braak, with his mission. He was a brave man, but unfortunately has not survived, and if you're reading these backup details without having heard from me, it will mean I've failed in my bid to fly to Lisbon and make direct contact with you, via your embassy there.

Now to business. Maud is not a person, but a cover name for a committee dealing with research into nuclear fission. The Cavendish Laboratory in the centre of Cambridge houses a number of eminent scientists, all with experience in this field. One of the most prominent is Dr Hans von Halben. Another is Alan Nunn-May. I can only assume that they're building an atomic bomb.

I think that completes Fukken's mission. It's tragic that he didn't live to see the victory which will surely follow your own development of such a weapon.

Heil Hitler

Professor Audrey Carpenter

PS I nearly forgot. It seems there is a decoding centre at Bletchley, staffed by virtually every boffin in the country, where machines are being developed to decode your Enigma machines. There are also radio intercepting stations, certainly at both Hanslope and Shefford. There will no doubt be others, presumably taking down your transmissions for decoding.

PPS. Please give my best wishes to Mary, Klaus and Katherine.

Canaris read the letter several times and realised this was something he had to discuss with his deputy. Pressing a button on the intercom on his desk, the admiral spoke softly to the crisp military voice which responded. 'A word with you as soon as is convenient.'

The recipient of this invitation, Oberst Hans Oster, correctly translated this message as 'in here immediately', and when he saw the look on the admiral's face, he knew this was not a social call. The Oberst felt a flicker of fear. They both had a mutual loathing of the Fuhrer but were biding their time, waiting for the chance to move against him. In the meantime, they had turned a blind eye to various warning signs involving their spies in England. Perhaps this had been spotted.

'What's the problem, Herr Admiral? Have the British realised that we're on to their double agents?'

'Not as far as I'm aware. They're all still churning out transmissions with a signal strength far greater than those of the puny sets we sent over, not to mention the length of their messages, which would enable any half-decent detection system to get a bearing on them.'

Oster frowned. 'I find it odd that our own spy-master didn't smell a rat.'

'Ritter did, but that wasn't part of my plan, so I made it very clear that any such comments would be treated as defeatism and rewarded with a firing squad. He's now fallen in line. No, my friend, it's much worse. Read this.' Canaris slid the letter from the professor across his desk.

Dumbstruck by what he had just read, Oster forced himself to remain calm. 'I presume that this man, Engelbertus Fukken, was one of Ritter's men in England. Did you know about him?'

'Indeed I did. In fact, I manoeuvred Ritter into sending him, and I also made sure his documentation was suitably flawed, in addition to the deliberate mistakes MI5 included in the samples brought back by *JOHNNY*. However this damned professor has undone all of our good work.'

'Who the hell is she?'

'Someone Ritter got to know during his pre-war time in America. He hadn't used her until I had this tip-off about a new super weapon being developed in Cambridge by someone called Maud. However, it seems Maud isn't a person but a codename. I've no idea what it might stand for. Any suggestions?'

'Knowing the English, I'd say it was most probably an acronym.'

'You could be right, although it doesn't really matter, not right now. What does matter is the possibility that our Enigma codes are being broken.'

'I find that difficult to believe. Surely there are millions of combinations to work through.'

'Yes, but if they're using some sort of machine, they might be able to go through all the permutations quickly enough for the information to be of value. Just think what a benefit that would give to the enemy.'

'It doesn't bear thinking about. But, how did this letter reach you?'

'The accompanying note from Hamburg explains that the professor handed this envelope in at the Spanish Embassy in London, with instructions to treat it as top secret and very important. The second secretary took it with him on one of his regular trips to Lisbon, where it was passed over to our people. When it reached Hamburg, they didn't know where Ritter's latest posting was, so they sent it to me.'

'Just like the proverbial hot potato. Thank heaven for supposed Spanish neutrality. But, why didn't they just send the letter to Lisbon in their diplomatic bag, rather than go to the trouble of delivering it in person?'

'Because they suspect; no, they're sure that since the start of the war the British have been intercepting all diplomatic bags and reading the contents.'

'I wonder if they'd have let this letter go through if they'd discovered its contents? Where's Ritter now?'

'I had to be seen to be doing something when he disobeyed my direct order not to involve *JOHNNY* in checking on Jakobs. He's now in charge of a searchlight battery in Dresden, but I softened the blow by promoting him to Oberstleutnent.'

'That was generous of you, Herr Admiral. I presume the postscript to the letter refers to his family, with Mary being his wife and Klaus and Katherine his two children?'

'Yes, although our clever professor obviously doesn't know that Mary was traded in for a younger model, and Ritter now has a third daughter with his secretary.'

'So, Herr Admiral, what are we to do with this information, which undoubtedly must be acted on.'

'My dear Hans, I don't think we have any choice.' Canaris picked up his cigarette lighter, lit it and held the flame beneath the letter and envelope and looked questioningly at his deputy. Oster nodded, and within seconds the document that could possibly have won the war for Germany became a pile of blackened fragments in the ashtray on the Admiral's desk.

Oster rose to leave, but then paused, turned to Canaris and announced in a voice heavy with emotion, 'I suspect we've just handed victory to the allies.'

The admiral nodded. 'I agree, but will either of us live to see the day?'

POSTSCRIPT

On the morning of 9th April 1945, with allied troops not far away, Wilhelm Canaris, Hans Oster and three other German 'traitors' were stripped naked, led to a hastily erected gallows in Flossenburg concentration camp, and hanged for their crimes against Nazi Germany.

ACKNOWLEDGEMENTS

Researching and writing this story has been a fascinating journey and I am indebted to all those who took the time and trouble to respond to my questions. I am particularly grateful to Mike Moran for pointing me in the right direction, and to Jann Tracey and Ellie Stevenson for their advice, support and guidance.

In addition to the details found in the files of the National Archives at Kew, the Cambridge Archives and the Cambridgeshire Collection, I have been fortunate to have had the assistance of Bob King, veteran of the Radio Security Service, and also Stan Ames, their tireless researcher. Dutch writer Jan-willem van den Braak very kindly shared with me the results of his research into Engelbertus Fukken. Special thanks must also go to Dr Giselle 'Gigi' Jakobs, who took time out from writing the biography of her grandfather, Josef, to provide me with information, comments and encouragement.

Finally I must thank my family and especially my wife for putting up with what has turned out to be a marathon.

FICTION FROM APS BOOKS
(www.andrewsparke.com)

HR Beasley: *Nothing Left To Hide*
Lee Benson: *So You Want To Own An Art Gallery*
Lee Benson: *Where's Your Art gallery Now?*
Nargis Darby: *A Different Shade Of Love*
Jean Harvey: *Pandemic*
Michel Henri: *Mister Penny Whistle*
Michel Henri: *The Death Of The Duchess Of Grasmere*
Michel Henri: *Abducted By Faerie*
Ian Meacheam: *An Inspector Called*
Tony Rowland: *Traitor Lodger German Spy*
Andrew Sparke: *Abuse Cocaine & Soft Furnishings*
Andrew Sparke: *Copper Trance & Motorways*
Phil Thompson: *Momentary Lapses In Concentration*
Paul C. Walsh: *A Place Between The Mountains*
Michael White: *A Life Unfinished*

WORLD WAR II NON-FICTION

Alex Merrill *Who Put Bella In The Wych Elm? Vol.1 The Crime Scene Revisited*
Pete Merrill *The Devil's Cauldron*
Andrew Sparke *Bella In The Wych-Elm*
Andrew Sparke *Rear Gunner*
Andrew Sparke *Stutthof*
Andrew Sparke *War Shadows*

Printed in Great Britain
by Amazon